KINDNESS OF STRANGERS

"Look, Holly, I can just as easily drive you to Santa Rosa in my car. I'll go shopping or something while you see the doctor. Come on, this will give me something to do with my time." Celia watched Holly's face carefully as she spoke. She could see the younger woman's resistance lessening.

Holly fought against a feeling of being overwhelmed. She didn't even know this woman who'd barged into her life with one of the best coffee cakes she'd ever tasted. She'd always been a loner, and she didn't want some stranger moving in on her. Holly knew what Alex would tell her to do. He'd always admired her independence—to a point. But he'd often told her she carried her independent streak too far at times, that she needed to learn to accept help from other people. Maybe, Holly thought, by stubbornly refusing to accept the offer of help, she really was risking her baby's life, and that was the last thing she wanted to do.

Books by Nancy Baker Jacobs

Rocking the Cradle*

Daddy's Gone A-Hunting*

Cradle and All*

See Mommy Run

The Silver Scalpel

A Slash of Scarlet

The Turquoise Tattoo

Deadly Companion

*Published by HarperPaperbacks

ROCKING
the
CRADLE

Nancy Baker Jacobs

HarperPaperbacks
A Division of HarperCollinsPublishers

HarperPaperbacks
A Division of HarperCollins*Publishers*
10 East 53rd Street, New York, N.Y. 10022-5299

This is a work of fiction. The characters, incidents, and
dialogues are products of the author's imagination and are not to
be construed as real. Any resemblance to actual events or
persons, living or dead, is entirely coincidental.

ISBN 0-06-100893-1

HarperCollins®, 📚®, and HarperPaperbacks™
are trademarks of HarperCollins*Publishers* Inc.

Cover illustration by Donna Diamond

First HarperPaperbacks printing: September 1996

Printed in the United States of America

Visit HarperPaperbacks on the World Wide Web at
http://www.harpercollins.com/paperbacks

❖ 10 9 8 7 6 5 4 3 2 1

DEDICATION

*This one is for the women writers of the
Monterey Peninsula: Adele,
Dianne, Mary, and Pat.*

And the king said, Bring me a sword. And they brought a sword before the king.

And the king said, Divide the living child in two, and give half to the one, and half to the other.

1 Kings 3:24–25

Chapter

1

The rented Toyota, its headlights dark, moved slowly and almost soundlessly through the night toward the secluded country airstrip. The vehicle turned onto an unpaved side road and stopped behind a low rise. The engine shuddered once and went dead.

A tall, slim woman in a black sweat suit and black sneakers emerged into night air pungent with a mixture of salt-laden fog and winter grasses. Standing very still, the dark figure listened for several minutes, but she heard only the wind whistling through the grass and the pounding of the distant surf. She pulled the hood of her sweat jacket over her flaxen hair, tucked an errant strand inside, and pulled the drawstring tight. The left pocket of her jacket yielded a pair of surgical gloves, which she pulled over her long, carefully manicured fingers.

Her senses alert, the woman crept toward the deserted runway. She crouched low in the tall grass, shivering slightly as damp, cold air sweeping in from the sea crawled along her back. She hugged herself for warmth and waited until the windows in the farm-house across the field went dark. Then she approached the row of small airplanes parked at the side of the blacktopped airstrip. Her destination was third in the line of six, a Cessna Skyhawk painted white with red markings. It was just as she'd remembered it.

Pulling a key from her pocket, she ducked under the wing strut on the pilot's side of the aircraft and unlocked the cabin door. She climbed inside, perched on the pilot's seat, and silently pulled the door closed behind her.

By the glow of her penlight, the cabin appeared to be exactly as it had been nearly four years ago, when she'd last been inside. The Cessna's owner remained a meticulous man. She had to admit he'd always taken excellent care of his toys . . . right up until he tired of them. Then he discarded them without mercy. But it was obvious he still cared about the airplane. No gum wrappers or maps were strewn about here. As usual, everything was clean, precisely in place, and in tip-top condition.

The intruder found the blue metal box lodged behind the passenger seat, right where the pilot always kept it. And his assortment of supplies was still inside: an opened pack of Doublemint gum, a roll of Tums, the wild cherry Life Savers he'd been addicted to ever since he kicked his smoking habit, a packet of Dramamine, a small yellow tin of Bayer aspirin, matching glass salt and pepper shakers, the two small jars he kept filled with sugar and Cremora, and, finally, a white plastic spoon. The box's contents all looked the same, except that the salt shaker was now filled with one of those herb salt substitutes, probably a concession to the heart attack the pilot had detailed in his court petition. But she didn't care about the salt shaker; the sugar jar was what she sought.

Noting its exact location in the box, she removed the sugar jar and unscrewed its cap. With steady hands, she pulled a small plastic bag from her jacket pocket, opened it, and carefully emptied a white powder into the sugar. She gently stirred the powder—thirty finely crushed Halcion tablets—into the sugar with her gloved index finger, screwed the cap back onto the jar, and replaced it in the metal box.

The intruder executed her tasks with precision. Before she crept back to her car and headed it toward the Coast Highway, she made certain that the Cessna looked exactly as it had before her visit. Neither the farmer who owned the remote landing strip nor the plane's pilot would ever suspect anyone had been there. At least not until it was far, far too late.

Chapter

2

Holly Sheridan raised her head from the pillow and squinted at the digital clock radio next to the bed: five-fifty-nine. She turned off the alarm before it sounded, ran her fingers through her short golden-brown hair, and lowered her feet to the bare floor.

"Stay in bed, hon," Alex told her. "No need for you to get up this early." He reached for his wife and pulled her gently back onto the bed.

"Don't be silly." Holly turned to face him. "I'll make you a good hot breakfast and drive you over to the airstrip."

"No need. You and junior need your rest. Besides, I'm not sure I can stand any more of that oat bran you've been feeding me. I'm in danger of turning into a horse."

"Fine, you had your steak last night. Now you'll just have to choke down some oat bran to make up for it." Alex wrinkled his nose. Holly kissed him gently on the lips, then placed his hand on the bulging mound of her belly. "Feel. 'Junior's' been chinning himself on my ribs for the past hour. I couldn't sleep through these calisthenics if I wanted to."

"They say a baby always knows when its mother is tense."

"Me? What have I got to be tense about? You keep telling me this court thing has nothing to do with me."

Alex yawned. "Right, and I can see you really take me seriously. You've been a regular model of relaxation lately." He kept his tone light, but he couldn't help feeling that Holly's obvious anxiety during the past few weeks was entirely his fault. He'd tried to handle his request that the court lower or, better yet, terminate his alimony payments to Celia without pulling Holly into what should be his own private fight, but she always knew when something was bothering him. If Alex had a problem, Holly was likely to lose sleep over it before he did. And he'd had more than his share of problems during the short eleven months they'd been married. "Sorry you married an old fart like me, sweetheart?"

"You're not an old fart, you're the best thing that ever happened to me."

"I only wish." On mornings like this, when he felt every one of his forty-nine years, Alex Sheridan couldn't help wondering what a vital young woman like Holly could possibly see in a guy like him. He'd suffered a minor heart attack only a month after their wedding, and then he'd moved her away from Los Angeles, where she'd had a promising career going, so they could start a new business together here in Bodega Bay. Now they were both struggling financially, and the business, Ecobay Housing, was threatened with bankruptcy. The scenery was gorgeous here on the Northern California coast, and the air was clean.

But there was still plenty of work to do on the house they were living in, and Alex was spending money they couldn't afford on a court battle with his ex-wife. If there was one thing he had always vowed never to do, it was to taint Holly with the incredibly bitter residue of his first marriage. But he hadn't even been able to keep that promise.

"Come on, lover, stop feeling sorry for yourself." Holly pushed her feet into a pair of blue terry-cloth slippers. "Things'll look a lot brighter once you get this hearing behind you."

"If I win."

"You will." Holly couldn't imagine a judge who would uphold the ridiculous divorce settlement Alex had made with his ex. "Just the fact that the baby's coming next month ought to cinch things."

Alex shrugged. "Too bad you're not the judge." He knew the judicial system could be maddeningly arbitrary and, truth was, he hadn't dared mention the expected baby in his court petition. Celia would be incensed enough about his hauling her back into court. If she found out about the baby, she might go completely off the deep end. Although he hadn't loved her for years—if he ever really had—Alex had never stopped feeling guilty about Celia. He realized now he'd been an idiot to give her the Bel Air house and sixty grand a year in spousal support when they divorced three years ago, even if they *had* been married twenty-five years. What hadn't helped matters was the way Celia'd always played the role of helpless child bride to the hilt; she hadn't earned a dime since their wedding day.

The last time he'd been in court, Alex had figured the settlement was a small price to pay for his long-awaited freedom. Back then, he'd thought he could afford it. He'd been earning six figures, and he'd been certain he'd never want to marry again. But everything was different now; now he couldn't imagine *not* being married to Holly.

Despite his current troubles, Alex considered himself incredibly lucky to have found Holly—this intelligent, attractive, independent career woman fourteen years his junior, a woman who showed him every day that, for some reason he'd couldn't quite fathom, she was crazy about him. She had become his best friend as well as his lover. And now she was about to give him a son or a daughter; Alex honestly didn't care which it turned out to be. If only he could get his financial life straightened out and put Celia far behind him, he'd be the happiest guy alive.

"Here, try one of these," Holly said, thrusting a plateful of steaming blueberry muffins in front of Alex. "I promise you'll never even notice the oat bran." She refilled his coffee cup.

Alex measured a heaping teaspoonful of sugar and stirred it into the steaming brew. He broke off a piece of the muffin, spread it with margarine, and chewed it. "Not bad," he admitted, washing it down with a swig of coffee. "You make this yourself?"

"Right." Holly arched an eyebrow. "I sneaked out of bed at five, threw on my designer maternity apron, whipped up the whole batch, and sneaked back into bed before you even knew I was gone."

Alex chuckled at the mental image.

"Truth is, they're from the health food store in Sebastopol. But I did reheat them all by myself."

"Like I said, they're not bad."

"See? Keep me around long enough, and your cholesterol will be so low you won't recognize yourself. And, who knows, you might even get to like healthy food." Holly smiled and sipped her orange juice.

"If it'll keep you around, sweetheart, I'll learn to eat straw. And like it."

"Hmmm, hadn't thought of straw. . . ." Holly poured the remainder of the pot of coffee into a steel thermos bottle and packed it into a maroon vinyl zippered bag. "Want me to put in a couple of leftover muffins in case you get hungry?"

"Save them for yourself, hon. My stomach's too jumpy to eat anything else this morning." Alex stifled a yawn. "All I need is plenty of java. Bet I didn't sleep more than two hours."

"You won't get a bet out of me. I felt you tossing and turning all night." Holly studied her husband's face. His strong jaw line and handsome nose were unchanged, but his blue eyes seemed duller and the hair at his temples grayer. He looked exhausted. She knew these past few months had been terribly hard on him. They'd come here to Bodega Bay to live at a slower pace and have more time together, but neither of them had done much relaxing so far. Alex had changed after his heart attack. He'd decided he couldn't spend the rest of his life designing mini-malls and office buildings. He wanted to do something more worthwhile with his architectural talents.

Holly was a hundred percent in favor of her husband's plan to design and build ecologically sound single-family houses, and she'd fallen in love with this tiny seaside community the first time she saw it. She adored its quaint fishing pier and its lovely homes with their sweeping views of the Pacific. She even loved the world-class golf course, despite the fact that she didn't know a putter from a wood.

But now she wasn't so sure it had been a good idea to come here. Alex loved designing the houses, and she'd learned to adapt the varied talents she'd once used as editor of *Stately Homes* magazine to participate usefully in the business. She'd even been studying for her real estate broker's license, so that she could legally sell Ecobay's houses once they were completed. In addition, the Sheridans had found a dependable building contractor to bring into partnership in the company.

But times were tough and, while they now had three houses under construction, they hadn't found buyers for any of them. Holly often worried that the stress of starting Ecobay Housing during an economic recession and trying to keep it afloat, and now the added pressure of this court case, might be pushing Alex toward another heart attack . . . maybe one from which he'd never recover. She couldn't help worrying about him. "I'll throw on some clothes and drive you over," she said, placing her empty juice glass in the top rack of the dishwasher.

Alex did his usual careful preflight check of the Cessna. Although he'd filled up on Friday, after he'd last used the plane, he climbed up on the wings and eyeballed the fuel level in both tanks. He took samples of the turquoise-colored gasoline to check for water or other contaminants. Finally, he ran his finger along the edge of the propeller blades, to assure himself that they remained smooth and free of nicks.

"Guess I can't avoid it any longer, Hol," he said. He pulled his wife close and buried his nose in her hair. She always smelled so clean, so natural. God, he loved her! "Don't know how I'm going to stand sleeping all alone in that hotel bed tonight," he told her.

"You *better* be all alone," Holly teased.

"You know there's nobody else I ever want to be with," Alex said. There was a time in his life when such a statement would have been a lie. But that was a long time ago, during another marriage, another life.

"Call me tonight and let me know how it went?"

"Soon as I get to the hotel." Alex bent down, covered his wife's lips with his own, and gave her a lingering kiss. "You take care of yourself and don't go anywhere near that stepladder. I'll finish painting the baby's room when I get back. Promise? And, if you have any pains, even so much as a twinge, get Greg to drive you to the doctor, okay?"

Holly nodded. "Don't worry about me. I still have to finish pricing the materials list for the kitchen of the Gull Drive house. You'll probably come back tomorrow and find me bleary-eyed, still punching numbers into the calculator." She clung to Alex a moment longer, fighting to keep her lower lip from quivering. She wasn't going to let herself indulge in tears. She couldn't understand why she'd been so weepy lately. It had to be her crazy hormones.

Holly straightened her spine and lifted her chin. Sure, she'd miss Alex, she told herself, but he'd be back before she knew it. "I just wish I could go with you," she said. "I love you so much I hate being without you for five minutes, never mind two days. Especially now." The baby kicked, as though to second her statement.

"I love you too, sweetheart, more than you know. But you know the doc says you can't fly till after the baby comes. Besides, like I keep telling you, this really isn't your problem."

*   *   *

As the Cessna gained altitude over the green mound of Bodega Head and then banked to the left, Alex radioed the nearest air traffic control tower that he was heading for the Santa Monica Airport, flying under Visual Flight Regulations. He usually loved skimming over this coastline, the brilliant blue Pacific on his right and the rugged green and gold Northern California hills on his left. But today all he could think about was his two o'clock court appointment, when he'd have to come face to face once more with Celia's hatred and bitterness. He wished he felt sharper, more alert, but he hadn't had a decent night's sleep in the past week.

As he leveled the plane at eleven thousand feet, Alex yawned and his ears popped. He checked his watch; it was just before eight. There was plenty of time. He should make Santa Monica by noon. He'd take a cab to the Third Street Mall, where he could grab a quick lunch—nothing heavy that would make him groggier—and walk over to meet his attorney at the courthouse well before two o'clock.

Alex rubbed his eyes. As he flew south, past the mouth of San Francisco Bay, he unzipped the maroon vinyl bag and reached for the thermos. Taped to its cap was a note. He opened it and read:

> Maybe we agreed when the justice of the peace advised us to
> ". . . let there be spaces in your togetherness, And let the winds of heaven dance between you," but that doesn't mean I have to like it. Come back quick. I miss you already.
> Love, H.

Alex's spirits lifted. He had a wife who wrote him love letters quoting Kahlil Gibran and made him feel life couldn't possibly be any richer. Holly made him want to fight dragons to protect her. He folded the note and tucked it into his shirt pocket; he would carry it over his heart today. Maybe it would bring him luck.

Alex screwed the cap off the thermos and poured himself a cup of coffee. He took the jar of sugar from the blue metal box, opened it, and dumped a generous portion into the coffee, stirring it well. The brew was strong and sweet, just the way he liked it.

He quickly put the coastline west of San Francisco behind him and skirted the western edge of the Monterey Bay sanctuary, heading south toward the Big Sur cliffs. He yawned again. Despite his case of nerves, he didn't ever remember feeling this tired. He poured another cup of coffee, sweetened it, and downed a large gulp. Why the hell didn't the caffeine kick in? Maybe some cold air would revive him. He turned off the heater switch and cracked his window open. A frigid blast hit him full in the face. He shivered and took another sip of coffee.

Alex stared at the control panel, but the dials and numbers were blurry. His eyelids grew heavy and he felt himself losing muscle coordination. His body swayed forward against the shoulder harness. Something was wrong, very wrong. He needed help. He reached toward the radio controls, knocking over the thermos and sending scalding liquid down his leg. But before he could scream out in pain, he blacked out.

Alex Sheridan never even saw the rocky Big Sur coastline as his little Cessna dove toward it.

Chapter

3

Celia Sheridan and her attorney, Leland Klein, arrived at the Santa Monica courthouse at precisely two o'clock. The room was already half filled with attorneys—identifiable by their nearly identical dark suits, white shirts, red-striped ties, and monogrammed leather briefcases—and battling couples. Leland whispered to Celia that they probably would have to wait while other family court cases were being resolved. He wasn't certain what position *Sheridan v. Sheridan* held on this afternoon's docket.

Celia proceeded down the center aisle, her chin high and her spine straight, the way she'd been taught to walk in modeling school so many years ago. She felt curious eyes upon her as she moved, and she was pleased with herself. She had dressed carefully for this event—tastefully but not pretentiously. She was wearing the new silk suit that matched the azure color of her eyes. She'd struggled to get used to wearing the blue-tinted contact lenses, but it was worth it. A gold dog collar and matching earrings, along with a pair of high-heeled taupe shoes and a small shoulder bag, completed her ensemble. Celia had had her hair tinted this morning, too, so there was no hint of gray among its pale gold strands, and she'd spent an hour and a half carefully applying her makeup.

She knew she looked her best—as attractive as any woman could expect to look at forty-eight, that is. She was pleased that her eyelid surgery last summer had subtracted a good five years from her face, and she'd been able to keep her body in shape with a strict diet and daily strenuous exercise. With a regimen that required rigid self-control, she had managed to maintain her fashion model's figure. Still, she knew all too well that her most marketable years were behind her. That bastard Alex had stolen them. No matter how hard she tried to keep her looks, her youth, Celia was convinced that she was used goods now. Men might say they didn't care if a woman gained a little weight, or looked a little older, or had been divorced. But they didn't really mean it. Most of the men Celia was interested in—men with money—had no use for a woman who'd been around the block a few times. Oh, they might claim that older women were really more interesting, that they were smarter than the younger ones, but Celia had learned long ago that most men didn't really want bright women. If a woman didn't learn to hide her brains and convince her man he was her intellectual superior, she'd end up alone.

As she and Leland Klein took seats near the front of the courtroom, Celia glanced nervously toward the back of the room and noticed Bryce Cannon standing near the heavy oak door. She recognized Cannon as the barracuda of an attorney Alex had used for the divorce. She hated the man's guts. Cannon was unusually tall, a good two inches taller than Alex's six feet one inch. The lawyer would have been handsome, except for his receding hairline and his tendency to scowl.

Celia looked around the room, surveying the other people seated in rows on the worn oak benches, but she could not locate Alex. It was after two o'clock now. If the son of a bitch had taken the Cessna, odds were he'd never be here. She only hoped he'd taken his child bride with him. Celia prayed that Alex and his new wife hadn't decided to drive down to L.A.

Bryce Cannon remained standing at the back of the courtroom, periodically checking his watch and cracking open the door to peer into the hallway outside. As time progressed and Alex still did not appear, Celia became more and more convinced that *Sheridan v. Sheridan* would be dismissed today without being heard, that her plan was succeeding and she would actually be the winner this time.

She tried to reduce her anxiety by listening and watching as other cases were called and Judge Schultz ruled on them. But observing this judge at work did little to reassure her. A pompous, humorless man, he obviously had already read the legal documents the various attorneys had submitted. Celia watched as the judge issued one ruling after another, quickly and with minimal questioning of the parties involved. Her neck muscles tightened as she heard a dumpy, fortyish woman in a shapeless pink dress trying to argue with the judge. Although her young female attorney had already offered the same arguments, the woman was repeating that she possessed no marketable skills with which she could be expected to support herself.

"You've had five years in which to acquire those skills, Mrs. Garcia," Judge Schultz said sternly. His impatience was obvious. "According to your own deposition, you've made no effort whatsoever to do that since your marriage ended. You can't expect your former husband to pay your bills indefinitely when you're not willing to work toward becoming independent. He has minor children to support now."

"But your honor—"

"I've made my ruling, Mrs. Garcia." The judge rapped his gavel, silencing her. "Next case."

The woman's chin quivered and Celia watched as tears began to roll down her plump cheeks. The judge's unsympathetic treatment of the Garcia woman did not bode well for what he might do with her own case. Sure, the Garcias had been married only seven years, not twenty-five as she and Alex had, but it was clear to Celia that this judge was a typical male chauvinist, the kind of guy who claimed the feminist movement had really given women equality. Everybody knew equality between the sexes was a farce. It didn't exist. The men called all the shots and no woman could expect life to be fair. If she was too dependent on her man, she was condemned—like Mrs. Garcia—as an old-fashioned parasite. But if she became independent, able to fend for herself, it just made it easier for her man to leave her.

As a child, Celia had watched her mother learn that hard lesson. Her mother had run her own small business. She'd been an independent woman long before it was fashionable. But she'd died all alone. All three of her husbands had let her pay their bills, and then they'd turned around and walked out on her. They hadn't wasted a good-bye glance on little Celia, either. She'd never forgotten that; she'd vowed she'd never be a sucker for men like her mother.

Celia watched as Mrs. Garcia left the courtroom,

looking defeated. If somehow Alex managed to show up today and this judge actually reduced or cut off *her* spousal support, Celia decided, she would appeal the decision all the way to the Supreme Court. If Alex got off the hook on paying her alimony, she would force his legal bills straight through the roof. There was no way she was going to let him spend "her" money on that bimbo he'd married.

The next case called involved a father, a skinny, pockmarked young man in soiled jeans and a plaid shirt, who was behind on his spousal and child support payments. Judge Schultz was as abrupt with the errant father as he had been with Mrs. Garcia, ordering him to pay what he owed in full within ten days or face jail time.

Celia felt a little better. She hadn't received this month's support check from Alex yet. With luck, the judge would hold that against the son of a bitch . . . if he ever made it here. And—unless Alex had lost his sweet tooth or given up coffee—that was becoming less and less likely as the minutes crawled by.

"Sheridan versus Sheridan."

Celia jumped as she heard her case called.

Her attorney rose and gestured for her to accompany him to the bench. "Leland Klein for the respondent, your honor."

Bryce Cannon approached the bench as well. "Bryce Cannon for the plaintiff, your honor. I'm sorry, but my client has not yet arrived. He lives in Northern California, and he had rather a long journey to—"

"You had a two o'clock court date, counselor. It's now ten after three and, as you can see, my calendar is full."

"If the court pleases, your honor, may we have just a few more minutes? I'm sure Mr. Sheridan must have been delayed unavoidably."

Judge Schultz nodded. "I'll take the next case. But if your client isn't here by the time I'm finished, counselor, you can forget about my hearing your case today."

"Thank you, your honor." Bryce Cannon returned to his post by the courtroom door.

Celia repressed a smile as she and her attorney took their seats. She couldn't help feeling a little smug, but she couldn't afford to let it show.

Another thirty-five minutes passed. *Sheridan v. Sheridan* was called a second time, and Alex was still absent.

"Your honor, at this time, in view of the fact that my client has not arrived, I would like to request a continuance," Cannon said.

Celia nudged her attorney. "Object," she whispered in his ear. "I want this thing thrown out of court."

Klein shook his head and remained silent.

Celia wondered why the hell she was paying this shyster if he wouldn't object when she wanted him to. She stepped forward. "May I say something, your honor?" she asked. She felt Klein's hand on her arm, attempting to pull her back. Annoyed, she brushed him away.

"Go ahead."

"Your honor, this kind of behavior is completely typical of Alex Sheridan. The man has treated me like dirt for nearly thirty years. He moved me across the country half a dozen times, he expected me to play the executive wife to help his career, he got rich because I was willing to stand behind him. He took the best years of my life and now he's trying to take away my last means of support. I strongly object to being put through this kind of stress all over again." She dabbed at the corners of her eyes with a linen handkerchief, being careful not to smudge her mascara. "The way I see it," she continued, "we made a deal when Alex dumped—I mean, when our marriage was dissolved. There's no reason he should be allowed to welsh on it now."

Judge Schultz leaned forward. His narrow brown eyes revealed no compassion. "I understand your obvious distress, Mrs. Sheridan, but Mr. Sheridan has the legal right to bring changed circumstances—either yours or his own—to the court's attention. If the court determines that any of these circumstances have, indeed, changed, I am authorized to modify your original—uh, 'deal' to take that into consideration."

"But, your honor, I—"

"Counselor." The judge addressed Leland Klein. "Explain the law to your client, please, *outside* the courtroom." He turned to the taller attorney. "I'm going to grant you a continuance, Mr. Cannon, but your client had better have a very good reason for his absence. When you locate him, I suggest you explain the law to him as well."

"Yes, your honor. Thank you."

Judge Schultz consulted his calendar. "February tenth, two o'clock," he said.

Both attorneys consulted their date books and agreed to the new date.

Holding her handkerchief across her mouth, Celia turned to leave. The crumpled linen hid the small, self-satisfied smile playing across her lips. Celia was by now virtually certain Alex Sheridan would not be in this courtroom on February tenth. Or on any other date.

It had been a long, bloody battle, this war of the Sheridans, but Celia was beginning to smell victory.

Chapter

4

~~~~~

Holly sat bent over her supplies lists in the third bedroom of the unfinished house where she and Alex
lived. This extra bedroom, like most of the rest of the
house, lacked carpeting and wallpaper. Still, it had four
walls and a roof, and it would have to serve as their
home office until they had the funds and the time to
finish it.

She faxed the German company that sold pure cotton carpeting, ordering sixty yards in a pale ivory
shade for the house Ecobay was constructing on Gull
Drive. The price of the carpet was astounding—more
than fifty dollars a yard, wholesale—but building
materials that were completely free of toxic chemicals
were both expensive and hard to find. The main thing
making Ecobay Housing different from its competitors
was its promise to provide healthy, ecologically sound
housing. That commitment meant a religious avoid-
ance of the thousands of building materials derived
from petroleum products. Those cheaper products
often leaked toxic fumes into the air, causing sick-

building syndrome and eventually making the house's inhabitants ill.

As Holly added up her figures, she wondered not for the first time whether such expensive materials were really worth the extra cost. Natural tiles from Mexico, formaldehyde-free lumber from Oregon, cement and seawater roofing slate from Belgium: those things added an additional third to the cost of each house's construction. Would customers really appreciate—and be willing to pay for—the result?

The question might be moot, she knew, unless Alex was successful in court today. Without a major reduction in his hefty spousal support obligations to his former wife, the Sheridans wouldn't have the money to keep Ecobay Housing afloat long enough to find customers for the houses they were building.

Holly was finding it difficult to keep her mind on her work. Her thoughts kept drifting back to Alex and the Santa Monica Courthouse. If she weren't eight months pregnant, she wondered, would she be with Alex now, sitting beside him to lend him moral support? She wasn't sure whether he would want her there in any case. Alex seldom spoke of Celia, and Holly knew precious little about what had gone wrong with her husband's first marriage. Alex had already been divorced when they met at one of *Stately Home*'s annual open houses for builders and architects. And he'd been tight-lipped ever since about that portion of his past.

Holly had never even seen a photograph of her predecessor; Alex said he'd destroyed them all at the time of the divorce because he didn't want to be reminded of "the biggest mistake of my life." Since he and Celia'd had no children, there seemed little need for him to contact her after the divorce—except to write the monthly alimony checks.

Holly supposed the decision not to have children must have been Celia's, or maybe the woman had had a physical problem. Certainly Alex had nothing against children; he was eager for the arrival of their own baby.

All Alex was willing to tell Holly about Celia was that the woman had always been a big spender and that she was extremely bitter about the breakup of the marriage. "Good old Celia figured I'd be her meal ticket for life," was the way he put it. He predicted she would fight his efforts to reduce the money he was paying her with every resource she had, but he felt he had no choice but to take her on.

Holly had to admit she was curious about Celia. From friends of Alex's, she'd learned that his first wife was a beautiful woman, a tall blonde who once worked as a fashion model. Knowing that made Holly self-conscious. Her body was strong and healthy, a little taller than average, and slim, when she wasn't pregnant. She had green eyes, brown hair, and a fresh, freckled face, and many people had told her she was pretty. But beautiful was not an adjective often used to describe Holly Sheridan.

Except by Alex, of course. He frequently told Holly she was the most beautiful woman he'd ever known, but she never believed him. Not when his first wife had actually been a fashion model.

Laying down her pencil, Holly stood up and stretched, one hand pushing into the ache in the small of her back. Gazing out the window across the golf course, she saw that the sea in the distance was choppy and white-capped, a sign that the inevitable afternoon winds had picked up. She glanced at her watch; it was four-fifteen. Alex's ordeal might already be over by now. She longed to hear from him.

The phone's bell split the silence. Maybe Alex had sensed her thoughts. Smiling, she grabbed the receiver. "Hello?"

"Hi, Holly. It's Bryce Cannon. May I speak with Alex, please?"

Holly's smile wilted as she recognized Alex's attorney's name. "Alex isn't here, Bryce. He's in court with you . . . isn't he?"

"Nope. He never showed up. Thought maybe he got his dates mixed."

Holly's hand froze on the telephone receiver and her heart skipped a beat. "No, he—Alex flew the Cessna down to L.A. this morning." She'd stood at the airstrip, watching until the white dot of the little plane disappeared over the horizon.

"Do you know what airport he was heading for?"

"Santa Monica. Said he was going to tie down there and grab a cab straight to the courthouse. I don't under—"

"Listen, Holly, don't worry. Not yet, anyway. I'll call Santa Monica Airport. If Alex was delayed, he probably radioed somebody there."

"Of course. Of course, he would radio the airport tower, wouldn't he?" And then he'd have somebody call her. Or at least call Bryce to tell him he wasn't going to make the court date. Their whole economic future depended on that court hearing. Holly knew something was terribly wrong.

"Call you back, soon as I find him," Bryce Cannon said.

"Yeah. Okay, thanks."

"And don't worry, really. I'm sure everything'll turn out fine." The line went dead.

Don't worry. Sure. The lawyer might as well have told Holly not to have green eyes or not to breathe. She stared out at the sea, searching the horizon for clues to her husband's whereabouts. How many other women had stood as she did now, she wondered, searching the empty gray waves for some sign that their husbands would soon be home? Some of the houses in Bodega Bay featured New England-style widow's walks, small balconies on the upper floors where sailors' wives once watched for their husbands' ships to sail over the horizon and back to the safety of the harbor.

Holly shuddered. Bryce Cannon would call soon, she told herself. He would call and tell her that Alex'd simply had plane trouble, that he was safe and sound, and he'd be home tomorrow, right on schedule. She had to believe that. She had to.

It seemed hours that Holly had been standing rigid, staring out the window, her thoughts churning. But when the telephone rang again, she was surprised to see that a mere twenty minutes had passed.

"Holly, it's Bryce again." She tried to sense good news in the tone of his voice, but it was flat, revealing nothing.

"Did you find him?"

"Not yet, I'm afraid. Listen, Santa Monica Airport hasn't heard from him. They say Alex must've been flying under Visual Flight Regulations, because he never filed a flight plan. He could've had plane trouble and landed at another airport somewhere, but Santa Monica doesn't know anything about him."

Holly's stomach clenched and the baby kicked.

"Alex would call one of us if that happened, wouldn't he?"

There was a pause on the line. "Probably. Unless he thought he could get the plane fixed and still make it to court on time. Maybe he had to land in a field somewhere, and he just hasn't been able to get to a phone."

"Yeah. Yeah, I'll bet that's it." Holly grasped at the straw Bryce was offering her. Alex was all right . . . somewhere. He was a good pilot, an excellent pilot. He'd be able to land that plane on a roadway or in somebody's pasture if he had to. Wouldn't he? "We'll hear from him soon, I know we will. Unless . . . "

"Unless?"

"What if he's hurt, Bryce? Maybe the plane crashed somewhere and Alex needs help." She had a vision of the Cessna, lying broken in a remote forest or on the peak of a mountain. Alex could be hurt, bleeding, unconscious. "Somebody should be looking for him." Holly heard the note of panic creeping into her voice. "Somebody should be looking for him right away."

"Just try to stay calm, Holly. I'll find out what has to be done here and contact the FAA, get them working on finding him as soon as possible."

Holly thanked Bryce and put the receiver down. Her eyes returned to the horizon, searching for a sign. A speck of silver in the afternoon sky grew larger and larger until finally she could make out its shape. But it was only a commercial jet, bound for Santa Rosa or San Francisco.

Hugging herself for warmth, she stood at the window, keeping her lonely vigil.

Chapter

5

"Waiter! I'll have another one of these." Celia tapped a crimson fingernail against the rim of her empty vodka tonic glass. "But have the bartender go a little lighter on the ice this time."

"Yes, ma'am."

"Ready for another one, Buffy?" Celia asked her friend. The two women were sitting at a table in the darkened barroom of their Brentwood tennis club. Celia had come directly from the courthouse, while Buffy had spent the afternoon playing tennis at the club. Cocooned here amid the barroom's dark oak furnishings and in its subdued lighting, the few occupants never had to know that the sun was still high in the smoggy sky outside.

"Not just yet." Buffy Lewis had barely touched her glass of chardonnay. She twirled her glass by its slender stem and shivered a bit in the room's air conditioning. "It's a little early for me."

The waiter put Celia's empty glass on his tray and walked away.

"It's pretty early for me too. But I need a jolt of something in my veins, after the day I've had." Celia plucked an invisible piece of lint off the sleeve of her azure suit.

"I just don't get it, Cele. Why wouldn't Alex show up in court? This whole thing was his idea, right?"

"Sure wasn't mine. Bastard wanted to cut me off with nothing. I tell you, Buff, Alex won't be happy till he sees me starve. After all the years I gave him!" Celia's mouth was a bitter red line. "The son of a bitch."

"So why wasn't he there? You think he changed his mind, decided not to pursue it after all?"

"Fat chance! I wouldn't put anything past that bastard. He wasn't satisfied with using up my best years and then dumping me for someone half his age. You'll never know how much I gave up for that man, and still he's not satisfied. Now he wants to break me, see me living in the street." The waiter delivered Celia's fresh drink. She grabbed it and gulped thirstily.

"Come on, Cele. It's not really *that* bad. These things happ—"

"The hell! Never thought I'd hear that kind of crap from you, Buffy, of all people. Shit, you'd think Charlie hadn't dumped you for that idiot typist with the big boobs."

Buffy flinched at the painful reminder. Sometimes she wondered whether keeping up her friendship with Celia Sheridan was worth the toll it took on her nerves. Yet they'd known each other for more than twenty years and, truth be told, she felt a little sorry for Celia. Like many divorced women, Celia'd lost half of her friends when her husband left her. Then she'd managed to alienate the rest of them with her perpetual bitterness and self-absorption. If Buffy dumped her too, Celia would have nobody left.

"There's one big difference between you and me," Buffy said coolly. "I've decided to move on with my life. If Charlie's happy with his dim little secretary, more power to him. I'm not going to waste the rest of *my* life obsessing about what Charlie's doing, what he's feeling, what he's eating, whether he had a goddamned bowel movement this morning. Maybe he's miserable about what he did to me, maybe he's not. But I basically just don't give a damn about Charlie anymore."

Celia drained her glass and signaled the waiter for another.

"Don't you think you should slow it down a little, Cele?" The anger had left Buffy now, replaced by concern for her old friend, who looked like she was quickly losing control. "It's not even five o'clock."

"Why shouldn't I get drunk if I want to? After what I've been through—"

"Maybe because drinking's not going to make you happy. Maybe because you're wasting your life. I know you don't want to hear it, Celia, but I really think you'd feel better if you'd just see that therapist I told—"

"So now I'm crazy!" Celia's voice rose, echoing against the paneled walls. "Is that what I'm hearing from my best friend? That I'm a crazy woman?"

"No! Just shut up a minute and listen. *I* went to counseling, and *I'm* not crazy. All it did was help me realize I'm a person too, worth every bit as much as Charlie. I don't need him. I'm okay without a husband. And the truth is, I've never been happier than these last couple of months."

"Yeah, well, that's you, not me." Therapy was a particularly sore subject with Celia. Alex had tried to push her into it for years, but she'd resisted. She'd been certain all he wanted out of marriage counseling was ammunition to use against her in divorce court, and there was no way she'd give him that.

Buffy sighed. "So tell me this. How long're you going to let Alex do this to you? Honestly, Cele, ask yourself. Is the man worth all the grief you keep putting yourself through?"

Celia's index finger rhythmically dunked the wedge of lime up and down in the fresh drink the waiter brought her. "Tell you the truth, I don't think it'll be all that much longer," she said.

Buffy ran her fingers through her short-cropped auburn hair; she'd stopped dying it six months ago, and now it was streaked with gray at the crown. "Hey, good girl. That's the right attitude. Let your lawyer get you the best deal he can. Then just let Alex go and start living your own life."

"Yeah, well, with luck I won't need either Alex or my lawyer much longer." Celia folded her cocktail napkin in half, then quarters lengthwise, then bent the sides upward to form a paper airplane shape.

"What do you mean?"

Celia looked directly at Buffy. "With a little luck, Alex and that bimbo he married cashed it all in this morning. That'd sure as hell keep him out of court."

Buffy stiffened. Celia sounded serious. "I don't understand."

Celia leaned forward and lowered her voice. "'Member Alex's plane, Buff? The Cessna?"

Buffy could smell liquor on her friend's breath; it wasn't true that you couldn't smell vodka on a person. "Yeah, sure, I remember it."

"Well, he kept it."

"So?"

"So . . . any bastard can afford to keep his own personal airplane, he sure as hell can pay his alimony. That's not too much to ask, right?"

Buffy now felt certain that Celia was drunk. "You're not making sense. What does Alex's keeping his airplane have to do with his not showing for the court hearing?"

Celia folded an end of her napkin into a point. "I figure he took the plane to get down here from Bodega Bay. Maybe—maybe he had a heart attack at the controls. Or ran out of gas. Wouldn't take much." She held her completed paper airplane aloft, pushing it around in circles in an imitation of flight. "*Bzzzzz* . . . " Suddenly her wrist arched downward and headed directly toward the table. The napkin crumpled as her knuckles crashed against the hard surface with a thump that rattled the ice in her glass. "Splat! There. No more Alex, no more bimbo wife. Serves 'em right."

"Celia! Don't even kid around like that. That's a terrible thing to say."

"Is it really? I don't think so." She chugged down the vodka tonic. "This is war, Buffy, don't ever forget it. Alex and that bitch of his are out to kill me, but they're not gonna get away with it."

Buffy pushed away her half-finished glass of wine. "Come on, Celia. You've had enough to drink. I'll drive you home." She stood up and tugged on Celia's elbow. "Come on, now, let's go."

Celia pushed back her chair and stood up, quieter now and noticeably shaky on her feet. She allowed the shorter woman to take her by the sleeve and guide her across the floor.

The bartender spotted the two club members as they

neared the bar. "Want this put on your tab, Mrs. Sheridan?" he asked.

"Yeah, right, jus' put everthin' on my tab." Celia leaned toward the bar and tossed what she'd been holding in her hand onto its polished surface. The bartender scooped up the crushed napkin and tossed it into the trash.

Chapter

6

Celia's head throbbed as she swallowed two more aspirins with half a glass of bottled water. She stared at her face in the mirror. Her eyes were still bloodshot and her newly sculpted eyelids a little puffy. She'd never been a good drinker; she had no tolerance for alcohol. It had been foolish to indulge herself this afternoon. Now she was in the bathroom of the Bel Air house, already hung over, and it wasn't even midnight. Even getting her makeup off had been hell. Her head seemed to be caught in a slowly tightening vice. Sleep would be out of the question for hours.

Celia tied her mint-green silk dressing gown tighter at the waist and walked slowly back into the bedroom, doing her best not to jar her aching head as she moved. She put one foot in front of the other, walking in a gliding motion. She lowered herself gently to the bed, holding her head level and steady.

The television set was already tuned to the eleven o'clock news on Channel Three, its volume low. Celia seldom was interested in watching the news, but tonight was different. She wouldn't sleep for hours anyway, so she figured she might as well see whether Alex would get his very own fifteen seconds of fame. With any kind of luck, the son of a bitch would get it posthumously.

The blond anchorwoman read a downbeat story about the leading economic indicators. The story didn't particularly interest Celia, but the anchorwoman did. Celia'd found out her own plastic surgeon had redone the broadcaster's face three times in the past dozen years, and she had to admit the woman still looked pretty good under the harsh lights. If the rumor that she was fifty-six years old was true, she looked *damned* good. Whenever Celia watched the news, she liked to watch Channel Three, because of the blonde. The competing stations, with their younger newscasters, always depressed her.

Celia fell back against the pillows, her eyes closed, half listening as the bald meteorologist gave the weather forecast: Santa Ana winds tomorrow, which meant it would be hot and dry, with an increased danger of fire. The winds were expected to shift by the weekend, returning the more typical cloud cover to the west side of Los Angeles.

Suddenly, there it was! Celia bolted upright and her eyes shot open. She pressed down on the remote control to increase the volume.

"Former Los Angeles architect Alexander Sheridan is feared lost somewhere along the California coast tonight," the anchorwoman reported. An old picture of Alex at some political function, smiling broadly while he shook hands with then-Mayor Tom Bradley, came on the screen. "Sheridan set out from Bodega Bay for Santa Monica Airport in his single-engine Cessna this morning, but he never arrived. Lynne Eckles of our sister station in Santa Rosa has the story."

A film clip shot a few hours earlier in Bodega Bay flashed on the screen, and Celia's hand froze on the remote control. A young woman identified as Holly Sheridan, "wife of the missing architect," was shown being interviewed about her husband's departure. So Alex hadn't had his bimbo with him after all.

"I'm afraid my husband might've had to land in a remote area and that he needs help," Holly Sheridan said into the reporter's hand-held microphone. The woman was plain-looking, Celia thought with a self-satisfied smile, actually mousy. Her hair was an undistinguished shade of brown, cut short in no particular style, and her freckled face wore no makeup whatsoever. The woman must have no pride if she could allow herself to be seen on TV looking like that, missing husband or not. Celia judged her successor's face somewhat chubby; going by the head shot on Channel Three, Holly might well have a weight problem. Celia felt irrationally cheered by this possibility.

Then the camera moved back to include both Holly Sheridan and the interviewer in the frame together, as the reporter did her summary. Celia's breath caught. "That fucker! That fucking bastard!" she screamed, throwing the remote control across the room, where it smashed against the opposite wall and fell to the carpet. Tears welled in her eyes as she realized that Holly Sheridan wasn't fat after all; Alex's new wife was just very, very pregnant.

Celia's rage was palpable now. Unable to sit still, she paced the bedroom, muttering obscenities under her breath. If the son of a bitch wasn't already dead, she was ready to kill him with her bare hands. Of all the atrocities he'd performed on her over the years, this was the worst, the absolute worst. The divorce, even his remarriage, paled alongside this final betrayal. Alex, the man who'd sworn he never wanted children, who felt so strongly about it he'd forced Celia into an unwanted abortion all those years ago . . . now the faithless Alex had fathered this homely bitch's baby.

The telephone rang. Celia stared at it. It was eleven-thirty, far too late for a casual call. Maybe Alex had been found and the police were calling to notify Celia. Maybe the authorities thought they were still married, that she was the widow. She sucked in air and sat back down on the bed, reaching for the phone on the nightstand.

"Celia, did you see it?"

"Oh, Buffy, it's you."

"Yeah." Buffy's voice was anxious, frightened. "Did you see Channel Three, Cele? Alex is missing, just like you said. They think his plane went down, and—"

"Yeah, I saw it, all right. I saw Alex's whore, too. Looks like she's about to pop."

There was a pause on the line. When Buffy spoke again, she sounded more compassionate. "It must be hard for you to see—"

"Hard? *Hard?* That should've been *my* baby, Buffy. My baby! I wanted it so bad. If we'd had our baby, we'd still be married, but that son of a bitch lied to me. He said he didn't want children, wouldn't have them. He said he'd leave me if I didn't get rid of it."

"What're you talking about, Cele? What baby? I thought you told me you had a problem, that you couldn't have kids."

Celia made a spitting sound. "Yeah, right. Because of Alex. *He's* the reason I couldn't have kids. Son of a bitch practically killed me. Probably wishes he had."

"Celia, don't talk like that. Your marriage just went sour, that's all. You know you weren't any happier than Alex was."

"But I was willing to stick it out, Buffy, that's the difference. I was willing to make it work. All Alex wanted to do was split and run. Well, I showed him, didn't I?"

"What do you mean, Cele? What're you talking about?"

Celia caught herself. Had she said too much? "All—all I meant was, it serves him right if his plane went down. It serves him right if he's dead."

Holly dragged herself into the kitchen. She was wearing Alex's loosely belted blue terry-cloth bathrobe, which she could barely close over her bulging belly. But it was warm and comforting. She'd hardly slept at all last night, and now she had a throbbing headache and an acid stomach, and the insides of her eyelids felt like coarse sandpaper.

Last night had been the worst night of Holly's life, no contest. As she lay alone and awake for hours in the big king-size bed, imagining Alex injured and bleeding in a farmer's field or on some remote mountainside, her fears grew darker and darker.

She'd had other difficult times in her life, of course; what woman of thirty-five hadn't? Last year, when Alex had his heart attack, Holly had been half scared to death, but it had turned out to be a minor one. She sometimes believed the heart attack might actually have been a kind of gift—after all, it had served as the impetus for Alex to quit a job he'd grown to despise and try something he'd always dreamed of doing.

Despite the many problems they'd had starting up Ecobay, Alex had been a much, much happier man since they'd made the move to Northern California.

The only other really big crisis in Holly's adult life had been her mother's death five years earlier. Watching cancer eat away at her once-strong parent's body had been excruciating, and in the end she'd prayed for her mother's agony to be over. She still missed her mother, of course, particularly now that her own child was about to be born. But parents were supposed to die before their children, and Holly felt she'd adjusted to her loss.

Now, however, it wasn't a parent; it was Alex who could be—Holly halted herself in mid-thought. She couldn't think of Alex as dead; she *wouldn't* think of him that way. He simply had to be alive. His first child was due in just a few more weeks. She needed him now more than ever, and the baby needed a father. *Alex had to be alive.* If not . . . but that possibility was far too cruel to contemplate.

Holly poured cold water into the coffeemaker and, with a shaky hand, measured six scoops of ground decaf into the brown paper filter. Today, she thought, she could use some real coffee, a strong jolt of caffeine to cut through her grogginess, but she'd abstained ever since her pregnancy was confirmed. Decaf would have to do.

When the coffee was brewed, she spread butter on one of yesterday's leftover muffins, bit off a chunk, and chewed, but the blueberry-studded muffin tasted like Styrofoam. The sharp, painful memory of fleeting joy as she'd served these same muffins for breakfast yesterday morning—could they have been Alex's last meal?—brought the sting of tears to Holly's eyes. She tossed the rest of the muffin into the sink, turned on the cold water, flicked on the garbage-disposal switch, and watched the soggy gray-brown mass disappear down the drain.

You're going to have to eat something, Holly scolded herself as she leaned against the edge of the sink. The baby needs food. She straightened her spine, pressed both hands against her belly, fingers spread apart, and closed her eyes.

"It's going to be okay, baby," she said out loud. "Daddy will come back . . . soon. I know he will." She tried to believe what she was saying, with her body as well as her mind, but as each hour passed, she knew the chance that Alex was alive was growing dimmer and dimmer.

After forcing down a glass of orange juice and a vitamin pill—she tried, but she couldn't manage to swallow even a bite of buttered toast—she headed back to the bedroom. Tossing off the warm bathrobe, she stepped into the shower, leaving the glass door ajar so she could hear the bedroom phone if it rang with news of Alex.

Ten minutes later, her hair still damp and hanging straight and limp around her puffy face, Holly dressed quickly in a pair of black maternity slacks and one of Alex's comfortable old shirts. Wearing his clothes, with his familiar masculine scent still clinging to them, made her feel closer to her missing husband. As she was buttoning the soft blue chambray shirt over her belly, the doorbell rang. Her pulse quickened and she moved to the door as fast as her bulky body would let her, half expecting to see Alex standing there with a sheepish grin on his face.

But it was not Alex on the doorstep. Through the

strip of glass next to the door, Holly saw Greg Garrison, their partner in Ecobay Housing. "Hi, Holly," Greg said, when she pushed the door open. His gray eyes focused on her chin, as though he couldn't bear to meet her gaze.

The tall, lanky building contractor had never been particularly comfortable around Holly—or around any woman, for that matter. She'd often noticed that Greg chose his words with extra care whenever she was within earshot, as if he thought females were too fragile to be exposed to authentic male conversation. But this morning his discomfort was even more pronounced.

"Hello, Greg," Holly said, opening the door wider and trying to hide her disappointment that he wasn't Alex. "Come on in. Have you heard anything?"

"'Fraid not. Just came to check on you, see how you're holding up."

Greg Garrison was a few years older than Holly, just shy of his fortieth birthday, but he looked far older. His sandy hair was not yet turning gray, but his tan face was leathery and lined from years of working outdoors in the relentless California sunshine. He wore tight, faded jeans with a tear in one knee, a wide leather belt with extra loops for hanging hand tools and his telephone beeper, and an old paint-spattered gray sweatshirt.

"Truth is, I'm not doing all that well," Holly told him, certain this came as no surprise. She knew she must look every bit as anxious and haggard as she felt. "How about a cup of coffee?" she offered. "I've got some decaf made."

Greg nodded shyly and followed Holly as she padded barefoot into the kitchen. After he was seated at the kitchen table with his hands cradling a cup of the steaming brew, he met Holly's exhausted green eyes directly for the first time. "FAA alert hasn't turned up anything yet?" he asked.

Holly shook her head, and tiny droplets of water dripped from her hair onto the blue shirt. "They say they've checked with all the airports between here and the Mexican border, and nothing. Nobody knows anything about either Alex or the Cessna. The Civil Air Patrol's supposed to be out looking for him."

"That's good. Sooner they start searching the hills and the back roads, the better. If Alex made an emergency landing somewhere, we're gonna want him found as fast as possible." Greg, like Alex, was a licensed general aviation pilot. Unlike his Ecobay partner, however, Greg did not have his own airplane. All of his in-flight hours had been chalked up either in Alex's plane or in rental aircraft. "Try not to worry too much, Holly," he said. "I mean, it can't be good for you, with . . . with the baby and all." He went back to watching the steam rise from his cup of coffee.

"I'm trying my best to keep my mind occupied during all this—this damnable waiting," Holly told him. "Thought I might try to do a little work on the company accounts this morning."

"Good idea. We can't afford to get behind on that stuff, not with the shape Ecobay's in."

Holly hardly needed to be reminded. "Got another fax from the roofing tile company yesterday afternoon," she reported. "Until we pay the twelve hundred due on the last shipment, they're not going to fill our new order."

"We got twelve hundred?"

"Not if we're going to satisfy the rest of our creditors, plus make this week's payroll."

"Shi—I mean, shoot. We're gonna have to finish one of these houses and sell it fast, Holly, or this whole thing's going right down the drain." Greg glanced around at the Sheridans' kitchen. Of the three houses Ecobay had under construction, this one, where Alex and Holly had been living for the past few months, was closest to being completed. It even had blue-and-cream patterned wallpaper on the kitchen walls and a full set of the latest electric appliances. This was hardly the time to suggest putting it up for sale, however.

Greg's visual survey of her home did not escape Holly's notice, but she chose to ignore it. She could deal with only one crisis at a time, and right now Alex was it. "What's left to do on the Pelican Loop house?" she asked, in an attempt to divert Greg's attention away from this one. "Haven't been over there in a couple of weeks."

Greg pulled on his leathery chin with its dark blond stubble. "Drywall's almost all taped and ready for painting. Cash flow as tight as it is, Alex and I had figured on doing the painting ourselves, saving the cost of a crew. But now . . . " Catching Holly's stricken look, he realized he'd mentioned Alex in the past tense, as though his partner wouldn't be back to help with the painting or anything else. He could have kicked himself for causing her more pain. The woman had enough to bear. "All I mean is, I'll get started on the painting myself," Greg said quietly. "When Alex gets back, he can catch up to me."

Holly bit down on her quivering lower lip. She poured herself another cup of coffee and sank down onto a kitchen chair. The baby was kicking harder now, battering her insides as though it was as anxious and upset as she was. She cradled her arms around her belly in an attempt to comfort her unborn child.

" . . . ready to install the stove and the dishwasher, soon as we finish with the floor tile," Greg was saying.

Holly's eyes glazed over as the contracter rambled on about the bathroom wallpaper and the brick facing for the prefab fireplace in the Pelican Loop house. She knew Greg's chatter was only an attempt to take her mind off Alex, to keep her from worrying, but all she wanted was to be left in peace. She didn't really give a damn how much work had to be finished on any of Ecobay's construction projects. She didn't give a damn about Ecobay. All she cared about, all she could think about, was Alex. . . .

"Thanks for stopping by, Greg," Holly said a few minutes later, as she abruptly cleared the cups and saucers from the table. Stacking them in the sink, she didn't offer to brew a second pot of coffee. "I shouldn't keep you from the job," she said, hoping he would take her hint and leave.

Greg inspected his work-scarred hands. A fresh plastic bandage circled his left thumb, where he'd mashed his thumbnail with a hammer last week, the latest of dozens of similar injuries over the years. "Is there somebody who can come over here and stay with you until—just until we hear?"

Holly ran her fingers through her hair, pulling at it absentmindedly. It was almost dry now, but still stick-straight and shapeless. She neither noticed nor cared. "I don't know many people around here," she said. "I've spent all my time with Alex or else working. I— I'll be all right by myself, really." The fact was, the Sheridans didn't have many neighbors, especially right now. Bodega Bay's plush houses were largely weekend and summer retreats for professionals from San Francisco and Sacramento. Many of the owners made their homes available for weekend rentals through local agencies, too, so Holly was never certain who might be in residence down the block or across the street. Now, in midwinter, most of the houses near hers were locked and empty.

"I don't think it's good for you to be alone just now," Greg told her.

"It's okay, Greg, don't worry about me. Please. I spent my whole life alone before I met—" Holly's throat closed and she couldn't force any more words out. After the wave of tears had passed, she took a deep breath and found her voice again. "I'm used to being alone, honest I am. And I've got plenty to do around here to keep myself busy. I've got those accounts payable to work on, a couple of loads of laundry in the hamper, my broker's exam to study for, the baby's bedroom." Holly knew she was probably protesting too much. She reached over and gently took hold of Greg's bandaged hand. "The truth is, I do appreciate your concern, but I really need to be alone right now."

The deep lines in the contractor's forehead eased. "At least let me take some of the pressure off you," he offered. He felt a quick stab of guilt; it wasn't seemly for him to be so relieved at the chance to leave Holly to her own resources. "Let me deal with the newspeople and the sheriff. You shouldn't have to talk to the public."

"I'd appreciate that, Greg, really I would. Thank you very much."

Greg pushed himself to his feet and stretched to his full six feet two. He wasn't sure whether it was more appropriate for him to give Holly a hug and a shoulder to cry on or to beat a fast retreat, which was what he really wanted to do. He settled for the middle ground, squeezing her hand self-consciously. "I'll just get on back to work then . . . if you'll promise to beep me if you need anything, anything at all." He pulled his hand away from hers and rested it on the black plastic telephone beeper hooked to his belt.

After Greg had left for one of the construction sites, Holly spent the rest of the morning fielding calls from old friends in Los Angeles who had heard last night's news report about Alex. She cut each call short, however, explaining that she didn't want to tie up the line in case the Civil Air Patrol was trying to reach her.

But that wasn't the only reason she didn't want to talk. It was just too hard, telling the same story over and over again. Besides, the calls reminded her far too much of the ones she'd received immediately after her mother's death—friends expressing regret and saying flattering things about a person who was gone forever. She didn't want to believe Alex wasn't coming back.

Between calls, Holly stared at Ecobay's account books, writing down a number here and a number there, until the figures began to blur before her eyes and she couldn't remember whether she was working on a pricing list or the accounts payable.

Her mind kept wandering away from her work, picturing Alex biting into that blood-rare steak she'd broiled for his dinner the night before last. Had his cholesterol level soared while he was flying south yesterday and given him another heart attack? If the meal she'd cooked had caused her husband's death, Holly doubted if she'd ever be able to live with her guilt.

If only she'd insisted he follow his doctor's orders, she chided herself. If only she hadn't indulged him.

Her thoughts grew darker. If she weren't pregnant, Holly told herself, she could have flown to Los Angeles with Alex yesterday, maybe managed to land the plane herself if he'd had a heart attack at the controls.

Or she could have ignored her own doctor's orders and taken that flight along with Alex.

If only she'd been with him yesterday, she felt certain, things would be very different right now.

If only, if only, if only. . . .

Chapter

8

At the Pelican Loop house, Greg Garrison dropped his paint roller back into the pan of Winter Wheat water-based paint and picked up a narrow paintbrush. Carefully dipping no more than a third of its bristles into the paint at a time, he transferred the creamy color to the seam that joined two perpendicular living room walls. When most of the brush's paint was on the wall-board, he dipped it again, repeating his motions until the seam blended invisibly into the rest of the wall's surface.

The telephone beeper sounded. Greg glanced down at the black box attached to his belt and was aware of a quick sense of relief as he read the number on the display. The number wasn't one he recognized, so it couldn't be Holly Sheridan calling him for help. It wasn't that Greg had anything against Alex's pregnant wife; he liked her as well as he liked any of his friends' wives. It was simply that he felt helpless around Holly, inadequate, as though he was lacking in manhood if he couldn't somehow fix things for her.

Greg had been trying to fix things for the women in his life ever since he was twelve and his father died. "You're the man of the house now, Greg," his mother had told him all those years ago. "I'm depending on you."

And depend on him she had. When the money ran out, Greg got a part-time job nights while he went to high school and later to trade school. To this day, he still supported his mother, who was spending her last years in a Sacramento nursing home. A penniless victim of Alzheimer's disease, old Neva Garrison no longer recognized her only child during his occasional visits. Still, Greg refused to let the state of California take over his mother's financial support. After all, he was the man of the house and she was depending on him.

"Hey, Lou, gotta return a call," Greg said, balancing the paintbrush on the edge of the paint can.

Lou Flint, one of the small crew of carpenters who'd worked on this job for the past two months, was in the kitchen, installing the last of the solid oak cupboards. Soon the cupboards would be ready for finishing with the special natural wood stain made of linseed oil, berries, and citrus peels that Holly Sheridan had tracked down somewhere. Greg and Alex had planned to do that job themselves too.

"Be right back," Greg said, heading out the door.

"No hurry," Lou called after him.

As soon as his boss had left the site, the carpenter put down his hammer and lit up a cigarette. He was relieved that it was only Greg Garrison on the job today. His other boss, Alex Sheridan, was far tougher to work for, a man with rigid rules, such as absolutely no smoking on the job site. Alex claimed Ecobay had a

pact with its future customers to keep all toxic sub-
stances away from the building materials, or some
such nonsense. Lou found that patently ridiculous.
How in hell would a buyer ever find out somebody'd
smoked a cigarette in this house while it was under
construction? Lou's compromise with the rules was
that he followed them part of the time—whenever Alex
was around. When he wasn't, Lou did as he damn well
pleased. Now he took a deep drag on his cigarette and
exhaled slowly.

As soon as Greg reached his pickup truck parked at
the curb, he unlocked the glove box, pulled out the cellular telephone he'd forgotten to bring into the house
that morning, and quickly punched in the phone number displayed on his beeper.

"Sheriff's office," a woman's voice answered.

Greg stiffened as he realized this was an official call.
"This is Greg Garrison," he said. "I'm returning a call
from this number."

"Oh, yes, Mr. Garrison. Hold on, please. Sheriff
Wills would like a word with you."

A moment later, a gravelly older man's voice came
on the line. "This is Sheriff Wills, Mr. Garrison.
Understand you're standing in for Alex Sheridan's
wife on this lost plane thing."

"That's right. Have you got news about Alex?"

"Can't say for sure just yet, but I did get a call from
the sheriff down in Monterey County that could mean
something. Fishing boat out of Monterey's spotted
what looks like pieces of a small aircraft in heavy surf
off Big Sur."

Greg's grip on the telephone loosened and he sank
down onto the driver's seat of the truck as he felt the
starch go out of his legs.

"You still there?" the sheriff asked.

"Yeah, I'm here," Greg replied with a sigh.

"Don't know for sure whether this's got anything to do with our man," Sheriff Wills went on. "Coast Guard's sending out a search plane, gonna try and see what they can find."

"Do they have reason to believe it's Alex's Cessna?" Greg wasn't sure he wanted to hear the answer.

"Like I said, it's gonna be awhile before we know anything for sure. Just thought I better let you folks know. You'll contact Mrs. Sheridan?"

Greg swallowed hard. He would rather eat broken glass for a week than relay the sheriff's message to Holly Sheridan, but he would do it. It was his duty. "I'll go see her right now," he said.

"Give you a call, soon's I hear anything more," Sheriff Wills said, ringing off.

Turning off his cellular phone, Greg sat silently in his truck for a few minutes, staring out at the rough, unfriendly sea beyond the hillside and picturing Alex's small plane diving into its frigid waters. When the images in his mind grew too vivid to bear, he shook his head to clear it and headed back to the house.

"Gotta take a run over to the Sheridan house," Greg told Lou Flint. His nose wrinkled as he recognized an unwelcome odor in the air.

Startled by his boss's sudden reappearance, Lou stubbed out his second cigarette in the stainless steel sink and picked up his hammer. "Sure, Greg, take your time," he said. "No need to rush back."

"And Lou," Greg said, the crease between his eyebrows deepening into a crevice.

"Yeah?"

"You want to hang onto this job, lose the goddamned cigarettes. You knew this was a clean site when you signed on. Alex's not being here doesn't change things." He owed his missing partner that much, Greg figured. The least he could do was keep faith with Alex's dream.

Feeling Lou Flint's resentful gaze boring into his back, Greg headed out the door to talk to Holly.

Chapter

9

Celia got behind the wheel of her gold Mercedes 350SL and started the engine. She was only going next door, but she'd decided that showing up at Pieter Vanderbilt's mansion on foot, standing in the street like a peddler until one of his servants opened the gate, might well diminish her status in the Dutch movie mogul's eyes. If there was anything Celia Sheridan had no intention of losing, it was status. Particularly now, when status seemed so integrally connected to money.

She backed the Mercedes out of her driveway and into the street and drove uphill for all of five hundred feet. Her own house was much more modest than Vanderbilt's place next door. Clearly visible from this tree-lined street high in the Bel Air hills, hers was a traditional Spanish-style two-story stucco house with four bedrooms and four bathrooms. Its thirty-five hundred square feet of living space were complemented by an attached triple garage, only a third of which she used.

The movie mogul's place, on the other hand, was a pseudo-Tara structure hidden from the street by hedges and iron gates. Vanderbilt had originally bought a much smaller house on the site, five years ago, and then knocked it down and built a more opulent one, complete with white stone pillars along the front and statues of naked Rubenesque women bordering the driveway. Celia had never seen more than glimpses of the new place, but she'd heard the main house alone was close to twelve thousand square feet. There was a pool house, too, one corner of which she could spot from her master bedroom, plus servants' quarters over the garage. Yet all that still wasn't enough to satisfy the greedy, eccentric Vanderbilt, a fact Celia intended to use to her own advantage.

Braking the Mercedes to a stop, Celia rolled down her window and announced herself to the black iron box set into a stone pillar attached to the Vanderbilt mansion's gate.

"Drive on through, please, Mrs. Sheridan," an English-accented male voice told her over the intercom. "You may park anywhere in the circular drive." The electric gates slowly began to open inward.

Celia did as she was told, smoothing the front of her periwinkle raw-silk tunic and slacks as she stepped out of the car. Acutely conscious of the impression she wanted to make, she had dressed with particular care this morning, down to her diamond rings, chunky gold bracelets, tanned cleavage, and violet contact lenses. She wanted to appear rich and pampered, like the very best of the crop of wealthy Bel Air matrons. She felt quite pleased with the result she'd achieved.

The last thing Celia wanted was for Pieter Vanderbilt to get the impression she was finally willing to sell him her house because she was desperate for money. If he thought she needed the money, Celia knew, he would offer her less. And she had absolutely no intention of settling for less. Less of anything.

The truth was, she didn't really have to sell her house at all, not with Alex's hefty life insurance money sure to be paid soon. Certainly the wrecked plane and Alex's body would be found before long. As soon as they were, she intended to file for her insurance benefits.

She didn't need the money from the house sale, but she also didn't plan to continue living in this house once she'd begun her new life. So Celia'd decided she might as well liquidate her Bel Air home now, while she had the chance. She would simply stash the money away someplace where she could get her hands on it in a hurry if she needed it.

"Well, Mrs. Sheridan, don't you look lovely this morning," Vanderbilt told her as he entered the claustrophobically overdecorated parlor where the English manservant had seated her.

Vanderbilt had kept his guest waiting precisely four minutes, long enough not to look overly eager but nowhere near long enough to be insulting. The movie director was a short man, pudgy-faced and nearly bald, with a gray-streaked brown goatee. Celia's research had told her he was only forty-six years old, younger than she was, but he was portly and didn't carry his age particularly well. She'd learned from the Hollywood trades that Vanderbilt had made half a dozen wildly successful movies, most of them action films starring internationally famous bodybuilders and all of them financed with large amounts of cash from unknown sources. The speculation among some of the neighbors here in Bel Air was that Vanderbilt used illegal funds laundered through offshore Dutch-owned banks to make his films.

Celia didn't give a damn where he got his money; she simply wanted a hunk of it for herself. "Good morning, Mr. Vanderbilt." Tucking a strand of blond hair behind one ear so that her dangling diamond earring became a little more visible, she smiled regally, as though her neighbor's compliment about her appearance was no more than her due.

"Call me Pieter, please," the little man said. Despite his pointedly casual attire—he was wearing tennis shorts, a white knit shirt that strained slightly across his midriff, and custom-made athletic shoes—he bent slightly at the waist for a moment, then straightened up rigidly.

Celia thought he probably would have clicked his heels if they hadn't been rubber. The man's physical movements seemed more appropriate to someone dressed in full military regalia than someone who looked like he'd just stepped off a tennis court.

"Certainly we can dispense with formality," Pieter Vanderbilt said. "We're neighbors, after all."

"For now we are." Celia cocked an eyebrow. She figured this oh-so-European routine must work well for the director in his business and personal dealings. Americans often treated wealthy Europeans like nobility, and Vanderbilt certainly had money—at least he did now. That hadn't always been the case. Celia'd learned he was born in poverty in Amsterdam a few years after World War II and had pulled himself out of the gutter with a combination of talent, an eye for public tastes, and sheer chutzpah.

"Please call me Celia, Pieter," she told him, smiling.

The manservant brought an ornate silver tray with a

pot of coffee, a pitcher of cream, and a bowl of little sugar cubes shaped like rosebuds. He served while Celia and Pieter made small talk and continued sizing each other up. Finally, when the manservant had left the room, Vanderbilt shot a less-than-subtle glance at the jeweled gold clock on the marble fireplace's mantel and broached the point of their meeting. "I'm really delighted to hear you've finally decided to sell me your house, Celia," he told her.

"*If* we can come to acceptable terms I'm willing to sell, Pieter." Celia set down her coffee cup and dabbed at the corners of her mouth with a blue linen napkin that had pink-and-white flowers hand-embroidered around its edges. "My mother is quite ill," she told him, "and I've decided to move back east to be closer to her for . . . for whatever time she has left." Celia lowered her eyes as though saddened by her mother's decline. In truth, her mother had been dead for many years, but she figured Vanderbilt had no way of knowing that.

"Ah, a dedicated daughter. How wonderful in our increasingly callous society."

Celia wondered whether Pieter Vanderbilt meant to mock her, but she decided to give him the benefit of the doubt. "I could lease my place out furnished while I'm gone, I suppose. Then I'd still have it in case I ever wanted to move back to L.A. But I thought, since you're so interested in annexing my property to your own . . . "

Vanderbilt pulled on his goatee. "The timing is good for me just now," he said, as though it might not be in a month or two. "My sister is coming over from Holland next month with her three small children. It would be convenient to have a more private place for them to stay." He gestured around the oval room at his fussy satin brocade and gold-painted hand-carved furniture, the gilded lamps modeled on those in the Palais de Versailles, and the gaudy paintings of winged cherubs flitting through the air over the heads of naked maidens with their eyes demurely cast down. "I have plenty of room for visitors in my own home, of course," he said, "but privacy is always so much nicer, don't you think?"

Celia nodded her agreement. "I'll tell you one thing up front: I'm interested in selling only if it can be done within the next thirty days," she said. "I don't want to have to come back from the East Coast to settle things. Also, because I'm moving out of the area, I might consider selling my furniture along with the house." As her gaze followed Vanderbilt's gesture around the crowded room, she couldn't help thinking it looked like something out of an old Vincent Price film. But letting her host guess that she found his home hideous would hardly help her cause, so she keep her disapproval well hidden. Celia Sheridan had had plenty of practice at keeping her thoughts and opinions well hidden. "My furnishings are not in the same—er, style as what you have here," she told him, "but they're appropriate for what is really a much different house. My place, as you know, is an authentic early California mission-style home."

Pieter Vanderbilt indicated that he could fix that easily enough, given time and money. "I'll have my architect see what he can do with it, as soon as my sister and her family have returned to Holland. If he doesn't think it can be remodeled to fit with the rest of my estate, I can always knock it down and start over, the way I did with this place." Celia had to fight hard against an impulse to cringe, if not to go running from the room in horror. "In the meantime"—Vanderbilt threw her a crumb—"I'm sure my sister will find your house and furniture quite serviceable."

Celia couldn't bear to think about the house she'd fought so hard for in her divorce ending up transformed into a monument to bad taste like this one, even if she was selling out. So she didn't. She simply mentally raised her bottom-line price another twenty-five thousand to compensate herself for future mental distress. "Why don't we get down to business, Pieter," she said. "I'm sure you have a price in mind."

"I'm sure you do too, my dear."

Celia raised her chin. "Of course I do, but I want to hear yours first."

Vanderbilt laughed indulgently. "So, a pretty lady like you has a head for business also."

Celia wasn't flattered. "My father taught me to handle money when I was just a little girl. And how not to let people take advantage of me because of my sex," she said, inventing a wise parent who might have done just that. In truth, the only thing any of her deserting fathers had taught her was that men could never be trusted to give women a fair deal. That was one lesson she'd learned well.

Vanderbilt's eyes twinkled with amusement. "I can tell when I've been beaten," he said, turning his palms upward. "I was thinking somewhere in the neighborhood of eight hundred thousand."

"Surely not including all of my furniture?" Celia asked, trying to look mildly offended. Secretly, she was immensely pleased; in today's tough real estate market, she'd have been willing to settle for seven-fifty.

In the end, they settled on a price of eight hundred fifty-five thousand dollars. Pieter Vanderbilt agreed to assume Celia's mortgage in the amount of slightly more than a hundred and fifty thousand dollars and to pay the difference in cash upon closing.

"Not literally in cash," Celia warned the director, picturing federal drug agents freezing her bank accounts and confiscating hundreds of thousands of dollars in illicit funds. "At closing, I'll expect a cashier's check drawn on a United States bank for the balance of the sale."

Vanderbilt waved his hand as if to dismiss his neighbor's concern. "No problem whatsoever, my friend. I'll have my attorney draw up the papers for you to sign tomorrow."

Celia forced herself to wait until she was in the driver's seat of the Mercedes and heading back downhill before she broke into a broad grin. With what Vanderbilt was paying for the house and the money from Alex's life insurance policy, she would soon have almost a million dollars in the bank.

Even for a woman with Celia Sheridan's tastes, a million dollars in cash was enough to start a completely new life.

Chapter

10

Holly carefully measured a strip of imported cotton wallpaper, sliced it off the roll with a single-edge razor blade, and dipped it in the bathtub, which she'd filled with lukewarm water. When the wallpaper had soaked for the specified period of time, she folded it in two with the good side out so that the prepasted backing could cure, then laid it flat on the bathroom floor. This wallpaper, which she and Alex had chosen for the baby's bedroom, was bright and whimsical, picturing a gathering of golden lions, silvery elephants, orange-and-black-striped tigers, rust-brown monkeys, and black-and-white-striped zebras. A horizontal strip of this jungle design, hung along the top edge of the walls adjacent to the ceiling, would form a border of cheerful color and action for the baby to see from the crib.

The previous day, Holly had spent ten hours papering the lower portion of the nursery's walls with a coordinating vertical-striped pattern, a combination of gold, orange, rust, and gray against a creamy white background. With her big belly getting in the way, the job had taken twice as long as it should have, but she'd refused to quit until it was done. After she finished adding the jungle animal border, the bedroom would need only the soft gray cotton carpeting now stored in rolls in the garage to be ready for the baby's arrival.

Holly's lower back ached painfully and her sore arms and shoulders fiercely protested the hard physical work she was forcing herself to do, but she kept at it. It was as though exhausting herself physically was the only way she could find relief from the malignant pain growing in her mind.

It had been two days since Greg had come to tell her about the small airplane that had crashed off Big Sur. Two days of endless waiting and agonizing about whether the doomed aircraft was Alex's Cessna, about whether he could possibly have survived. Two days of pushing her body to its physical limits and of constant prayers—for Alex's survival, for the baby's health, and for the strength to make it through these endless days.

Now, however, Holly felt herself nearing complete exhaustion. She couldn't take much more of not knowing whether the husband she loved so much was dead or alive. Her situation gave her a strong feeling of sisterhood and compassion for all the women whose husbands were missing in action in wartime or lost on marine expeditions. How could they stand years of uncertainty?

Carrying the wet strip of wallpaper, Holly dragged herself back into the nursery and slowly climbed the stepladder. The phone rang once, then a second time.

She was tempted to let the machine answer the call, but what if it was Alex trying to reach her? She draped the sticky strip of wallpaper across the top of the stepladder and climbed down again, barely managing to catch the telephone on the fourth ring.

"Hello?" Holly's voice revealed her exhaustion.

The line clicked once and went dead.

She swore under her breath and felt the sting of angry tears come to her eyes. There had been half a dozen calls like this one in the past three days, and they pushed her patience to its limits. Surely people must know she was waiting to hear news of her missing husband. How could anyone be so cruel as to keep calling her, tying up her line, only to hang up when she answered?

Unless it was Alex trying to call, she told herself, hoping against hope: Alex trying to call and something going wrong with the connection each time. Or maybe it was her younger sister, Heather, trying to reach her from New Zealand. Heather had married a Kiwi six years ago and emigrated to Wellington, where her husband's family owned a chain of stationery stores. Holly and Heather weren't particularly close anymore, but Holly had telephoned to tell her sister about Alex's disappearance a couple of days ago. Maybe Heather was calling to offer her sister support.

Yet, with today's modern communications technology, Holly knew it was highly unlikely that either Alex or Heather would be unable to get through to her for three full days. More likely, these hang-ups were just somebody playing a cruel joke.

The phone at the Sheridan house had been ringing a lot since Alex's disappearance. Some calls were well-intended, from Southern California friends who wanted news, sent their best wishes, even offered Holly a place to live until the baby was born if she could manage the trip to Los Angeles. Determined to stay here in case Alex came home again, she'd turned down all those generous offers. Even if Alex never returned, she had a business to run here, and the last thing she wanted was to make a grueling five-hundred-mile trip, only to feel she was imposing once she'd moved into someone else's home.

There were other calls too, some that Holly bitterly resented. These came from people she categorized as vultures—an ambitious funeral director soliciting her business, a Los Angeles–based TV talk show producer who wanted her to appear on a show about women whose spouses had disappeared, a handful of creditors obviously worried about how Alex's unexplained absence might impact on Ecobay's payment of their bills. Holly herself had slammed down the telephone receiver in response to two of these particular calls.

She was back on the stepladder, leaning precariously off to one side as she brushed the sticky wallpaper border into place, when the doorbell rang. "Great timing," she said under her breath, feeling irritated.

"Be right there!" She yelled as loud as she could, hoping that whoever was ringing the bell would hear her through the closed door and windows and wait. It took several more minutes before she was able to anchor the wallpaper strip securely enough that it wouldn't slip down the wall as soon as she left it.

"There," she said, as she laid down her brush and climbed down the ladder. "Don't you dare move!"

Wiping her paste-covered hands against the old paint-spattered shirt of Alex's that she'd put on this morning, she hurried to answer the door. Greg Garrison was standing outside on the steps with a hang-dog look on his face. He was clean-shaven and dressed in crisp khakis and a light blue oxford-cloth shirt under a tan corduroy jacket. Obviously he had not come straight from the construction site.

Holly's heart plummeted as she took in the significance of Greg's appearance. "What's happened?" she asked, dreading his answer.

"Can't say for sure yet, but the Coast Guard's found some more pieces of the plane that went down near Big Sur. It—I'm really sorry, Holly, but there was a man's body in the cockpit." Greg looked at his shoes, unable to bear watching Holly's last shred of hope dissolve before his eyes. "They think it's probably Alex."

Holly's legs suddenly gave way and she felt herself sinking. As her vision blurred, Greg stepped across the threshold and grabbed her before she hit the floor. He half carried and half dragged her into the living room and set her down on the sofa.

Greg waited until Holly seemed fully alert again and then went into the kitchen and brought her a glass of water before telling her about his plan. "I've already talked to Clarence Pomoroy out at the airstrip," he explained. "He says I can borrow his plane to fly down to Monterey and take a look."

"Take a look? You mean at the wreckage? Or the . . . the body?"

"Somebody's got to identify him, Holly, and you certainly can't do it, not in your condition."

"But I'm Alex's wife." She took a small sip of the water, felt her sense of control begin to return, and handed the glass back to Greg. "I should be the one."

All her life, Holly had been the strong one, the person who could cope with virtually anything. The daughter who, at age eleven, had taken over running the household after Heather came down with rheumatic fever and required their mother's constant attention. The friend who talked a lonely neighbor whose husband had left her out of committing suicide. The editor who never missed a deadline at *Stately Homes*, even when half her staff was out sick with the flu.

The one thing Holly had never been good at was accepting help from other people. She'd always been extremely tolerant of weakness—in everyone but herself. Holly Sheridan was nearly incapable of asking anyone for help or of accepting it when it was offered to her. The thing she hated most in the world was feeling weak or beholden to others. Only with Alex had she been able to lower her emotional barriers, to let herself be vulnerable. "I should identify the body," she said once more. "I'm Alex's wife."

"You're also better than eight months pregnant and your doctor said you weren't to fly until after the baby comes." The woman Greg saw sitting next to him was extremely stubborn, there was no mistaking that, but she also seemed close to breaking down. Her hair was disheveled, she wore no makeup, the man's shirt she had on was paint-stained and covered with wallpaper paste. She even had some of the sticky stuff smeared across her left cheek and a blob sticking to her right eyebrow.

But worst of all, her green eyes held a fear so primitive it was unlike anything Greg had ever seen before. "Let me call somebody to come and stay with you while you wait," he said, setting the water glass on the coffee table.

"No," Holly said. "Absolutely not. I don't want anybody here." She began scratching a hunk of dried wallpaper paste off her shirt. "I don't know anybody anyway," she said. "I should really be doing this myself, Greg. I should be the one to look at the—at the body."

"No way. You're going to have to let me do this much for you," Greg insisted. "There's no possible way you can go down there yourself. Your job now is to take care of yourself and of your baby. I'll fly down and find out if it's Alex. Then I'll come back here, just as soon as I can."

Holly felt caught. She knew Greg was right, but she could hardly stand it. Her thoughts racing, she stared out the big picture window, across the golf course at a sea of whitecaps. Today, the bay was a frigid gray, almost black in spots, and the sun was hidden by a thick cloud cover that threatened rain. She shivered involuntarily, thinking of Alex in that freezing water.

"I'll be back as quickly as I can," Greg reassured her, patting her shoulder gently. He wasn't comfortable leaving this woman alone here, but what was the alternative? He certainly couldn't take Holly Sheridan in the plane with him, not with her baby due so soon. And somebody had to go look at that body; somebody had to end this thing once and for all. After he and Holly knew whether Alex was dead or alive, they could move forward, they could make plans. Certainly this state of suspense had to be far worse than knowing the truth, however terrible it might be.

"All right," Holly said, with a sigh of resignation, "I'll wait here." Hugging herself for warmth, she stared straight ahead at the sea. "And Greg?"

"Yes?"

"Thank you."

Holly glanced at Greg only briefly as he went out the front door and headed for the airstrip up the highway. Then she returned her hypnotic gaze to the dark view out her window. It was nothing like the vivid gold and blue of the sky and sea on that morning she'd stood at the edge of the same airstrip, watching the white speck that was Alex's Cessna disappear over the horizon.

Was it possible that was only four short days ago?

11

Celia peered into the round mirror the saleswoman placed on the counter in front of her. "I don't know," she said. "This color seems awfully harsh on me, doesn't it?" She frowned at the reflected image of her pale oval face, which was now surrounded by straight, shoulder-length, jet-black hair.

The geriatric saleswoman—Maisie, according to her name tag—nodded agreement. "Problem is, you're so fair-skinned, dear. You want my opinion, black's way too much contrast for a girl with your light complexion—unless maybe you're willing to go with a darker makeup. You going for a more exotic look, dear, that the idea?"

Celia's idea was to change her appearance drastically, so Holly Sheridan would never recognize her, just in case Alex's new wife had seen photographs of her predecessor. But Celia certainly wasn't going to confess that to this wrinkled and bent Cinema Wigs clerk, who called everyone "dear" and referred to women in their forties as "girls."

Instead, Celia told her, "I'm auditioning for a

commercial, and they're looking for a brunette. I always try to look the part when I audition. Can't leave much to the imagination anymore, not if you want the part."

"Some of these casting people don't seem to *have* much good old imagination these days, you ask me." Little ash-blond Maisie—Celia felt certain the clerk's own coiffure was from the shop's vast supply of wigs—moved behind the counter and pulled open a drawer. For the past thirty-five years, Maisie had worked here at this small West Hollywood wig shop, supplying wigs and hairpieces to the major movie and television studios, as well as to people who'd lost their own hair for one reason or another. She knew her stock well. "Here's a beauty," she said, pulling a reddish-brown number out of the drawer. "One hundred percent human hair from Taiwan, all hand tied. These red tones might help brighten up your face. Here, dear, try it on, see how you look in it."

Celia did as she was told and had to admit that the result was far more flattering. The dark auburn wig wasn't exactly natural-looking, but she didn't look nearly as washed out as she had in the black one. The question was, did she look different enough from the old Celia Sheridan? She'd always worn her blond hair smooth—in a loose side-parted pageboy, pinned up in a French twist, or tied into a low chignon or ponytail. This wig was a much darker color than her own hair, but its smooth style was quite similar.

"How about something in this same color, only maybe curlier?" she asked.

"Sure," Maisie said, anxious to please as always. "We got plenty of curly ones. Give you a whole new look, dear. If that casting director's only seen your composites, he's not gonna recognize you."

Celia tried on three more wigs before settling on one with a thick mass of shoulder-length dark auburn curls. It made her look like a country western singer or a truck stop waitress, she thought, amused by the reflected image. With some cheap new clothes from someplace women with neither her taste nor her money shopped, something synthetic in black or navy or dark green instead of the springtime colors she usually wore, even good old Buffy wouldn't recognize her. Not that Celia intended to let her best friend see her looking like this.

"I'll take this one," she decided, removing the curly wig.

Celia paid three hundred ten dollars plus tax in cash for it. As she left the shop, Maisie chirped happily at her. "Good luck with that audition, dear. Hope you get the part."

Celia's next stop was at a nearby Thrifty Drug, where she bought a dark auburn eyebrow pencil and a gold metal compact filled with face powder two shades darker than her own skin. Sitting outside in the store's parking lot, she tilted the rearview mirror of the Mercedes until she could see her reflection and carefully applied the makeup. Finally, she took the new wig out of its box and put it on, meticulously tucking each blond strand underneath its snug cap.

As she surveyed the results of her efforts in the mirror, she was pleased. "Hello there, Pat," she whispered to her reflected image, trying on the old name for size.

Half an hour later, Celia was at a used car lot on Santa Monica Boulevard in West Los Angeles, buying a two-year-old brown Buick station wagon, the kind of utilitarian vehicle so common on American highways that it wouldn't stand out in traffic. She handed the salesman her personal check for ten percent of the purchase price and told him, "I'll be back with a certified check for the rest in the morning. I'll expect the car to be checked out and ready to go by then."

"We'd be happy to arrange financing for you, Mrs. Sheridan," he said, reading her name off the check. "Approval only takes about twenty minutes if you have a major credit card, and you can take the car with you today if you want." He didn't mention the fact that selling Celia financing for the station wagon would bring him an additional commission on the sale.

Celia held up her hand in protest. "My name is Patterson now, not Sheridan. I'm going back to my maiden name, now my divorce from that sonofa—from my husband is final. I want the car titled in the name of C. J. Patterson. And I don't want financing."

"Well, fine, then Mrs.—er, Ms. Patterson. It's been a real pleasure doing business with you."

"Eleven o'clock," Celia told him, allowing herself time in the morning to go to the bank for the check, then take a cab back here to the car dealership to pick up the car. "I want the paperwork ready to sign and the car ready to drive when I get here. Understand?"

"No problem." The salesman gave her an ingratiating smile.

Celia strolled back to her Mercedes, which she'd parked around the corner, out of sight. After she slipped behind the steering wheel, she pulled off her wig and put it back into the round Cinema Wigs box before driving home to Bel Air.

As she drove through rush-hour traffic, she began adding to her mental list of things she had to do before she began a much longer drive—to Northern California.

12

It took Greg Garrison five hours to fly to Monterey, go to the county coroner's office to identify the body that had been found in the wreckage of the small plane, and return to the Bodega Bay airstrip. The sun had already disappeared behind the thick cloud bank, and it was rapidly growing dark by the time he reached the Sheridan house.

As he knocked on the front door of the house, it swung open, so Greg let himself in. "Holly!" he called, closing the door behind him as he stepped into the tiled entryway. "Holly, it's me, Greg. I'm back." The house was cold; obviously Holly had not bothered to turn up the furnace as the afternoon's heat began to dissipate.

A few steps farther inside, Greg spotted her—sitting alone on the sofa, just as he'd left her well before lunchtime. Holly Sheridan's arms were wrapped around herself for warmth as she stared outside at the angry, churning Pacific.

As Greg entered the living room, she turned her

head in his direction, an expression of sheer agony on her pale face. The moment she spotted the pitying look in his eyes, Holly knew her husband was dead.

She stiffened, and her fingernails dug deeply into her upper arms. She didn't notice the pain. "Did he have another heart attack?" she asked, in a small, frightened voice.

Greg shook his head. "Don't know yet. I'm afraid there has to be an autopsy," he explained, sitting down on the sofa next to Holly. "They should know more by tomorrow afternoon." He watched as Holly's face crumbled. "It—it might have been the plane, Holly. Something could've gone wrong with the Cessna. The FAA will do an investigation, but it's going to take a few weeks before we'll know anything."

Holly bit down on her lower lip until she tasted blood. Slowly, her body began to shake all over. Somewhere deep inside herself, she'd known this moment was coming. Yet that made it no easier. Alex was dead. She would never get over that terrible blow.

Feeling incompetent to handle the emotional situation, Greg, in his tentative way, tried to reach out to the grieving woman. "They said Alex didn't suffer long," he told her, laying his work-worn hand awkwardly on her trembling shoulder. He could think of nothing more comforting to say.

Holly twisted away from his touch, buried her face in her hands, and broke into gut-wrenching sobs.

Greg turned his face away, uneasy about being a witness to this woman's deep, private grief. Yet leaving her alone in this cold, dark house seemed wrong. Finally, he rose, turned up the thermostat until he heard the furnace kick in, and went into the bedroom to find a blanket. When he returned to the living room, he gently wrapped a soft blue-and-white quilt around Holly's shoulders.

By that time Holly Sheridan was physically exhausted and her sobs had faded to a faint whimper, the sea outside the window was no longer visible through the blackness of the night.

Chapter

13

Celia smiled at her reflection in the glass door of
Bodega Bay's Bayside Realty as she pushed it open.
The smile was not because she looked particularly
good—in her opinion, she'd seldom looked worse—but
because she now bore so little resemblance to the old
Celia Sheridan. She was wearing the dark wig she'd
bought in West Hollywood, with a slightly baggy black
pants suit she'd found on sale for sixty-nine dollars at
Sears in Santa Monica. When she dressed this morning,
she'd resisted a strong temptation to brighten up the
drab outfit with a colorful scarf at the neck, telling herself that new widows shouldn't be concerned with how
they look.

It had been four days now since the *Los Angeles
Times* had run Alex's brief obituary notice, causing
Celia to breathe a long sigh of relief. The same day the
obit appeared, she'd filed for the life insurance benefits
that had been part of the divorce settlement. The face
value of Alex's policy, two hundred fifty thousand dollars, would be paid as soon as Celia's lawyer obtained

a copy of Alex's death certificate and forwarded it to the insurance company. As far as Celia was concerned, that quarter of a million was money in the bank.

Now she was taking the next step in her plan, a move she had to make well before that bitch Alex had married gave birth.

Celia entered the small real estate office and introduced herself to its sole occupant, a woman who was sitting at one of the three desks working at a computer terminal. "Hello, I'm Pat Patterson," Celia announced. "I called earlier about renting a house in the area."

"Oh, yes, Mrs. Patterson, I took your call." The woman rose and thrust out a hand. "I'm Margaret Melby," she said, shaking Celia's hand. Margaret Melby was a bleached blonde whose navy skirt pulled around her ample hips. At thirty-nine, she was already a grandmother twice over. She'd started a new career in real estate three years ago to help with the family bills. "Sit down a minute, Mrs. Patterson," she said, "and I'll tell you what we've got."

Celia did as she was told. "Call me Pat, please, Margaret."

"After you called, Pat, I printed out a list of houses that should be available for longer leases," Margaret said. "There's not as many to choose from as for the weekend rentals, but I'm sure we can find you something. You know how it is—some people don't like to let their houses go for more than a week or two at a time."

Celia frowned. "I'm definitely going to need a place for a month or more. There's been so much upheaval in my life lately." She cast her glance downward and let her chin tremble just slightly. "I don't remember if I told you on the phone, but my husband—I'm a new widow."

Margaret Melby nodded sympathetically. "That's what you said. I'm very sorry."

"Maybe it sounds strange," Celia said, "but I really need some time to myself just now. I don't know how long—a month maybe, three or four at the most. You know, a chance to get away from people, think about what I want to do with the rest of my life. Back home . . . well, it seems like there's always somebody trying to give me advice about something, trying to tell me what to do."

"Well, you're not going to have people bothering you around here," Margaret promised, opening a map of the region and spreading it flat on the desk. She picked up her computer printout of houses for rent. "Winter's our slow season in Bodega Bay, and most of these homes are empty, so you're in luck. You've got a much better chance of finding the kind of place you want this time of year."

The two women discussed the type of house Celia was seeking; she kept her requirements as flexible as possible, being careful not to allude to her real agenda— renting a house located as close as possible to Alex's.

"As long as everything is furnished, it doesn't matter whether the house has two bedrooms or three or even four," Celia said. "Basically, I just want it to have the right vibes."

Margaret raised an eyebrow.

"What I mean is, I'll know the right house when I see it," Celia explained. "It'll *feel* right to me, no matter how big it is."

"Vibes. I see. Okay, then." The saleswoman began to mark the available properties on the map. "Right here on Heron Drive I have an adorable little house that might be just right. Two bedrooms, two baths. Backs up to the golf course, and it has a wonderful ocean view. Rents for two fifty for a weekend, seven fifty for a week. The owner's out of the country for a couple of months, and I think he'd probably be willing to rent it on a monthly basis for somewhere around twenty-five hundred, maybe a little less." Margaret's voice was full of enthusiasm.

Studying the upside-down map, Celia listened with one ear as the rental agent extolled the virtues of more than a dozen other houses on the list. Finally she spotted Sandpiper Circle, the street whose name was printed on Alex's alimony checks. It was a cul-de-sac in what was called the south section of the Bodega Harbour golf course and housing development.

"Do you have anything in this section?" Celia asked, circling the area with her finger. "Looks like it might be more private over here."

Margaret checked her list. "We've got two places in that section that might work for you. One's on Owl Court. You can get it for twenty-eight hundred a month." She placed another red X on the map to mark the house's location. "It's a two-story, with two large bedrooms and a den, partial ocean view. Then there's a three-bedroom right here."

Celia caught her breath as Margaret placed another red X on the map, right on Sandpiper Circle. "How much?" she asked, trying to remain cool.

Margaret chewed on her pen as she ran her finger down her list of houses and their corresponding rents. "Three hundred for the weekend, nine hundred for a week," she said. "Monthly rental's not specified here, but my guess is it would go for around three thousand, thirty-two hundred, tops."

"Why is it priced so high?" Celia asked. She didn't

really care, but she didn't want to look too eager. She wanted Margaret Melby to think she'd talked her into renting this house.

Margaret searched in a file drawer for a few minutes. When she'd located the right file folder, she pulled it out and removed some photographs. "Looks like it's the view, mainly," she explained as she inspected the pictures. "This house is perched on the edge of a ravine; the way it's built, you get a full ocean view from all the bedrooms, as well as from the living room and family room. It's big, too, over twenty-eight hundred square feet."

Celia leaned forward in her chair. "I'd like to see these four to start with," she said, indicating houses of varying sizes on Loon Court, Heron Drive, Condor Court, and Sandpiper Circle. She already knew which one she would take, but in order to obscure her true intentions, she had to look at more than one. The last thing she wanted to do was raise Margaret Melby's suspicions.

Because it was farthest from the real estate office, the Sandpiper Circle house was the last one Margaret took Celia to see. Celia vetoed the first house outright. "I don't like that narrow little staircase to the master bedroom," she said, wrinkling her nose. "Gives me claustrophobia."

The second house had been nixed because Celia disliked the idea that golfers playing the course behind it might be able to see into the house. "Not my idea of privacy, to have a bunch of men in plaid pants staring into my bedroom at six in the morning," she said peevishly.

By the third house, Celia had decided not to be quite so blatantly negative. "This one's not bad," she admitted. "It might work for me, even if it does have a pink kitchen. But I'd like to see the one on the ravine before I make a final decision."

Now the two women were in Margaret's Cadillac, pulling into quiet, deserted Sandpiper Court. Celia looked around quickly, tensing as she spotted number twelve—the address printed on Alex's checks. So this was where he'd been living. It was a single-level ranch-style house on the right side of the cul-de-sac.

Number twelve appeared to be locked up tight. Was Alex's knocked-up whore hiding behind those walls? Celia wondered, feeling a sharp wave of bitterness course through her. But one thing she noticed about Alex's house made her feel much better. In the drive-way sat four identical cardboard cartons with the name of a ceramic tile company stamped on the outside, as well as two large open boxes filled with castoff building debris. There was not a shred of landscaping around number twelve, either, and it had no light fixture above the front steps. Celia could see red and black wires sticking out of a round hole to the upper right of the front door, precisely where a porch light belonged.

It was with a deep sense of justice that she realized the house Holly Sheridan was living in was still under construction. Served the bitch right, Celia thought. If she had anything to say about it, that house would never be finished . . . not during Holly Sheridan's life-time, anyway.

"What do you think, Pat?" Margaret was asking.

Celia was staring openly at the unfinished gray house, paying no attention to the real estate woman's pitch. "Huh?" she said finally, realizing that Margaret expected some kind of answer from her. "Sorry, didn't hear what you said."

"I said this is it, number seventeen, the big brown house. I asked whether you think it's too big for you. If you do, we could skip looking at it and see a few of the others while we still have some daylight."

"No, no, I'd like to see the inside," Celia said, "as long as we're here."

The interior of number seventeen was attractive, Celia thought, for such a modern house. Her own taste ran more to the traditional. This house had none of the elegant touches of her classic Spanish-colonial home in Bel Air, but she knew she had to forget about that house. She wouldn't own it much longer anyway. She'd authorized her attorney to handle the closing of the sale to Pieter Vanderbilt. By the end of next week, the Bel Air house would be Vanderbilt's property, not Celia's. All she could do now was try not to think about what might happen to it after that.

"This view is wonderful," Celia said, walking to the living room picture window. She meant it. The room had sliding glass doors opening onto a wide balcony that ran the entire width of the back of the house. The view from here was private, too—a wide expanse of ravine and grassland that swept two thousand feet to the sea beyond. She could see the full curve of the bay from here, with its tiny fishing harbor and Bodega Head on the northern edge. "Okay if I take a look out here?" Celia asked, unlocking the glass door and sliding it open without waiting for Margaret's permission.

Out on the deck, it was windy and cold, typical of Bodega Bay on a winter afternoon. Celia walked the length of the wooden balcony. Two large bedrooms, in addition to the living room, had sliding glass doors opening onto this deck, while the third bedroom was located around the south side of the house. Directly below the deck was a small brick patio, reached from the family room on the lower level. At the edge of the property, which extended only a few feet beyond the patio, was a downhill slope that dropped steeply into the ravine.

"I'd like to see the kitchen," Celia said, coming inside again. She was shivering in her thin pants suit. As a longtime resident of Los Angeles, she'd grown unused to chilly winds like the ones that plagued Bodega Bay on a daily basis. She would have to buy some warmer clothes to wear during the next few weeks. After that, she could go back to being Celia Sheridan, wearing her own beautiful, expensive clothes, wherever she decided to live. It definitely would not be here.

"This house has all the modern conveniences," Margaret told her, pointing out the microwave, the trash compactor, the instant-hot-water spigot on the sink, the seamless sand-colored Corian countertops.

Celia poked around the place for half an hour— checking to see that dishes and linens were supplied as promised, testing the firmness of the king-size bed in the master bedroom, checking the water pressure in all three bathrooms, checking the view as she sat on the living room sofa and at the dining room table, turning the two television sets on and off—all the while pretending to let Margaret talk her into renting this place.

"The house does have a good feeling about it," Celia said finally. She sat down at the kitchen table and opened her purse, removing a red checkbook and a pen. "I'll take it. How large a deposit do you need?"

"I'll need the first month's rent and an equal amount as a damage deposit," Margaret told her. "But since I'm not sure of the exact monthly rent, why don't you just give me a check for an even thousand now? You can give me the rest tomorrow, after I talk with the owners."

Celia made out a check for a thousand dollars, payable to Bayside Realty. "Sorry, this is a new account," she explained as she handed Margaret the check. "My checks don't have my name printed on them yet." Celia had opened a checking account in the name of C. J. Patterson at a Santa Rosa bank this morning, using her birth certificate as identification and depositing eight thousand dollars in cash. "Go ahead and call the bank to make sure it's good, if you want to," she offered.

Margaret shrugged off the suggestion. "I'll have the lease agreement ready first thing in the morning," she said, folding the check and attaching it to the list of rental properties on her clipboard. "Providing I can reach the owners tonight, that is. I'll get a cleaning crew in here tomorrow afternoon, too, so you can probably move in on Friday, if that's okay with you."

Celia nodded. "The sooner the better. My room at the Lodge is nice enough, but"—she made a sour face—"you know how it is. It's still a hotel, not a real home."

As Margaret drove her back to the Bayside Realty office where she'd left the Buick station wagon, Celia couldn't help feeling extraordinarily pleased with herself. By Friday, she would be in a perfect position to get to know Holly Sheridan.

Holly measured six scoops of ground decaf into the unbleached paper coffee filter and switched the coffeemaker on. She hadn't felt like having company lately; these past few mornings, she'd had all she could do to get out of bed and force herself through the day. But this morning, she felt almost eager to talk to the inspector from the Federal Aviation Agency, who was due at the house in less than fifteen minutes.

Holly was optimistic that the FAA man would be able to answer the many questions that haunted her days and nights, that he would finally tell her what had happened to Alex.

She'd received the Monterey County coroner's preliminary autopsy report in yesterday's mail, but it revealed nothing she hadn't already learned from Greg. In its dry, scientific language, the coroner's report said that Alex had died from injuries to his head and neck that were "sustained in the crash," not from a heart attack—exactly what Greg had told her. According to the letter, however, final toxicological reports on "tissue and fluid samples taken during the autopsy" would take another one to two weeks, whatever good they would do. Nothing told her why her husband was dead.

Reading the coroner's letter had upset Holly badly. It hurt to think of Alex as a collection of mutilated body parts and tissue samples under the coroner's knife. Alexander Sheridan had been her husband, the man she loved, the father of the child she was carrying—not some kind of specimen for scientists to dissect and study. She realized that everyone who reads an autopsy report on a family member must feel the way she did, but that didn't make it any easier.

The hardest thing for Holly to accept after she'd forced herself to read the coroner's report from beginning to end was that she'd learned nothing new. Perhaps today's meeting with the FAA man would be different. Perhaps today she would finally find out why Alex's Cessna had failed him. Then she could begin to get on with the rest of her life.

When the coffeemaker had stopped making its gurgling sounds, Holly took two cups and saucers from the kitchen cupboard and set them on the counter next to the glass coffeepot. She felt a little embarrassed that all she had to offer the inspector was a cup of coffee. Other than canned and frozen foods and a few fresh vegetables, she had virtually nothing in the house to offer him, not so much as a stale cookie. Coffee would have to suffice.

The doorbell rang precisely at ten o'clock. Holly took this as a positive sign, an indication that FAA inspector Fred Pruitt was a prompt and efficient man. As she ushered him inside, the inspector introduced himself and explained that he'd been assigned to investigate Alex's case.

"Can you tell me why my husband's plane went down?" Holly asked, as soon as they were seated in the living room, each holding a cup of her steaming coffee. She perched nervously on the edge of the sofa while Pruitt selected a chair facing her.

Fred Pruitt was in his mid-thirties, a tall thin man in a shiny black suit who seemed to be constantly in motion, even while seated. As he stirred his coffee, he twirled his spoon impatiently between his fingers. When at last he rested the spoon on the saucer and set the coffee down, he began doodling in his notebook. Holly noticed that his feet shuffled back and forth silently on the soft gray cotton carpet, too, raising little balls of fuzz and reminding her that she hadn't vacuumed in more than two weeks. Her mother would have said Fred Pruitt had ants in his pants.

"I wish I could tell you exactly what happened to your husband, Mrs. Sheridan," Pruitt told her, "but my job is simply to help gather the facts and forward them to Washington. The experts there will put all the pieces of the puzzle together and come up with a final conclusion about what caused the accident."

Holly felt her heart plummet as she realized that there was more waiting in store for her. "How long is all that going to take?" she asked, certain she would not like the answer.

"Anywhere from a couple of weeks to several months. But you can help us hurry things along."

"Me? How? I've only flown in the Cessna a few times, and not recently. Not for two or three months, anyway. I don't know the first thing about airplane mechanics."

Pruitt continued to doodle in his notebook, sketching a seagull in flight with his mechanical pencil while simultaneously sizing up Holly and her house. "The condition of the airplane isn't what I want to talk to you about, Mrs. Sheridan," he said. "We've got aviation experts to handle that part of the investigation. They'll interview the airstrip owner and the mechanic and reconstruct as much of the aircraft as possible from the parts that have been recovered. They'll be able to tell whether mechanical failure caused the crash."

"Then what do you want from me?" Holly balanced her coffee cup on her knee. She'd poured herself some of the dark liquid only to keep Inspector Pruitt company, not because she really wanted it. Lately her stomach was too queasy for coffee. Now the brew was quickly growing cold and unpalatable.

"I want to ask you some questions about your husband and about the day his plane went down," Pruitt explained. "My job is to collect more pieces of the puzzle to send to Washington."

"Sure, I'll tell you whatever I can." The baby kicked suddenly, causing Holly's knees to jerk. Her coffee sloshed from side to side in the cup, spilling over onto the saucer. She set down her cup and saucer on the lamp table before the coffee could slop onto her maternity slacks or the carpet.

Pruitt quickly flipped a page in his notebook and read from a list of prepared questions. The first several were about Alex's age, profession, and general physical health. Holly answered them as completely as she could.

"Let's talk a little about that day," Pruitt said, when he'd finished with the basics. "You said Alex was bound for Santa Monica Airport?" Holly nodded. "What was his reason for going there?"

"He had a court hearing scheduled at two o'clock."

"At the Santa Monica courthouse?"

"That's right."

"For what purpose?"

Holly sighed. "Is that really important?" she asked. She didn't like the idea of discussing Alex's court case with this stranger.

Pruitt poked at his chin with the eraser end of his pencil. "I'm sorry if this seems too personal, but I really have to ask these questions. Sometimes the psychological profile of the pilot can be the most important part of our investigation."

Holly was confused. What was this man trying to say? As far as she could see, the only important pieces of this investigation were the mechanical condition of the Cessna, the weather conditions that day, and Alex's physical health. Anything else was irrelevant and none of the government's business. "If you must know," she said, "Alex was petitioning for a change in the terms of his divorce agreement. But I don't see what that has to do with anything."

Pruitt wrote something in his notebook. "It all goes to the pilot's state of mind," he said, as though that made everything clear to Holly. "We never know in advance what might be important. Now, this divorce agreement you say Mr. Sheridan was trying to alter. I'd like to know exactly what the dispute was about."

"I don't know all the details," Holly said. "This hearing had nothing to do with me; it was about Alex's first wife, Celia. He—Alex really didn't talk much about her, not to me, anyway. He always said his divorce was very bitter and he didn't want to taint his relationship with me by talking about it all the time, the way lots of divorced people do. All I know is that we couldn't afford to keep paying the alimony anymore. We just plain didn't have the money."

Pruitt looked around at the house and the panoramic view of the Pacific Ocean through the living room window. "Why was that?"

"Because Alex used to earn a lot more, before he had his heart attack and we moved up here. Back when he and Celia separated, he agreed to pay her five thousand dollars a month alimony. Gave her their house, too.

"I guess Alex didn't figure on getting married again. He definitely didn't figure on his health changing the way it did. Anyway, lately—" Holly felt her chin begin to quiver. She stopped talking until she'd regained her composure. How long would it be, she wondered, before she could speak of Alex without feeling the urge to cry? She took a deep breath and continued. "Lately Alex and I weren't earning five thousand a month between us."

She told Inspector Pruitt about Ecobay Housing and its financial problems.

"Are you saying Ecobay is on the verge of bankruptcy?" he asked.

"No, not really. I'm sure we'll turn it around soon. It's just that we were undercapitalized to begin with, and the housing market is in a slump right now. No one wants to give us credit. But Alex and I—" Holly stopped herself, realizing she'd spoken of Alex as though he might still walk in the front door any minute, as though he remained the driving force behind Ecobay Housing. "I mean, before Alex died, I was sure we would make a go of Ecobay. Now—well, I just don't know. The main problem then seemed to be to cut down the alimony payments and stop the drain on our savings."

"Got any more of this coffee?" Pruitt asked. "It's very good."

"Uh, sure, I'll get you—" Holly started to get up off the sofa.

Pruitt sprang to his feet. "No, don't get up, Mrs. Sheridan. I can wait on myself. Can I bring you a fresh cup?"

Holly sat back down and glanced at her coffee cup; it was still full. "No, thanks." She felt tired and discouraged enough not to care whether her guest had to serve himself. "The milk's in the refrigerator, if you want some," she called after him as he headed toward the kitchen.

The inspector's sharp eyes took in a variety of details about the Sheridans' still-uncompleted home as he refilled his cup and carried it back to the living room. "Did your husband carry any life insurance, Mrs. Sheridan?" he asked, after he'd sat down again.

Holly stiffened, her sense of violation rapidly increasing. "I don't see why that matters," she said.

"We can query every insurance company in the country if we have to," Pruitt said, stirring milk into his coffee until it was an even light-brown color, "but it sure would be a whole lot easier if you just answered my question."

Holly thought it over. She didn't like caving in to what seemed like government intrusion into her private life. Still, her husband was dead and she wanted to find out why as soon as possible. If she stonewalled Pruitt, the FAA would undoubtedly delay its report. "There are a couple of insurance policies, I think," she said. "Ecobay Housing has one, for fifty thousand dollars. Key-man insurance, I think it's called."

"The kind of policy that pays the business if one of the crucial partners dies, right?"

Holly nodded. "It would pay the same amount if

Greg Garrison died, too. Alex designed the houses and Greg's in charge of the actual construction. He's our general contractor."

"And the other policy?"

"I'm not sure how much that one's for. Alex's attorney could tell you—Bryce Cannon, he's in West Los Angeles. All I know is it's a policy Alex took out years ago, when he was still married to Celia. I guess it became part of their divorce settlement. I wouldn't even know he had it, except—well, when we found out I was pregnant, Alex tried to take out a life insurance policy for me and the baby, in case—" Holly swallowed hard. "Just in case."

"Did he buy that policy?" Pruitt asked.

Holly shook her head. "The insurance companies turned him down," she said. "After his heart attack, Alex couldn't qualify for regular life insurance anymore. Too high a risk, I suppose. Anyway, he said he was going to try to change the beneficiary on the old policy . . . if the court would let him, that is. That was one of the things he planned to ask for at the court hearing in Santa Monica."

Pruitt made a few more notes and then abruptly changed direction. "What medications did Alex take, Mrs. Sheridan?"

"Aspirin," she said. "One baby aspirin each morning, as a blood thinner. Vitamins, too—all the antioxidant ones."

"Any prescription drugs? Heart medications, blood pressure medicine, tranquilizers, antidepressants, sleeping pills?"

"No, nothing else. He was on heart medication for a while—Tenormin, I think—but he went off it at least six months ago."

"What about liquor? Would you say your husband was a heavy drinker?"

Holly bristled again. "Absolutely not," she said. "And Alex was adamant about never drinking any alcohol within twenty-four hours of flying."

Hearing the growing irritation in Holly Sheridan's voice, Pruitt raised both hands in a calming gesture. "I know some of what I'm asking sounds a bit accusatory," he explained, "but it's all part of our standard investigation. I really do have to ask you these things."

"My husband was not a drunk." Holly's body had gone rigid with resentment.

"Did your husband use any illegal drugs?" Pruitt asked, avoiding Holly's angry green eyes. "Marijuana, cocaine, speed, LSD, cra—"

"No!" Holly heard her voice rising and felt tears coming to her eyes. "Look, Inspector, what are you trying to do here, make out that Alex was at fault? My husband was a good pilot, he was a careful pilot. He wasn't drunk or on drugs, that day or any other. It was the goddamned airplane that killed him! Why can't you understand that?"

"I didn't mean to upset you, Mrs. Sheri—"

"Then stop badgering me." Holly felt the baby kick again. No doubt the poor little thing could sense her rapidly increasing agitation. Willing herself to calm down, she folded her arms across her belly in an effort to protect and comfort her unborn child.

"I'm sorry," Fred Pruitt said. "Just one more question, and then I'll leave you alone."

Holly chewed on her trembling lower lip as she waited.

"I'm sorry, but I really do have to ask you this."

Pruitt crossed and uncrossed his long legs. "Did your husband ever mention having suicidal thoughts?"

Holly gasped audibly. Such an idea had never occurred to her. A heart attack, yes; some kind of mechanical failure in the Cessna; a bizarre quirk of the weather or air currents; even—what did they call it?—pilot error. Alex could have had a sudden lapse in judgment that caused the plane to crash; that sort of thing happened occasionally even to commercial airline pilots. Any of those things Holly could understand and accept. But that Alex would intentionally put his aircraft into a nosedive toward the Pacific was far beyond her comprehension.

"Absolutely not," she said, feeling defensive on Alex's behalf. "My husband had everything to live for. The baby coming, Ecobay, everything." Holly herself. Surely Alex had no reason to want to leave her, she thought, especially not now. Especially not that way.

"I had to ask," Pruitt explained. "Particularly when a pilot's been having financial problems and he's heading toward a difficult and emotional confrontation, like Mr. Sheridan was that day."

"You didn't know Alex," Holly said. "If you knew him, you could never suggest that. He could easily have died last year, when he had his heart attack. But he fought and fought; he refused to let go. After he got out of the hospital, he did everything he could to live the best possible life, to be healthy again. He started exercising every day, he changed his diet, he cut down on his workload, everything. That's why we moved here to Bodega Bay, Inspector, why we started Ecobay Housing. Can't you understand? We came up here so Alex could *live*!"

Pruitt closed his notebook and stood up. "Thank

you, Mrs. Sheridan. Don't get up, please," he said, as he saw her starting to rise. "I can find my own way out."

Holly realized she was trembling all over. She wasn't sure her shaky knees would hold her up, so she sank back down onto the sofa. "You'll let me know what they find out about the plane, won't you?" she asked.

"The agency will be in touch with you as soon as our report is completed. In the meantime, if you think of anything else that might be important, I'd appreciate your giving me a call." Pruitt pulled a business card from the inside pocket of his suit coat and placed it face up on the table in front of Holly. "Will you do that?"

"I—sure, I guess so." But Holly had no intention of sharing any more intimate details of her life, of Alex's private life, with this man. In her heart, she knew that Alex had not been responsible for the Cessna's crash, not on purpose anyway. In her opinion, that fact was all the government was entitled to know about him.

"Thank you, Mrs. Sheridan," Fred Pruitt said again, as he disappeared through Holly's front door. "I'll be in touch."

Chapter

15

⌒

The open boat tilted and its nose dipped as Greg cut the speed of the outboard motor. "How's this spot?" He had to shout to be heard above the engine's roar.

Holly brushed her golden-brown hair out of her eyes and looked around. Bodega Bay was unusually calm today and the sun was shining brightly, turning the Pacific a brilliant shade of azure. Bodega Head loomed large on the northern horizon; the swollen finger of earth jutting into the Pacific was now a vivid green, the result of winter rains. Instead of the strong afternoon winds common to the area, today there was no more than a light breeze, gently playing with Holly's hair. Alex's lightweight khaki windbreaker, which she'd grabbed on her way out of the house, gave her more than adequate protection from the weather.

Alex would have loved this day, Holly thought wistfully. "This is perfect," she called out to Greg.

Sitting on the hard bench in the front of the ten-footer Greg had borrowed from a friend for this occasion, Holly held the box containing Alex's ashes on her lap. "Can you shut off the motor, Greg?" she shouted. "I'd like it to be as quiet as possible."

"Sure." Greg switched the motor off and waited at the rear of the boat, giving Holly as much space, as much privacy as she needed. The only sound was that of water lapping against the sides of the old wooden boat as it rocked gently to and fro. Overhead, a dozen brown pelicans soared gracefully and soundlessly in *V* formation.

Holly sat still for a moment, feeling the warmth of the afternoon sun on her back and her head. She was grateful that Greg had offered to take her on this brief journey, appreciative that he'd been willing to help her put Alex to rest. In a month or two, after the baby was born and her life had settled down, she'd decided she would go to Los Angeles and hold a more formal memorial service for Alex there. She would plan a gathering that all of their old friends could attend, an event where everyone who'd cared about Alex could bid him good-bye. Perhaps her sister Heather might even be able to come from New Zealand. But for now, today's more personal ritual was all Holly felt she could handle.

She picked up her copy of *The Prophet* from beside her on the wooden bench and began to read aloud from it.

"If you would indeed behold the spirit of death, open your heart wide unto the body of life.

For life and death are one, even as the river and the sea are one."

Because she and Alex had included a quote from Kahlil Gibran in their wedding service last year, she thought it appropriate to select another from the same source for Alex's burial.

Neither Holly nor Alex had ever been particularly religious people. Holly's personal creed was a combination of Christianity and humanism, with a smidgen or two of Judaism thrown in for good measure. She believed in the essential goodness of humanity, that somehow, in some way, people would eventually come together and find a way to coexist in love and peace. She lived her own life according to the Golden Rule and expected others to do the same. That she was often disappointed didn't really matter; despite often-painful reality, Holly Sheridan had never lost faith in the future.

She read another passage from the book aloud.

"Only when you drink from the river of silence shall you indeed sing.

And when you have reached the mountain top, then you shall begin to climb.

And when the earth shall claim your limbs, then shall you truly dance."

Holly closed the book and set it back down on the seat of the boat. She shut her eyes for a moment, remembering Alex as he'd held her close and kissed her good-bye for the last time. Then she opened the sturdy brown box she held on her lap, reached into it, scooped out a handful of her husband's ashes, and scattered them in the breeze.

As handful after handful of ashes landed on the surface of the water and floated gently away, Holly began to feel an increasing sense of inner peace. "Sing, Alex," she said. "Sing loud, so I'll always be able to hear you. Sing and climb and dance."

When the box was empty, Holly closed her eyes again and said a silent prayer for Alex and herself and their baby. From this day forward, whenever she saw the vast Pacific, whether it was here or back in Los Angeles, she knew she would think of Alex, that she would feel his presence near her.

When her prayer was finished, Holly turned to Greg, who sat quietly gazing at the horizon, one hand on the outboard motor. "I'm ready to go back now," she told him.

Greg nodded solemnly, started the engine, and steered the little boat back toward shore.

Chapter

16

After they docked the borrowed boat, Greg offered to buy Holly dinner at the Lucas Wharf restaurant. But she thanked him and begged off, saying she preferred to be alone with her thoughts this evening. Secretly relieved that he wouldn't have to spend another couple of hours searching for words that might comfort the grieving widow, Greg drove her directly back to Sandpiper Circle.

"Thanks again for all your help today, Greg. I really appreciate it," Holly said, climbing out of his pickup truck. "Don't bother to get out. I'll be all right."

Greg watched as she approached her front door, keys in hand. He was just shifting his truck into reverse to back out of the driveway when he saw Holly turn around and hurry awkwardly back toward the driveway.

"Greg! Somebody's broken into the house!" she yelled, her eyes wide with fright.

In an instant, Greg switched off the truck's engine, released his seat belt, and bolted out onto the driveway. Holly was right. The narrow strip of glass next to the front door of the low gray house had been shattered from the outside, allowing an intruder to reach in and unlock the deadbolt. "Get back into the truck, Holly," he ordered. "You're not going inside until we're sure nobody's still there."

Holly did as she was told.

Greg grabbed his cellular phone out of the glove compartment and used it to call the sheriff's office. Then he took a crowbar from his toolbox and started back toward the front door.

"Don't go in there, Greg, please. Wait till the police get here," Holly pleaded. She felt both frightened and violated.

But Greg's adrenaline was flowing. That someone would break into Holly's house while she was off scattering her husband's ashes in the bay thoroughly infuriated him. How could anybody be so cruel? The front door was still unlocked. He pushed it open and headed inside, the crowbar held aloft in readiness.

Greg quickly searched the entire house, including the garage, but whoever had been there was gone. "Nobody's around," he told Holly, after he returned to the truck, his heart thumping hard in his chest. Now that his impulsive search had been completed, he began to realize what a foolish move it had been. What if intruders had still been inside the house, possibly armed with a gun? The crowbar he held in his hand would have given him no protection whatever. Although he would never admit it to a woman, particularly to a pregnant and newly widowed woman like Holly Sheridan, Greg was glad he'd found the house empty. He'd never thought of himself as the macho hero type, and he felt too old to change now.

"The TV's gone," Holly said a few minutes later, as

she surveyed her living room. "The VCR, too." She found the kitchen intact, except for eight place settings of Towle sterling silver flatware she'd inherited from her mother. She felt lucky that she'd been wearing her engagement and wedding rings, and she'd slipped Alex's wedding ring onto her left thumb before Greg had picked her up today. The rings were what she would have most regretted losing. Appliances and silverware could always be replaced. "Let's check the bedroom," she said to Greg.

With Greg following close behind, Holly headed straight for the oak triple dresser and pulled open the top left-hand drawer. Sighing deeply, she swore under her breath. The money was gone, every cent of it. "I had almost six hundred dollars in this drawer," she told Greg, tears welling up in her eyes.

"Six hundred bucks in *cash*?" he asked, stunned.

"Mostly, along with a few checks."

"Why on earth did you have all that money sitting in a drawer?"

"Friends and people Alex used to work with sent it to me with their sympathy cards. You know, twenty-five dollars here, fifty there. I was supposed to donate it to some worthy cause in Alex's memory." Holly slid the drawer shut again. "I never got around to choosing a charity," she said. "Now it's too late; the money's gone, stolen."

All of Holly's gold and silver earrings, along with Alex's good cuff links and his gold watch, were missing as well. But what seemed strangest of all was that she found Alex's sock drawer completely empty.

"What would a bunch of thieves want with my husband's socks?" Holly asked Sheriff Wills half an hour later. Surely they hadn't come in here barefoot.

The sheriff was a large man with a massive potbelly

and a florid complexion. He'd arrived at the Sheridan house in a squad car, with a skinny twenty-something female deputy at the wheel. Holly couldn't help thinking that the red-nosed sheriff's beer belly made him look almost as pregnant as she was. "I don't get it," she said. "Socks?"

Sheriff Wills lifted one of his rounded shoulders, as though shrugging both of them would take more energy than he was willing to expend. "These guys use socks to carry out the loot," he explained. Holly wrinkled her nose; the sheriff exuded a strong odor of liquor. "Prob'ly shoved your jewelry and silverware into the socks. Sometimes they work in pairs. Guy inside the house stuffs the goods into some socks, ties 'em closed at the top, and tosses the whole lot out the window to his accomplice."

While the sheriff slouched in front of the fireplace, one elbow resting on the mantel, his deputy was busily dusting a thick black powder on the front door, the kitchen counter, the bedroom dresser, and any other surface she thought the burglars might have touched. She was attempting to raise latent fingerprints. Discouraged by this further assault on her house, Holly wondered if she would have to clean up the sooty layer after the police were finished.

"I lived in Los Angeles for sixteen years and nothing like this ever happened to me," she complained, shaking her head. "I thought small towns were supposed to be safe." She watched as the deputy began applying the sticky black powder to the top of the stove and the handle of the refrigerator. "Why here?" she asked the sheriff. "Why now? Today of all days." She'd already told him about her afternoon's mission on the bay.

"You're an easy target, Miz Sheridan," the sheriff told her, his eyes shifting quickly between his deputy and his wristwatch and back again. "Local newspaper run some kinda notice about the funeral?"

"No," Holly said. "Today was a totally private ceremony, just Greg and me. I'll have a public memorial service down in L.A. in a few weeks."

The sheriff belched quietly and rubbed his stomach. Holly noticed that his beefy hands were trembling slightly. "Any strange phone calls the last few days?" he asked.

Holly sank into a chair, her mood growing blacker by the minute. "Just hang-ups, if that's what you mean," she said. "Lots of them." She'd answered two more of those annoying calls before Greg picked her up this morning.

"There's your man," Sheriff Wills said, hooking his thumb into his belt. "These guys hear about folks havin' a funeral or a wedding or somethin'. It's in the papers or on TV. Some event where a family's likely to leave money or gifts layin' around the house and then go out. Usually, what happens is the papers print where and when the big event's gonna take place, and that's when they hit the house. In your case, the thief prob'ly just kept callin' the house here, waitin' for the time when nobody answered the phone."

Greg walked over to Holly's chair and stood with his hand resting on its back, attempting to comfort her with his physical presence. "Sounds like you know who's behind these break-ins, Sheriff," he suggested.

"Wish we did, Garrison. If this's like the rest of 'em, Deputy Snyder here ain't gonna pull up one print don't belong here. These guys are smart enough to wear gloves. By the way, we're gonna have to take your prints, Miz Sheridan's too. Gotta know which ones we can rule out."

Deputy Snyder finished dusting the kitchen and closed the small wooden case that held her fingerprint kit. "All done in here, Sheriff," she announced. "Want me to print these folks now or do it later at the station?"

The sheriff checked his wristwatch again. "How long you figure it's gonna take?"

"Ten, fifteen minutes."

The sheriff's reluctance to stay here any longer was obvious to Holly. She caught him checking his watch again. It was almost five o'clock, the man's cocktail hour, she guessed; he wanted to get out of here so he could have another drink. She began to feel her anger shifting from the burglars to this sluff-off of a country sheriff. "I'd really rather not have to go down to the station," she said. She was a taxpayer and the sheriff was a public servant; Holly wanted some service, not just a lot of shoulder-shrugging.

"All right, we'll print you now," the sheriff said. "Let's move it along here, Deputy."

"What are my chances of getting my things back?" Holly asked as the deputy rolled her fingers on an ink pad and then pressed each finger on a white card. In the background, she could hear sounds of hammering as Greg began boarding up the broken window.

"The truth?" the sheriff asked.

"I wouldn't ask you if I didn't want the truth." Judging by the way this sheriff worked, Holly thought she could guess the answer.

"Even if we catch these guys, they're prob'ly gonna have fenced your stuff already," he told her. "Best thing you can do, Miz Sheridan, is call your insurance man first thing in the morning, get your claim in the works."

In other words, Holly thought, I can kiss my belongings good-bye.

"Deputy Snyder here'll type up a list of the things you're missin' for your signature, Miz Sheridan. You can stop by the station tomorrow or the next day and sign it." Sheriff Wills hurried out the front door, barging ahead of his deputy. "You're gonna need a copy for your insurance," he called to Holly over his shoulder.

"I'm really sorry about all this," Deputy Snyder said, shaking Holly's hand as they stood for a moment in the doorway.

Holly got the impression the young woman was talking about more than the burglary.

The deputy glanced over her shoulder and saw her boss standing impatiently beside the squad car, gesturing to her to hurry. "I'll do whatever I can to see you're not inconvenienced any more than necessary from here on out, Mrs. Sheridan," she promised. "Tell you what—don't worry about stopping by the station to sign those papers. I'll bring them over here just as soon as I have a chance."

"Thank you, Deputy," Holly said. "I really appreciate your concern." After watching the policewoman climb into the squad car and back it out of the driveway, Holly closed and bolted her front door, wondering whether she could ever feel safe here again.

Then she headed back inside to help Greg clean up the sticky black powder that was now clinging to every visible surface.

Chapter

17

The kitchen of Celia's rented house smelled strongly of cinnamon and apples, a warm, homey odor she remembered from her childhood. She transferred the coffee cake she'd just taken from the oven to a plate and covered it with a sheet of tinfoil. Celia was an excellent cook, the result of years of gourmet cooking classes. Along with interior decoration and art appreciation classes, she'd taken half a dozen cooking courses to keep herself occupied during her marriage. It wasn't often anymore that she allowed herself to bake, however; the older she got, the harder it seemed to be to keep off those extra pounds, and she didn't believe in tempting herself unnecessarily. She knew the resolution would have to change now, however, at least for a few weeks.

When the coffee cake was ready, Celia slipped her arms into a thick cobalt-blue cardigan sweater, checked in the mirror to see that her wig was on straight, and carried the cake across the street.

"Hello there," she said with a practiced smile, when

her neighbor's door opened a crack. The door was held in this position by a stout security chain. "I'm Pat Patterson, from across the street." Celia kept the smile frozen on her face to hide the raw hatred she felt for Holly Sheridan. This was the first time she had seen her husband's new wife in the flesh, and she understood even less why Alex had preferred this plain colorless woman to her. Holly didn't have half Celia's looks. "You and I seem to be the only ones living here on the circle," Celia told her, "so I thought I'd just pop over and say hello."

"Oh," Holly said, peering over the safety chain she'd installed earlier this morning. "I didn't realize anyone had moved in." Getting to know her neighbors was not high on Holly's list of recent priorities, particularly since most of them at any given time were short-term renters who preferred to keep to themselves. "I'm Holly Sheridan." She noticed that the tall, pale-faced, dark-haired woman was holding a plate with something wrapped in silver foil on it.

Celia thrust the plate forward, as though the chained door presented no real barrier and Holly could easily take hold of it. "Here, I baked this for you," she said. "Thought you might like some fresh homemade coffee cake. It's apple."

"How nice," Holly said, unlatching the security chain and opening the door. "This certainly wasn't necessary." Realizing that her hands were covered with sawdust, she wiped them off on her shirt, leaving streaks of light powder across her bulging belly.

"Nonsense. I believe in being neighborly," Celia said, quickly sizing up Alex's widow now that she could see more of her. What she observed left her with conflicting feelings. On one level, she was pleased that the woman she'd grown to dislike so much since Alex had married her looked disheveled, haggard, as though she were nearing the end of her emotional rope. Even the clothes Holly wore were a disaster: a man's blue shirt spattered with paint and a pair of baggy jeans. Good, Celia thought; she wanted Alex's bimbo to be every bit as miserable as she'd been for the past few years.

But on another level, she couldn't help worrying. She wanted the baby Holly was carrying to be born healthy, and that depended upon Alex's whore's staying in good physical condition right up until she gave birth. Carefully keeping her facial expression friendly, Celia handed Holly the plate.

"Oh, this is still warm!" Holly said, suddenly aware that she was hungry. Had she eaten breakfast this morning? She couldn't remember. All she knew was that she'd tossed and turned in bed all night, worried that the burglars might return. This morning, she'd thrown on the first clothes she could find, called the insurance agent to report the burglary, installed the security chain on the front door, and begun sanding the railing along the deck at the back of the house—anything to keep herself busy physically, so her mind couldn't wander off in too many painful directions. With the exception of time out to answer a brief phone call from Alex's attorney, who said he was coming up to see her tomorrow, plus a few trips to the bathroom, Holly had not let herself sit down since dawn.

"Sorry," she said. "I don't mean to seem rude. It's just that—well, come on in, Pat. I'll make us a pot of coffee." What else could she do? Holly wondered. She didn't feel like having company, but she could hardly slam her door in this woman's face, not after she'd gone to the trouble of baking something especially for her.

Celia followed Holly into the blue-and-white kitchen. "Why don't you just sit down and rest a bit," she suggested, taking off her heavy blue sweater and draping it over the back of a kitchen chair. "I know how tough it is to be on your feet when you're pregnant. Just tell me where you keep things, and I'll make the coffee."

Holly protested, but her guest insisted. In the end, she fell gratefully into a chair. Her back ached badly, and she truly was bone-tired.

"I noticed the police were over here yesterday," Celia said, as she measured water into the coffeepot. "I hope there's nothing wrong."

"Somebody broke into my house—in broad daylight," Holly told her. "Stole the TV and the VCR and my mother's silverware while I was—well, while I was out."

"How awful! I thought it was supposed to be safe around here."

"So did I. You didn't happen to notice anybody strange on the circle yesterday afternoon, did you?"

"'Fraid not. Didn't see anybody or anything until the sheriff's car showed up. Probably wouldn't have noticed the car either, except I went to put on my front porch light and there it was." In truth, Celia had been spying on Holly's house almost steadily since she'd moved in. She'd noticed an old black van parked in Holly's driveway yesterday afternoon; it had given her a moment's pause, worrying her that Holly might be moving out suddenly. But that van would stay Celia's secret; there was no way she was going to risk talking to the police, about it or anything else.

"I tell you, Pat," Holly said wistfully, "all those years I lived in L.A., I never had any trouble like this."

"So you're from L.A. too? What part?"

"Santa Monica, actually. How about you?"

"Pacific Palisades." Celia chose an area of Los Angeles that she knew well, one that was adjacent to Santa Monica, for her fictional home. "I've lived there for the past twenty years. I knew people who'd been robbed down in L.A., of course. One of my friends was even raped in her own home. But luckily nothing like that ever happened to me."

As the two women compared their impressions of Los Angeles, Celia was careful not to make Pat Patterson's phony background too similar to Celia Sheridan's real one. She had no way of knowing how much Alex had told his new wife about her predecessor, and she couldn't risk Holly's becoming suspicious of her. Still, Celia knew that sticking fairly close to the truth—substituting another nearby wealthy area of Los Angeles for Bel Air, for instance—would help her keep her story straight.

"I don't know about you," Celia said, "but I got to where I just needed to get away from L.A. for a while. The earthquakes, the fires, the floods, the incessant crowds, it was all overwhelming me." She paused a moment for impact. "Particularly since my husband passed away." Watching Holly's tired face for a reaction to what she'd just told her, she carried a cup of hot decaf over to the table.

"Your husband died?" Holly asked.

"Just this year," Celia told her, pleased to see a flare of interest come into the other woman's green eyes. "It was very sudden, a real shock. I—I guess I just wasn't prepared to be a widow." She looked away, as if momentarily overcome by sadness.

"My—my husband died too." Holly's eyes began to fill. She blinked rapidly until she regained control.

"Oh! You poor thing," Celia said, sliding into the chair across from Holly's. "I never dreamed you might be a widow too."

Holly nodded. "My husband Alex's plane crashed, and—"

"And you're pregnant!" Celia was all concern, reaching across the table to give Holly's hand a quick, comforting squeeze. "I thought I was bad off when my—but you're younger, and with a baby coming too."

"I'll manage somehow," Holly told her, studying the piece of coffee cake her new neighbor had placed in front of her. She reached for a knife and began to butter the apple-and-cinnamon concoction. The familiar motion distracted her from her grief, helped her to keep from crying in front of this woman. Pat Patterson seemed nice enough, Holly thought, but she was a complete stranger. Even if she, like Holly herself, was a new widow.

"I was alone for thirty-four years before I met Alex," Holly said. "I'll just have to get used to being alone again. This time I'll have the baby, though." She took a big bite of the coffee cake. It was delicious.

"Still, this has to be a horrible time for you." Celia picked an apple slice off the top of her piece of coffee cake and nibbled on it. Her sliver of coffee cake was less than half the size of the piece she'd cut for Holly. She would allow herself to eat at most a bite or two, without the added calories of butter. "Are you having a boy or a girl?"

"My husband and I didn't want to know ahead of time. We wanted to be surprised when the baby was born."

"Doing it the old-fashioned way. Can't say I blame you. Tell you what, Holly," Celia said. "I've got nothing but time on my hands for the next few weeks, and I could use a friend around here. You know, somebody to talk to. You can be my new project—at least until your baby gets here."

Holly's jaw dropped. She was appalled by the other woman's suggestion. She had no intention of becoming anyone's "project." "Oh, no. I can take care of myself perfectly well, thank you very much."

Celia pushed away her plate, leaving most of her coffee cake still uneaten. "Hey, don't take offense. All I meant was, I'd be happy to help you out any way I can. Only if you *want* my help, of course. Like—well, I thought I'd drive over to Petaluma this afternoon to go grocery shopping at the Safeway. Why don't you give me your list and I'll do your shopping at the same time?"

"That's not necessary, Pat, really it isn't."

"I know it's not *necessary*, Holly. But it's a good half hour's drive over country roads to Petaluma, and there's no supermarket any closer. Surely you can't be buying all your groceries at that little milk store up the road. Their prices are highway robbery! I'd like to help you out on this, really I would."

"I have to go to the doctor, day after tomorrow, in Santa Rosa," Holly said. "I'll get my groceries there."

"Santa Rosa." Pat refilled her coffee cup and added a splash of hot coffee to Holly's. "That's even farther than Petaluma. Do you really think it's a good idea for you to drive that far all by yourself? When's your baby due?"

"A little less than two weeks from now, but there's no reason I can't drive. I've been driving since I was sixteen years old."

"What if you go into labor and you're stuck out on

one of those deserted country roads? I sure wouldn't want to risk *my* baby's life that way."

"But—"

"Look, Holly, I can just as easily drive you to Santa Rosa in my car. I'll go shopping while you see the doctor. I won't poke my nose into your business, I promise. But if I'm doing the driving and you go into labor, you won't be alone. I'll be able to take you to the hospital. Come on, this'll give me something to do with my time." Celia watched Holly's face carefully as she spoke; she could see the younger woman's resistance lessening. "Please," she added with a wry smile. "I like to stay busy, and there doesn't seem to be all that much to do around here. Why not let me help us both out?"

Holly fought against a feeling of being overwhelmed. She didn't even know this woman who'd barged into her life with one of the best coffee cakes she'd ever tasted. She'd always been a loner, and she didn't want some stranger moving in on her like gangbusters. Yet it was tempting to have somebody around. She'd already leaned far too hard on Greg Garrison. Holly knew what Alex would tell her to do. He'd always admired her independent streak—to a point. But he'd often told her she carried her independence too far at times, that she needed to learn to accept help from other people. Maybe, Holly thought, by stubbornly refusing to accept Pat's offer to drive, she really *was* risking her baby's life. That was the last thing she wanted to do.

"All right," Holly said reluctantly. "If you really want to go to Santa Rosa with me the day after tomorrow, fine; we'll go together."

"Then it's all set." Celia rose from her chair, carried her plate over to the sink, rinsed it off, and put it into the dishwasher. She didn't want to overstay her welcome on this first visit and risk scaring Holly off. "What time's your doctor's appointment?"

"Eleven o'clock."

"I'll pick you up at nine forty-five. We can have a nice lunch together somewhere in Santa Rosa afterward, if you feel up to it."

"Thanks, Pat. I didn't mean to seem ungrateful a minute ago, really. It's just that—"

"Hey," Celia said, putting her sweater back on. "I lost my husband too, remember? I understand the kind of emotional roller coaster you're on right now. No apology required."

As Celia walked back across Sandpiper Circle toward number seventeen, she felt enormously pleased with herself. She had Holly Sheridan exactly where she wanted her.

Chapter

18

Celia sat in a comfortable pine rocking chair in the third bedroom of the big brown house with the morning *San Francisco Chronicle* spread across her lap. This room was the only one in the house that had a direct view of Holly Sheridan's smaller place across Sandpiper Circle, so Celia found herself spending much of her time here, alternately reading and looking out the window.

Holly hadn't left her house, and the leather-faced workman in the pickup truck who sometimes stopped by to visit her—Celia figured he had something to do with Ecobay Housing—was nowhere in sight. If the gray house across the street remained quiet for the rest of the morning, she could stop by to see Holly once more before their trip to the doctor tomorrow.

An excuse for another visit wouldn't be hard to concoct. She might even ask a minor favor of Holly—her advice about the best restaurant in town, perhaps, or where to get clothes dry-cleaned—so that the pregnant woman wouldn't begin to feel too beholden to her new neighbor. When people thought they owed debts they couldn't readily repay, Celia knew, they sometimes cut off contact with their benefactors, if only to avoid embarrassment. She definitely did not want Holly Sheridan to feel beholden. For now, anyway. After the baby was born, it would no longer matter. Holly would be in no position to feel—or do—anything.

Alone in her rented house with the front door locked, Celia wasn't wearing her dark wig. She was allowing her blond hair to air-dry after her morning's shower. If anyone came to the house, she would simply grab the wig and pull it on before answering the door. Until she absolutely had to, she didn't want to wear the confining mass of dark curls; after an hour or two, the warm tight wig always made her scalp itch fiercely.

Celia had already read the main news stories in the *Chronicle* and finished with the movie and television reviews in the Datebook section. Now she was searching through the classified ads for furnished apartments available for rent in San Francisco. She'd circled two ads that looked promising—one for a place in the city's Nob Hill section and the other for one near Opera Plaza—when, out of the corner of her eye, she spied a white Toyota turning into Sandpiper Circle.

As the car passed her house, she noticed it had an Alamo rent-a-car sticker on its rear bumper. Was somebody about to move into another of the houses on the circle? Celia wondered. Still holding the newspaper, she crept closer to the window and stared openly at the car.

The white Toyota turned into the driveway of the Sheridan house and parked. An exceptionally tall, balding man emerged from the driver's side, walked around the back of the car, opened the trunk, and removed a fat black briefcase. As she stared at him, Celia's long, slender fingers began to crush the newspaper she was holding, squeezing it harder and harder until her knuckles turned white.

She knew the man who was ringing the Sheridans' doorbell. It was Bryce Cannon, the shark of an attorney Alex had used to get the divorce, and his presence here in Bodega Bay could bring her nothing but grief. Celia had seen Bryce Cannon again at the back of the Santa Monica courtroom, waiting for Alex to show up at the spousal support hearing the two of them had forced on her. If Attorney Cannon had had his way, Celia would be back in Bel Air right now, trying to figure out how to survive on a small fraction of her previous income.

Her whole body shaking with a potent combination of rage and fear, Celia backed away from the bedroom window and hurled the balled-up newspaper to the floor. She ran frantically across the hall and into the bathroom and yanked the dark wig over her damp hair, as though somehow Bryce Cannon could see straight through the walls of her house, discover who she really was, and warn Holly off.

The face Celia saw reflected in the bathroom mirror as she tucked the last strands of blond hair under the dark wig looked haunted, terrified. Her hands were shaking so hard she could barely manage to get the wig on straight. She looked different now, it was true. But even with the dark reddish-brown hair hiding her own blond tresses and brown contact lenses to change the color of her eyes, Celia knew she could never risk coming face to face with Alex's sharp-eyed lawyer.

She hated Bryce Cannon almost as much as she hated Holly Sheridan.

When she was fully disguised once more, she

returned to her observation post in the extra bedroom and pulled the rose-colored curtains shut, except for about an inch at the center.

Half an hour later, Celia was still standing at the window, staring anxiously through the gap in the curtains at Bryce Cannon's rental car and Holly Sheridan's house. She was unaware that her hands were kneading the lower edge of the curtain, and she hardly noticed when the temperature under her wig rose and her scalp began its inevitable itching.

Chapter

19

"You didn't have to come all the way up here just to show me these papers, Bryce, really you didn't," Holly told Alex's attorney, after she'd served him a cup of coffee and a slice of Pat Patterson's leftover coffee cake. They were sitting at the dining room table, using it as a desk. "We could have handled this by mail and on the phone."

"Nonsense," Bryce Cannon said, picking up his square of coffee cake and taking a big bite out of it. "It's no trouble." He flashed Holly a smile; a crumb dangled precariously from his chin, then fell onto the lapel of his dark brown suit. "Truth is, I plan to use this trip for a little R and R as well. I'll play a round of golf on the course here this afternoon, stay overnight at the Lodge, and fly back to L.A. in the morning. Hey, this stuff is great. I love apple cake." He wolfed down the rest and washed it down with a gulp of black coffee.

"My new neighbor across the circle brought it over yesterday."

"Well, my compliments." After wiping his fingers

on a paper napkin, Bryce began to take a series of papers—Alex's will, three life insurance policies, and the Ecobay Housing partnership agreement—out of his briefcase. "I'm just sorry I couldn't bring you better news, Holly," he said, laying the papers out on the table. "As you know, Alex and I had been trying to change the terms of his divorce agreement with Celia when he died. It's a rotten shame, but because he died *before* the hearing, the court's got no choice but to let Celia have the proceeds of his main life insurance policy. She's still the official beneficiary. That just leaves you this smaller policy, for ten thousand dollars."

Holly tried to focus on the legal papers spread out in front of her, but the small black print just swam before her eyes. She'd seen some of these documents before, of course—namely, the Ecobay partnership agreement and the key-man insurance policy for the company, although she'd never actually read the boilerplate on the latter. She knew little or nothing about the other two life insurance policies, and she was stunned when Bryce told her the value of the larger one. It would pay Celia Sheridan a quarter of a million dollars as soon as the Monterey County coroner's office issued Alex's official death certificate.

"Things could be worse," Holly told the attorney. "I didn't know about the small policy. Figured I'd probably have to borrow money to pay for Alex's memorial service. But this should cover it, and maybe some of the baby's doctor bills, too." She brushed an errant strand of brown hair behind an ear. She hadn't bothered to dress up for Bryce Cannon's visit this morning, and now she felt awkward and shabby in her jeans and sweater, entertaining a visitor wearing a suit and tie.

She wished she had at least put on some makeup—and that all her earrings had not been stolen.

Bryce discovered the crumb on his lapel, picked it off carefully, and deposited it on his plate. "Ten thousand dollars isn't much, I'm afraid. Chances are Alex didn't even remember he had the policy. I don't recall his ever mentioning it." The attorney slid the papers closer to Holly's side of the table. "The architectural firm Alex used to work for took this out sometime in the mid-eighties—sort of a year-end bonus for its top employees. It's been paid up for years."

"I'm confused, Bryce. If Alex didn't remember he had this policy, how'd you find out about it?"

"The company's head human resources guy heard about what happened to Alex and gave me a call. Remembered me from our negotiations at the time Alex quit the firm, I guess. Anyway, he sent the policy right over. The way it's written, the beneficiary is the employee's next of kin. Luckily, that's you."

"It was nice of him to call you." Despite her financial circumstances, Holly couldn't get enthused about ten thousand dollars. The fact was, she probably wouldn't be a whole lot more excited if the proceeds of the larger life insurance policy were coming to her. Money would never bring Alex back. If she could have Alex back, Holly thought for the thousandth time, she would gladly live with him in a dirt hut.

"So the bottom line," she said, "is I get ten thousand dollars and I keep our half of Ecobay, right?"

"That's about it. The fifty thousand in the key-man policy goes directly to Ecobay Housing. If you and the other partner—" Bryce began to shuffle through the contract he'd drawn up for Alex last year, creating the construction company.

"Greg Garrison," Holly offered.

"Right, Garrison. If you and Garrison agree, he could use the fifty grand toward buying out your share of the company. I don't know how you feel about that."

Holly leaned back in her chair and sighed. It was ironic, she thought, that she might well end up selling her share of Ecobay Housing to Greg for a mere fifty thousand dollars; certainly he couldn't come up with any more right now. After Holly had sold her Santa Monica condominium last year, she'd invested her whole after-tax profit—pretty much her entire life's savings—in the company; her contribution alone had been sixty-five thousand dollars. Alex had put in another twenty-five thousand, plus all his years of experience as an architect.

Still, Holly had to face the fact that Ecobay was now on the verge of bankruptcy; until the three houses it had under construction—including the one she was living in—were completed and sold and the construction loans paid off, the company was worth much less than their original investment.

"Right now," Holly told the attorney, "I'm afraid I don't feel much of anything about Ecobay." Maybe if she sold her interest she could get her old job at *Stately Homes* back again. The magazine editorship had paid her fifty-four thousand a year. Would that be enough to move back to Los Angeles and raise her child in decent circumstances? It would mean child care, and eventually private school. She shook her head to clear it. Even thinking about her financial condition made her head ache. "I just want to have the baby," she said. "*Then* I'll worry about the company."

"Makes sense to me." Bryce leaned his long body toward his client's widow. His brow was deeply furrowed with concern. "Listen, Holly, be honest with me. Are you sure you really want to stay up here all by yourself? I'd be happy to take you back to L.A. with me tomorrow, if you need somebody to travel with. There must be people down there you could stay with."

"No! No, Bryce, thanks. Thanks for the offer, but I'm not up to seeing a lot of people just now. I'm much better off here, really I am."

"But what about the baby? Who's going to take you to the hospital when the time comes?"

"I can always call Greg," Holly told him. "And if I can't reach him, maybe my new neighbor. Besides, there's always nine-one-one. Don't worry about me, I'll be fine."

"Well . . . " Bryce was clearly skeptical. He didn't like the idea of Holly Sheridan's living alone in Bodega Bay at a time like this. What would Alex have wanted him to do about it? What *could* he do? Holly was no kid; she was thirty-five, plenty old enough to make her own decisions. He really had no choice but to defer to her wishes.

"Really." Holly forced a smile onto her pale lips. "I'll be fine. The baby will be fine. I don't want you worrying about us."

"If you say so. . . . I'll see what I can do to expedite the death certificate anyway, to get you your insurance money." He closed his briefcase. "Then I'll go ahead and file Alex's will for probate."

"Sure. Thanks, Bryce." Holly nodded her agreement, but her mind was already drifting away from the financial information the attorney had come all this way to give her. Her job right now, she knew, was to have a healthy baby; she would worry about money and jobs and Ecobay and whether she wanted to stay here in Bodega Bay later.

Chapter 20

"So what did the doctor say? Is everything all right?" Celia asked as she barged into the obstetrician's reception room, carrying two stout shopping bags. She had left Holly off at her doctor's office in Santa Rosa a little less than two hours ago and was returning to pick her up. The waiting area, which had been crowded with pregnant women earlier, was empty now except for Holly. Only the doctor's receptionist, a young white-uniformed woman sitting at a desk that was separated from the rest of the room by a wall with a sliding glass window, remained in the office. The rest of the doctor's staff had already left for lunch.

Holly nodded. "The baby's head is down, so everything's on schedule, maybe even a little bit early. The only problem is that my blood pressure's up a tad. The doctor's not too worried, though, as long as it doesn't go higher." She closed the copy of *Working Mother* magazine she'd been reading while she waited for her neighbor to return. Holly knew that articles about how other single moms managed to live full lives should give her confidence that she too could do a successful job of bringing up a child by herself, but she was having trouble remembering anything she'd read.

Celia set down her shopping bags on the low brown-tweed sofa next to where Holly was sitting and looked around. The doctor's reception room was unexceptional: basic brown institutional furnishings, beige walls, and a selection of the requisite baby and child care magazines cluttering the cheap-looking lamp tables. Only a red plastic child-size table and chairs in a corner—apparently intended for kids who'd been brought here because their mothers couldn't afford a sitter—broke the monotony. The receptionist, behind her window, was on the telephone, busily making appointment reminder calls.

"I'm not a bit surprised your blood pressure's up," Celia told Holly, "considering everything you've been through lately."

"That's what Dr. Moravian told me. Said I had to try to relax more." Holly rolled her eyes. "Like I haven't tried. Like it's that easy." She sighed. "If I weren't pregnant, I could tank up on tranquilizers or red wine for a few days. Find some way to knock myself out for a while and get some rest, no matter how churned up I feel inside."

Celia stiffened. "You certainly can't do anything like *that*!" She frankly didn't care whether Holly Sheridan ever got another full night's sleep, but the health of the baby Alex's bimbo was carrying was a different story. No way should Holly even think about drinking or taking drugs, not when she was almost ready to give birth. "You're just going to have to find some other way to relax and get some sleep," Celia told her.

"I'm doing the best I can!" Holly snapped back. But she was instantly contrite. "Hey, sorry, Pat, I didn't mean to take my frustrations out on you. I would never do anything to hurt my baby, no way. It's just I feel like I'm at the end of my rope these days."

Celia leaned over and placed a firm hand on the shorter woman's shoulder. "It's all right, Holly. I probably sounded like I was scolding you. I didn't mean to. I understand how you feel, really I do. I've been pregnant myself. And I'm a widow, just like you. I know how rough it is."

"Guess we should get going if we're going to have some lunch and still stop at the grocery store on the way home," Holly said, reaching for her purse. She glanced at the two shopping bags. "Looks like you were really serious when you said you were going shopping, Pat."

"I had a ball," Celia said. She meant it. Shopping was among her favorite pastimes, particularly when she could afford to buy whatever she wanted, the very best. With the money she had coming in, she could afford to furnish a nursery with nothing but Baby Dior if she felt like it.

"What'd you buy?" Holly wasn't really interested, but she knew it was time to begin taking some interest in other people. Perhaps, like the women's magazines advised, getting outside herself, empathizing with somebody else, would help lift her depression.

Celia flashed her a sly smile. "I decided to give a one-woman baby shower," she said.

"I don't get it."

"This is all for the baby." Celia opened one of her bags and pulled out a tiny yellow cotton nightgown. Its hem and cuffs were hand-embroidered with minuscule green-and-white lilies of the valley. "Isn't this the sweetest thing you ever saw?"

Holly's eyes widened. Momentarily speechless, she watched Celia pull more infant-sized garments out of the bags. She spotted a price tag still attached to the little yellow nightgown; it had cost thirty-eight dollars! Celia took two similar garments from her bag, one in white with orange-and-yellow flowers, and the last in mint green with white flowers. Holly couldn't believe it—well over a hundred dollars for three infant gowns! With one or two exceptions, she'd never spent that much on her *own* nightwear.

"This is my favorite," Celia said, her eyes alight despite the dark contact lenses she was wearing. The hooded sweater she took out of the shopping bag was hand-knitted of cloud-soft white yarn. "Look at these little buttons, Holly. Aren't they just precious?" Each of the miniature fasteners on the sweater was square, with rounded corners, and bore the image of a bright yellow baby duckling. "I bought a nice warm blanket sleeper too, for chilly nights, and a couple of those towel sets that have little hoods for drying the baby's hair. And look at this!"

Layette items were quickly strewn all across the reception room sofa. Celia removed a bulging cardboard box with a musical mobile inside it from her second shopping bag.

"You just fasten this rod to the crib and wind up the music box," she explained, "and all these little clowns dance around in the air. It gives the baby something to watch and listen to and supposedly helps develop good eye coordination." The clowns attached to the mobile were pudgy, hand-stuffed little dolls dressed in bright red, blue, green, and yellow costumes. Each clown had orange yarn hair peeking from under its peaked hat. They resembled a series of tiny Raggedy

Ann and Andy dolls dressed up as Bozo the Clown. "You *do* have a crib, don't you?" Celia asked. "Because if you don't—"

"I—I can't—" Holly pushed herself up off the couch and stepped away from the costly display, as though trying to escape from her benefactor. "I can't possibly accept all these things from you, Pat." Holly was stunned and embarrassed. Why on earth had this woman she'd met only a couple of days ago bought all this for *another* woman's baby? It didn't make sense.

"Don't be silly, Holly. Of course you can. You can't tell me the baby isn't going to need these things."

"No, of course not. That's not what I meant. It's too much, that's all, it's just too much." Holly had planned to supplement the baby gear she already had on hand with some inexpensive layette items from J.C. Penney and Target. She'd never envisioned having things like these. "I hardly even know you," she protested.

From behind her glass barrier, the doctor's receptionist was now staring openly at the two women. Holly felt her face growing warm with embarrassment.

"Just humor me, Holly," Celia insisted.

"But I could never pay you back."

"I don't want to be paid back," Celia lied. "Just let me do something for the baby, that's all I ask." Holly would pay her back eventually, of course, in spades, Celia thought; she just didn't know it yet. If Celia could play this out to the end, precisely the way she planned it, Holly wouldn't know what she was in for until the very last minute. And by then it would be too late.

Celia began refolding her purchases and stuffing them into the bags. "It's been years and years since I got to shop for a baby," she told the younger woman with an eager smile. "I'm getting a real kick out of it, and I can well afford it. That's all this is, nothing more."

Holly stood rooted to the carpet, shaking her head. There had to be two or three hundred dollars' worth of merchandise in the two shopping bags, maybe more—far more than Holly herself could possibly afford to pay for a few pieces of clothing and a musical mobile. She knew she was supposed to feel grateful for these pricey gifts, but she didn't. What she felt was embarrassed and increasingly claustrophobic, as though Pat Patterson were smothering her. Smothering her with kindness, perhaps, with unexpected generosity, but smothering her all the same.

"The only thing I regret is that I don't know whether it's going to be a girl or a boy," Celia said, as though Holly had made no protest whatsoever. "So I bought everything in white and yellow and green and nothing in pink or blue." She folded the last of the tiny garments and put it away. "You didn't ask the doctor which it is, did you?"

"Which what?"

"A girl or a boy?" Celia herself had a strong preference for a girl—boys could grow up to be such bastards. Still, she couldn't afford to be choosy.

"Uh—no, I told you," Holly said. "Alex and I want it to be a surprise. All we want—I mean, wanted—was for our baby to be born healthy."

Celia's smile faded and her eyes grew cold. "That's all I ever wanted too."

Holly glanced toward the receptionist. The young woman was grinning broadly, as though she found the scene in the waiting room very amusing. Holly looked away again, grabbed her jacket from the coat tree, and slipped her arms into its sleeves.

The woman in the white uniform slid open her little window. "See you next week, Mrs. Sheridan," she said.

"Uh, sure. Wednesday morning," Holly answered.

"Ten-fifteen."

"Right."

"Tell you what, Holly," Celia said, as the two women emerged from the doctor's office into the hallway of the medical building.

"What?"

"If you're so intent on paying for this stuff, you can buy my lunch."

"Lunch? Oh, sure. I'd be glad to. There's a Great Earth right down the street. That okay with you?"

"Whatever." Celia never ate more than a few mixed greens with lemon juice at lunchtime, anyway.

"Tell me about your children, Pat," Holly said, searching for a topic of conversation as they entered the elevator. "How many do you have?"

Celia shot her a puzzled look. "Children?"

"Yeah. How many do you have? How old are they?"

"I have no children," Celia said coldly, holding the shopping bags in front of her like a shield.

"But you just said—" Holly stopped herself, mortified to realize that her question had been insensitive. "I'm sorry. I didn't mean to pry."

"It's been a long, long time since my baby died," Celia said, her face grim. "Like my dear late husband was always telling me, I've had a lot of years to get over my loss."

She reached out and angrily punched the elevator button for the first floor.

Chapter

21

Greg Garrison recognized the familiar odor hanging in the air the instant he entered the Gull Drive house. That damned Lou Flint was at it again! The contractor walked slowly toward the master bedroom, where the carpenter, a lighted cigarette dangling between his lips, was hanging one of the folding closet doors.

"Pack up your tools and get the hell out of here, Flint," Greg said angrily. He stood in the bedroom doorway with his hands out in front of him, balled into fists, and his feet wide apart, as though physically ready to throw the other man off the construction site if necessary.

"What the hell!" Startled by his boss's unexpected appearance, Lou Flint spun around. He abruptly let go of the door he'd been lifting onto its metal track; it slammed against the wall, leaving a slight dent in the plasterboard.

"I've warned you about your goddamned smoking for the last time. Now I want you out. You're finished."

Shooting a defiant look at Greg, Lou Flint tossed his

lighted cigarette onto the plywood subfloor and ground it out with the toe of his black leather boot. The extinguished cigarette left behind a thick black smudge and a trail of ground tobacco.

"Fuck you, Garrison," Lou mumbled under his breath, as he tossed his screwdriver toward his open toolbox. It careened off one of the box's red metal corners and clattered onto the floor. "You owe me three weeks' pay, plus severance."

"Screw severance, Flint. You'll get paid for your time and not a penny more. And don't expect a reference."

Glaring daggers at his boss, Lou Flint gathered up his tools from the floor, threw them into the tool chest, and then slammed the cover closed and latched it. "Coulda fooled me. Here I thought Sheridan was the only tight-ass prick around this place," he said.

His eyes narrowing with anger, Greg tightened his fists but kept his mouth shut, stiffling a strong urge to reply in kind. If he did, he knew, this confrontation would surely come to blows, and he had far more to lose than to gain from a fistfight with an employee, even one as surly as Lou Flint.

Lou pushed his way past Greg and stomped down the hall into the kitchen. He put his toolbox on the countertop, grabbed his denim jacket from the corner where he'd left it this morning, and put it on. Before he picked up his tools and walked off the site, however, he pulled a half-empty pack of Camels from his shirt pocket, removed one, and inserted it between his lips. With one hand, he flipped open the top of his silver lighter, spun the flint wheel until it caught and flared, lit his cigarette, and inhaled deeply.

"Fuck you, Garrison," Lou repeated, exhaling a stream of thick, acrid smoke in his boss's direction.

"Fuck you and all your goddamned green-freak buddies." The man's heavy boots hammered across the bare plywood flooring as he stormed out of the house, leaving the front door open to the afternoon winds.

After Flint had driven his pickup off in a screech of tires, Greg went through the house opening windows. While the place was airing out, he took a rag and wiped up the evidence the cigarette had left on the master bedroom subfloor. Sure, carpeting would be installed in this room before the house went on the market, and probably no one would ever find out that cigarette ash had been ground into the plywood underneath it. But Greg knew if Ecobay didn't have a reputation for integrity, if people didn't believe its houses were environmentally clean and safe, they wouldn't pay an extra dime for an Ecobay house.

If Ecobay's product was no different from the competition, this whole experiment would go right down the drain. Besides, it was a matter of principle.

Greg scrubbed at the black spot until it was almost eradicated, then tossed the rag aside and began hanging the closet doors himself. From now on, he could see, he would be doing much more of this kind of work by himself. Without Alex to help out, and now without his main carpenter on the job either, Greg was elected. He could see the target completion date on the house moving farther and farther into the future.

Greg jimmied and shifted the second closet door into its track, then adjusted it until it met its mate perfectly. The master bedroom was falling into place, if slowly. The wallboard was completely installed now— although he would have to plaster over the dent Lou Flint had just put in it—and the taping had been completed. Now all the room really needed was a couple of coats of paint, nontoxic wood stain on the doors and door frames, and wall-to-wall carpeting. That could be done in a week. The house as a whole, however, would require at least another eight to ten weeks if Greg didn't hire more help.

On the other hand, he could get the house where Holly Sheridan was now living into shape to sell within a week, two at the most. If he could bring just one man in there to help him finish the back deck, add a few light fixtures here and there, and complete work on that third bedroom, the place could be finished and on the market by the beginning of next month.

"Goddamn it," Greg said out loud. Much as he dreaded it, he was going to have to talk to Holly about where Ecobay was headed. Very soon. Lou Flint had to be given his three weeks' pay right away. And maybe the horse's ass really *was* entitled to severance pay. Greg would have to check on that, or maybe Holly could make some calls to find out. It wouldn't pay to have Flint filing a complaint against Ecobay Housing with some bureaucratic state regulatory agency.

What Greg really needed right now was a new partner, an active partner, another hands-on guy like Alex Sheridan. Somebody with vision, an architect who could design these unique houses, yet somebody who wasn't too self-important to get his hands dirty along with the rest of the crew if necessary. But that simply wasn't going to happen as long as Alex's widow owned half of the company. Ecobay was too small to split three ways. There simply wasn't enough potential profit to support that many partners. Not for the foreseeable future, anyway.

Greg headed for the kitchen, closing windows as he went. When the house was all closed up again and the smoke odor was gone, he poured himself a cup of coffee from the thermos he'd brought from home. He tore off a section of brown paper that had been wrapped around a stack of floor tiles and spread it flat across the surface of the kitchen counter. Using the stub of a pencil he always carried in his shirt pocket, he began to write a column of figures on the paper, starting with the fifty grand payable from Alex's insurance.

Half an hour later, Greg's coffee was gone and his numbers covered most of the strip of brown paper. Clearly, if Ecobay was to survive, the insurance proceeds would have to be used wisely, and a new partner to replace Alex would have to be brought in within the next couple of months. Surely Holly Sheridan would understand that. He would have to make her understand.

Greg could see two possible ways to go. He could trade Holly the fifty thousand, plus the house she was living in, for her share of Ecobay. She would have to take over the mortgage payments on the Sandpiper Circle house, of course. But fifty grand plus the equity in the house seemed an eminently fair price for her half interest in Ecobay, considering its current worth.

If Holly didn't go for that deal, the only alternative was to complete and sell the Sandpiper Circle house she was living in and reinvest the proceeds in the company. Holly and her baby would have to move into a rental place somewhere. Luckily, there were plenty of rentals available in Bodega Bay, even if they did tend to be pretty pricey.

With the money from the sale of its first house, Ecobay might be able to hire an architect part time, Greg figured, along with a bigger construction crew to finish up the Gull Drive and Pelican Loop houses and then begin building one or two more. Holly could continue doing the company's ordering and billing, while Greg supervised the construction.

Greg knew which alternative he preferred. It was the first, no argument about it. Paying Holly off with a combination of cash and the Sandpiper Circle house would give him the two things he most wanted right now—control of Ecobay's future and the knowledge that Alex Sheridan's widow would have enough ready cash to get by, at least for a year or two.

It would also release Greg from the twin burdens that had weighed so heavily on him lately—his fear that Ecobay Housing wouldn't be able to survive Alex Sheridan's death and his piercing guilt over not being able to make things right again for Alex's young widow.

Chapter

22

Celia scooped half a dozen dress shirts off the higher pole in the closet and threw them into the open cardboard box with their hangers still attached. Reaching into the box, she savagely punched the shirts down to make room for additional clothing.

"Don't you think we ought to fold those shirts first?" Holly asked. Her helper's hasty, almost violent stripping of the closet made her uneasy. Holly was sitting cross-legged on the bedroom carpet, emptying the bottom drawer of the big triple dresser where Alex had kept his exercise clothes. Before she put each pair of jogging shorts or sweatpants into a box destined for the Salvation Army, she made sure it was clean and neatly folded. Then she placed its matching tank top or sweatshirt on top of it.

"Doesn't matter," Celia said, her jaw rigid and her hands tightly clenched at her sides. "Don't they wash everything before they sell it anyway? Unless you need to keep these hangers." She lifted the top shirt out of the box again, holding it by two fingers, as though it smelled bad and she didn't want to risk soiling her hands.

"No, no, I've got more than enough hangers." Holly closed the now-empty drawer and opened a smaller one, which held Alex's underwear and T-shirts. She reached in, lifted out a stack of multicolored Hanes briefs, and meticulously arranged them on top of the exercise clothes.

Celia let the shirt she was holding fall back into the box and then yanked a thick gray wool pullover sweater off its sturdy wooden hanger and tossed it on top of the mashed shirts. She did the same with a blue cardigan and a brown tweed sports jacket with suede patches on the elbows. "There," she said, wiping her hands against the backside of her jeans. "That takes care of the closet. Except for the shoes." She kicked her toe at a dozen pairs of shoes, ranging from black leather dress oxfords to an old pair of Birkenstocks to some nearly new Nikes, all neatly lined up on the closet floor.

"I think those better go into a separate box," Holly suggested. She didn't want to soil Alex's clothing so badly that the Salvation Army couldn't sell it. The point here, after all, was to help others less fortunate as well as to clear the house of Alex's personal belongings. She started to push herself up off the floor to get another box out of storage, but Celia quickly motioned her back down.

"Don't get up, Holly. I'll find an empty box. In the garage, right?"

"Right. Way in the back."

Celia's spine was rigid as she walked stiffly out of the room. She seethed with unexpected anger she couldn't afford to show. It had been her idea to help Holly with this nasty job, which promised to be emotionally diffi- cult for the young widow. "I didn't have any help at all when my poor Jeff passed away," she'd told Holly, spontaneously choosing a name for her fictional dead spouse. "Nobody should have to do this alone."

Holly had seemed eager for her neighbor's help, and Celia figured the task would give her a chance to snoop through the things Alex had left behind, plus gain a bit more of his widow's confidence. What Celia hadn't counted on, however, was how angry she would feel after being stuck for more than an hour in the bedroom that Alex and Holly had shared. Her rage grew every time she saw the king-size bed, with its cheap-looking beige-and-white plaid bedspread. She wouldn't have something so common-looking in *her* home, of course. Still, this massive love nest had to be where the fucking traitor who'd deserted her had impregnated his trophy wife. It made her blood boil.

Once inside the Sheridans' bedroom, Celia couldn't take her eyes off the looming piece of furniture. It became symbolic of everything that had gone wrong with her life in the twenty-nine years since she had married Alex Sheridan. And the more she stared at the bed, the more it infuriated her.

Celia knew she had to get out of the room before she said something she would later regret. Holly already sensed that something was wrong. She escaped to the garage and found an empty carton, big enough to hold Alex's shoes and perhaps a few other things as well. And before she returned to the bedroom, she took a deep breath, flexed her jaw open and closed a few times, and swiveled her head around on her stiff neck to help release some of the tension in her shoulder muscles. She couldn't afford to have Holly wondering why she was so emotional about packing up the personal effects of a man she'd supposedly never met. The widow might start asking questions Celia had no intention of answering.

"Here we go," Celia said, tossing the empty box onto the bedroom floor. It landed against the edge of the bed with a thud. Within two minutes, she had thrown in all twelve pairs of Alex Sheridan's shoes. "There, that's finished. What next?"

"I—I hadn't thought. This takes care of most of Alex's clothes." Holly took a mental inventory of her husband's belongings. She'd already thrown out most of the things he'd left behind in the bathroom—extra medications, an old hairbrush, and the like. His toilet kit with his electric shaver and all the other personal things he'd used daily had been in the Cessna when it went down. Now everything in the kit was either underwater or strewn across some faraway beach.

"Alex had a lot of books in his office," Holly recalled. "I don't know whether we should get rid of some of those too. I mean, I guess we might as well, if somebody could use them."

"Let's go look," Celia said eagerly. She was grateful that at least Alex hadn't kept his books in the bedroom. She had to escape this room that sparked so much pain and resentment, away from the bed that brought back so many rancid personal memories, before she blew her cover. She folded the flaps of the shoe carton closed and carried it out of the room, depositing it by the front door with two others she'd packed earlier.

Alex's office was in the third bedroom of the house. Celia saw that the room was half complete at best. Alex's big old desk—she recognized it as the one he'd taken with him when he'd moved out of the Bel Air house—was pushed against one still-unpainted wall. A much newer computer table stood at right angles to the desk, while a long low bookcase made of boards and cement blocks was on the opposite side of the room.

"I'll go through the desk later," Holly said. "Most of the stuff in there I'll need to keep for Ecobay anyway. It's these books over here on the bottom couple of shelves I thought I might donate to charity."

Celia knelt down in front of the bookcase and read some of the titles on the spines of the books: *Modern Architecture, Contemporary Design in Single Family Housing, Single-Story Construction Techniques.* She recognized a few that had once been in Alex's home office in Bel Air. "We'll need another box for these," she said, rising again. "I'll go get one."

"Thanks," Holly said, awkwardly lowering herself to the hard plywood floor next to the bookcase. Her belly felt heavier than ever today, as though a concrete watermelon were resting on top of her bladder.

"I'll pull the books I want to get rid of off the shelf and hand them up to you, okay?" she suggested, when the other woman had returned from the garage with the empty carton.

Holly emptied about half the bookcase. She had no use for the architecture books, and if Ecobay hired another architect, surely he'd have his own favorites. She hoped the Salvation Army could either sell them or give them to a needy architecture student. She didn't want Alex's favorite novels, either. His taste had tended toward war stories, while she preferred biographies and lighter fiction.

After checking each volume for any papers Alex might have tucked inside, she handed dusty hardcover copies of *The Young Lions, War and Remembrance,* and several other World War II novels to her neighbor, who stacked them in the book carton.

As she was sorting a group of books about soldiers' experiences in Korea and Vietnam, Holly came across three slimmer volumes with unlabeled spines. After handing over the war books, she set the smaller books on the floor and opened the cover of the top one. A sharp pang of loss struck her as she saw that the inside pages were covered with Alex's handwriting. Were these his notebooks from long-ago architecture classes? She turned over a few of the pages marked with blue ink and read a section at random, dated October 22, 1965, back when Alex would have been a college student and Holly was a small child.

It's been three weeks now since Dad died, and I can't stop thinking about him and the way he was always so hard on me. Why didn't he ever seem to approve of me or anything I did? Aunt Leah keeps telling me I'm off base, that Dad really was proud of me—in his way. But I just can't see it.

"What've you got there?" Celia demanded.

"I don't really know. Seems to be some kind of journal Alex kept a long time ago," Holly said. "Dates way back to the middle sixties." She picked up the second volume and opened it near the middle. It had been written in 1966 and 1967. The third of the three volumes was much more recent, however, dated in the early 1990s. "This one here is only three or four years old, though." Holly glanced up at her neighbor, a puzzled expression on her lightly freckled face. "I had no idea Alex kept a diary."

Neither had Celia. Her throat constricting, she thrust out a hand and grabbed one of the books lying by

Holly's side. Celia and Alex had been married in the middle sixties. Whatever the bastard had written in these books, it had to be about her and her life; she just knew it. The last thing she needed was for this pregnant bitch to learn her most intimate secrets—assuming Alex hadn't already blabbed them all. It was bad enough that her philandering husband had humiliated her while he was still alive; now the son of a bitch had figured out a way to make her suffer after he was dead.

"Hey, wait a minute!" Holly protested as the other woman snatched up the diary. "I'm not giving these books away."

"You really should throw them out, Holly," Celia said, grabbing the second of the three journals. "It—it's not good for you to dwell on the past." She knew she didn't sound logical, but she couldn't think of anything else to say. She could hardly blurt out the truth. "It's better just to put things like this behind you, get rid of them right off the bat," she insisted. "I know, I've been there."

"No way!" Holly reached over, wrenched the two slim books out of the other woman's grasp, and held them tightly and possessively against her chest. "I'm perfectly capable of making my own decisions about this, thank you very much."

Her neighbor was acting particularly odd today, Holly thought. She could sense a great deal of hostility in the other woman. Why, Pat's hands were actually trembling, and her pale lips were a thin, tight line; she seemed thoroughly enraged about something. Yet she'd volunteered to help with this depressing task, hadn't she? Holly certainly had never asked her neighbor to help sort Alex's things.

Holly was puzzled. Why on earth should Pat Patterson care whether or not she kept her husband's old diaries? Perhaps, she thought, the woman's almost palpable animosity was not about the diaries at all but about something else. She'd started to sense it back in the bedroom. Maybe, Holly thought, Pat was still angry because she'd refused all those things for the baby the other day. Sure, Holly had compromised by accepting the musical mobile for the nursery, but she'd also insisted that Pat return all the handmade clothing. Had the older woman felt rebuffed, so that now she was holding a grudge?

"Listen, Pat," Holly said, her thoughts reeling, "I think we've both done more than enough for one day. I can pack the rest of the books myself, when I get around to it."

"I'll help you. You shouldn't be lifting heavy boxes, Holly, you know that." Celia didn't want to leave without those diaries.

"I don't plan on lifting any boxes," Holly told her. "I'll leave them right here on the floor. The Salvation Army man can carry them away."

"No, really, I'll come back and help you." Celia was frantic. She had to have those diaries! She had to find out what Alex had written about her—*now*, before this colorless blimp of a woman had the chance to invade her privacy, maybe have another good laugh at her and the terrible, painful life Alex had forced on her all those years ago.

Holly slid the diaries back onto the bookshelf and awkwardly pushed herself to her feet. The simple motion of getting up off the floor was fast becoming all but impossible. "Let's go, Pat," she said. "We're both tired."

"But—"

"You can carry that box of books out to the front door for me if you want to help. It's almost full, anyway."

Celia picked up the box Holly indicated. It was all she could do not to reach out and grab the diaries off the shelf a few feet away, but Holly was watching her carefully, obviously puzzled by her behavior. "We certainly put in a good afternoon's work, didn't we?" Celia said, attempting to lighten the tension before their fledgling friendship was irreparably damaged. It was imperative that Holly Sheridan trust her if her plan was to work.

Holly swept her bangs off her brow. She could feel sweat trickling from her armpits, and her back ached more than ever. "I don't know about you, but I'm exhausted. Think I'll go soak in the bathtub for a while." She'd had more than enough of her new neighbor for one day. It wasn't that she was ungrateful for the help, but her patience was wearing thin. Maybe her emotions were on such a roller coaster because of her crazy hormones, Holly thought. Perhaps, between her pregnancy and her grief, she was going a little nutty, becoming too sensitive and short-tempered. Whatever the reason, she suddenly couldn't stand another minute of Pat Patterson's company. She simply had to be alone.

After Holly had ushered her helper out the front door, she stood and watched as the taller woman crossed Sandpiper Circle and entered her own house. Then she latched her front door and put on the chain lock.

As she ran hot water into the bathtub, added a squirt of liquid bubble bath, and watched fluffy white suds expand across the surface of the steaming water, Holly Sheridan could feel her exhausted body gradually beginning to relax. And as she lay back in the soothing warmth, she realized how much she appreciated the first real solitude she'd had all day.

Celia carried the two suitcases into the attached garage, loaded them in the back of the station wagon, and closed up the car before opening the garage door to let in the morning sunlight. She didn't want to risk Holly's glancing across the street and spotting her as she packed the car.

Before she started her day trip, Celia made two phone calls, one to confirm her noontime appointment and the second to her neighbor. "Sure there isn't something I can pick up for you in town, Holly?" she asked. "A carton of milk or some fresh fruit, maybe?"

"Thanks, Pat, but I really don't need anything right now."

Celia heard a note of exhaustion in the other woman's voice. "You feeling okay?" she asked. "You're not having labor pains or anything, are you?" She held her breath as she waited for Holly's answer. If the baby decided to come today, while Celia was away, all her careful plans would go right down the drain.

"I'm just a little tired from yesterday," Holly replied. "That's all."

As she hung up the phone, Celia decided she would simply have to hurry her trip as much as possible and hope that Holly was right. If she didn't get stuck behind some poky farmer on the curving country roads between here and San Francisco, she could do all her errands and be back in Bodega Bay by dinnertime.

Two hours later, Celia was in the maternity department at Macy's on Union Square, fingering a soft beige knit tent-style dress. She lifted it off the rack and carried it over to a mirror mounted on a pillar, then held it up in front of her. This color would be more flattering once she got rid of this horrible dark wig, she decided, as she examined her reflection.

"Beige goes with everything. You can dress this one up or down. It's very practical."

Startled, Celia looked around. A young saleswoman was standing next to her.

"Are you looking for a gift for somebody?" the clerk asked, her expression blank.

Celia's jaw tightened. Was this little snip trying to imply that she looked too old to be expecting a baby? Women in their late forties were having babies all the time lately. She'd even read about some Italian woman in her *sixties* who'd given birth—with the help of a donated embryo. This clerk couldn't possibly be that ignorant or that insulting, could she? Celia took a breath and got her temper back under control before she allowed herself to speak. She told herself that the woman probably meant only that, with her trim figure, she didn't look pregnant. No sense going out of her way to take offense.

"It's for my sister," Celia lied. "She's my height and build, but blond."

"This dress should be perfect for her then. It comes in black too, but beige is so much nicer on a blonde, don't you think?"

Celia bought the beige dress, along with a pair of brown maternity slacks and an oversized yellow sweater. After the clerk had folded her purchases and put them into a dark green shopping bag with a Macy's logo, Celia headed upstairs to the home furnishings department, where she bought a fat throw pillow, selecting it more for its oval shape and softly padded thickness than its pink color.

Twenty minutes later, as she emerged from the handicapped stall in the women's rest room, Celia looked completely different. The dark wig was stowed away in her shopping bag, but her body appeared even more changed than her hair. Now she wore the brown maternity slacks and yellow sweater she'd just bought, with the throw pillow stuffed underneath at her waistline to give her a rounded silhouette. She washed her hands at the sink, then began to brush out her hair. It felt wonderful to be free of that itchy wig.

"My youngest was a midlife baby too," confided a short elderly woman who was washing her hands at the next sink. "Your little one will keep you young, you can count on that."

Celia smiled at the woman, pleased that her altered appearance obviously had passed muster. She was even willing to ignore the woman's implication that Celia looked to be in "midlife."

Celia was right on time for her noon appointment. As she surveyed the fifth-floor apartment on Grove Street near Van Ness, a stone's throw from Opera Plaza, she reminded herself to move more slowly, as though her bulging belly weighed an extra twenty pounds. She tried to walk leaning a little backward, in that awkward way Holly did. It wouldn't do to have the building manager, a thin, sixtyish man with nicotine-stained teeth and fingers, suspect that she wasn't really pregnant. Fooling him was essential to her plan.

The apartment was very small, with only one bedroom and bathroom, a combination living-dining room, and a tiny in-line kitchen. Everything—the walls, the carpet, the furniture—was that neutral color halfway between beige and gray, and now that she saw it Celia realized why the newspaper ad had described the place as a "cozy 1 br., fully furn." It was cozy, all right, a far cry from either her house in Bel Air or the one she was renting in Bodega Bay. This whole apartment would probably fit into the living room of either house. Still, if she decided to rent it, this would be only a temporary address. All she really needed for now was someplace clean and fully furnished, and this seemed to fit the bill.

"I'm going to need a crib soon," she told the building manager. She spread her fingers over her soft belly and smiled in a way she believed made her look maternal. "Is that a problem?"

"Nope. Got a couple down in the basement. I can clean one up for ya, Mrs. Sheridan. But when we talked on the phone, you didn't say nothin' about a family. Rent's higher, ya know, the more people ya got livin' here."

"It'll be just me and the baby, Mr. Fraser. Surely an infant isn't going to do any damage to the furniture."

"No Mr. Sheridan?" The building manager glanced at Celia's naked ring finger.

Celia shot him a sly look and lowered her voice to a confidential level. "I'm not married, Mr. Fraser. My baby's daddy's a sperm bank. You know how it is. Biological clocks keep right on ticking, and you can't wait forever for Mr. Right to come along, can you?"

Fraser shrugged. This was San Francisco, after all, and Celia Sheridan's was far from the strangest story he'd ever heard from a tenant. "It's gonna be ten bucks a month extra for the crib. That's twelve hundred and ten each for the first and last months, plus five hundred for yer damage deposit. Comes to twenty-nine hundred and twenty dollars altogether to get ya moved in."

Celia signed the month-to-month lease that Fraser pulled from his pocket and wrote a check on her Los Angeles account for the full amount of the specified rent and deposits, showing her driver's license for identification. Although she'd taken pains to identify herself as Pat Patterson in Bodega Bay, here in San Francisco she wanted to be known as Celia Sheridan. Celia Sheridan, expectant mother.

After Fraser handed over the keys to the apartment and left, Celia went down to the garage and brought up her two suitcases. She quickly unpacked them, loading the clothes they held into the dresser drawers in the bedroom and hanging up a few things in the compact closet. Most of the suitcases' contents were her own clothes: dresses, slacks, and sweaters she planned to wear here in San Francisco after the baby was born. The rest of the things were for the baby—crib-size blankets and sheets, disposable diapers, a set of plastic nursing bottles. In the bottom of the suitcase were the tiny clothes she'd bought in Santa Rosa, the handmade gowns and sleepers that Holly Sheridan had so stupidly rejected when she'd tried to give them to her.

It was easier this way, Celia told herself, as she ran a finger across the delicate embroidery that circled the neckline of the small yellow sleeper. She lifted the tiny garment to her face and felt its softness against her cheek. It was better this way, to have the things the baby would need right here, all clean and ready, when she returned to San Francisco.

After she finished unpacking, Celia introduced herself to the neighbor across the hall.

"I'm Muriel Knack," the old woman told her, as she opened the door a crack. "Nice to meet you, Celia. I hope you're going to like it here."

"I'm sure I will. This building seems quite conveniently located, although it will probably be just a temporary home for us. With my baby coming and all—" Celia patted her belly again, just in case Muriel Knack's sharp old eyes hadn't taken proper note of her pregnancy. "In a few months, I'll probably have to find a place with a second bedroom. You know how fast babies grow."

Pleased with herself for having found an acceptable if not very plush San Francisco home, plus two witnesses to her near-term pregnancy, Celia rode the elevator down to the main floor. Leaving the station wagon parked in the building's underground garage, she walked the short distance to a bookshop on Opera Plaza's ground level, where she purchased two books about childbirth, one of which included photographs documenting each step in the birth of a baby, with clear directions for handling an emergency delivery. When she got back to Bodega Bay, she would study them thoroughly.

As she left the bookstore with her purchases, Celia noticed that the lunch crowd at Max's Opera Plaza Cafe across the courtyard had thinned out and realized that she was famished. She'd been up since six o'clock that morning, and now it was nearly two, well past her usual lunchtime. Besides, as an expectant mother, she had to eat to keep up her strength, didn't she? Certainly she could afford to take a few minutes for a quick lunch.

Celia climbed onto a tall chair in the bar section of Max's and ordered a Caesar salad from the handsome young waiter, then left her jacket folded across her chair and headed for a pay phone near the women's rest room.

She dialed a Los Angeles number. "This is Celia Sheridan, Charlene. I want to speak to Leland," she announced, when her attorney's secretary answered.

"Sorry, Mrs. Sheridan. Mr. Klein's on another line. Can he call you back?"

"This is long distance and I'm at a pay phone. I'm afraid you'll have to interrupt him."

There was a long pause. Finally, the secretary sighed audibly. "Okay, Mrs. Sheridan, hold on," she said. "I'll see if he can take your call."

She would have to speak to Leland about that stupid Charlene, Celia thought, as she listened to static on the line. Any client who paid Klein as much as she did should be treated like royalty.

"Hello, Celia, what can I do for you?"

Celia recognized her lawyer's deep voice on the line. "Hello, Leland. I'm calling for an update on the house sale and Alex's life insurance policy."

The attorney explained that the escrow on the Bel Air house was scheduled to close on Friday.

"Does that mean I get my money the same day?"

"Right. Either Vanderbilt or his attorney will bring a

bank check for the full amount of the purchase price to the closing. The escrow company will pay off the mortgage immediately and issue you a check for the remainder. That reminds me. I'll need the address where you want me to send your check."

"I don't want it mailed, Leland. Deposit it in First Western Bank as soon as you get it. You have my account number."

"Okay, if that's what you want. I'll have Charlene dig the information out of your file."

"Now, what about my money from Alex's life insurance? Do you have the check yet?"

"There's been a little bit of a delay on that."

"Delay? What kind of delay?" A note of panic crept into Celia's voice. "I don't understand."

"Because of the death certificate," Leland Klein explained. "The Monterey County coroner hasn't officially determined the cause of Alex's death yet, and the insurance company requires a death certificate before they pay off the beneficiary. That's standard industry practice."

"But that's not fair! It's not my fault the coroner's dinging around. Hell, the plane crashed and the man died, right? Where's the mystery in that? The insurance company's trying to pull a fast one, and I don't like it."

"Calm down, Celia, I'm negotiating with the insurance people right now, and I guarantee they don't want a lawsuit for bad faith. If I push them a little harder, I think they'll accept the preliminary death certificate and pay off the policy. After all, it's not like there's any question about it's being Alex Sheridan who died in that crash."

Thank God for small favors, Celia thought. "So how long is this thing going to take? I'm entitled to that money now."

"I know you are, but you're just going to have to be patient a little longer. My guess is you'll have your check by the end of next week at the latest."

"I guess I can live with that, as long as they don't try to stall. I'm counting on you to get me that check, Leland." Celia glanced at her watch. It was twenty after two. She could make it home by five o'clock if traffic wasn't too bad. "Have them send the check to your office. Then I want you to deposit it in my checking account with the money from the house."

"That's close to a million dollars altogether, Celia. Surely you don't want that much money just lying around in some checking account. It should be invest—"

"*I'll* worry about investing my money, thank you very much. Your job is to collect it for me. And to make sure nobody cheats me."

By the time Celia hung up the phone and returned to her table in the bar area, her Caesar salad, a basket of fresh crusty sourdough bread, and a giant glass of iced tea were waiting for her. She remembered to climb back onto the high chair slowly and awkwardly, as though she really were pregnant. When she caught two women at a nearby table eyeing her with obvious sympathy for her apparent discomfort, she felt thoroughly pleased with herself. She was really having fun here, basking in the sort of attention pregnant women always commanded, the kind of notice they deserved. The caring and concern that Alex had stolen from her so long ago.

But she'd shown him.

As she ate her lunch, Celia added figures in her head. With a million dollars in cash to pave the way, she and the baby could easily begin a new life anywhere she chose. The possibilities were deliciously endless.

Chapter

24

Holly lay flat on her back on the living room sofa with the oldest of her husband's journals propped up against her belly. She'd been resting here for the past hour, alternately reading the words Alex had written in his college days and gazing past her stocking feet at the fog that was slowly moving in to obscure her view of the golf course and seacoast outside the window.

Alex was so young when he began to keep this journal, she thought; he was a complete stranger to her. He'd been as self-absorbed as any other teenager in those days, obsessed with girls, cutting classes at UCLA to go surfing with his buddies, constantly battling with his controlling, disapproving father. Undoubtedly the fact that Alex's dad had died before the two had a chance to resolve their conflicts had severely impacted Alex's life. In the months after his father's death, the entries showed Alex quickly changing from a carefree youth into a young man who seemed to seek out personal burdens, perhaps as a form of punishment for his earlier lack of responsibility.

Neither the teenage Alex Sheridan who surfed and chased girls nor the slightly older Alex, with his overly developed sense of duty, seemed much like the mature man with whom Holly had fallen in love. But perhaps that wasn't so strange, she decided. Was she still the same girl who'd gone to USC to study journalism seventeen years ago? Or even the young woman who, four years later, had graduated with a respectable B average and started out as an editorial assistant at *Stately Homes*?

In those days, Holly'd thought that she would head some important general-circulation magazine by the time she turned thirty and that by the same age she would marry the man of her dreams. A year or so later, according to her girlhood plans, she would take time off to give birth to two perfect children—a boy and a girl—and when they were old enough for nursery school she would resume her skyrocketing career in magazine journalism without missing a stride.

But reality had intervened. As things worked out, Holly rose through the ranks of *Stately Homes* to the position of editor, a respectable enough job but hardly comparable to the same spot at *Time* or *The New Yorker*. She had married the man of her dreams, all right, but she hadn't met him until she was in her middle thirties. And now she was being forced to revise her dreams once more. The two perfect children she'd wanted would be only one child, and he or she would have to be raised by a widowed mother.

No, Holly Sheridan was a far different person from the naive student she'd been so many years ago. Real life had seen to that. Undoubtedly it had changed Alex in the same way.

Just as she felt herself beginning to doze off in the fading light of late afternoon, the doorbell rang. Holly jerked awake, tossed the journal onto the coffee table, swung her feet onto the floor, and slowly pushed herself up off the sofa. "I'm coming, I'm coming," she called out, as she heard the bell ring a second time.

Greg Garrison was standing on the doorstep with the worried look on his face that was becoming so familiar to her. "I—I just wanted to see how you're getting along, Holly," he said, avoiding looking directly into her eyes.

"Come on in, Greg. I'll put on a fresh pot of coffee."

A few minutes later, the two were sitting at the kitchen table, sipping steaming decaf from a pair of thick blue pottery mugs Holly had received as a wedding gift.

"I know I haven't seen all that much of you lately, Holly," Greg said, as he stirred sugar into his coffee, "but I really have been thinking about you. I know I should come around more often, help you out and all, and—"

"It's not a problem, Greg; honest, it's not."

"But I know Alex would've wanted—"

Holly held up her palm to silence her visitor. Greg looked so guilty she felt embarrassed. Clearly the man was uncomfortable around her, whatever his reasons, and his obvious distress made her uneasy too, as though it was up to her to quell his ever-present guilt. "Listen, Greg," she said, "my new neighbor across the circle, Pat Patterson—she's been over here two or three times a day lately, helping me out. Practically lives here. Yesterday, she even helped me pack up—" Holly swallowed hard as the reason for yesterday's job hit her once again. "Pat helped me put Alex's clothes in cartons for the Salvation Army. She's been a real godsend, so you don't have to feel guilty about neglecting me, really you don't."

In truth, Holly was beginning to feel smothered by

Pat. She wished the woman, as well-meaning as she seemed to be, would take more day-long trips like today's and give her a little breathing room. Until Greg's arrival, Holly had been enjoying some rare solitude, but she wasn't about to admit that to him. "Pat absolutely insists on driving me to the hospital when my time comes," she added. "Honest, Greg, the best way you can help me is to keep Ecobay Housing alive and on schedule. I don't need you hanging around the house to fetch and carry for me."

Holly couldn't help noticing the look of relief that crossed Greg's leathery face as he listened to her speech. She'd tactfully let him off the hook and he was clearly grateful.

"I'm doing the best I can with Ecobay, Holly," he told her. "I told you about what happened with Lou Flint. Surly bast—uh, I mean jerk, he had to be fired, no doubt about that. Still, Flint did manage to get the work done on time, and right now we haven't got either the hours or the money to train another carpenter. That'd take me longer than finishing the job myself."

Holly and Greg discussed business for a while. Once or twice, Greg came close to suggesting that they might sell the house Holly was living in to keep Ecobay Housing afloat. But whenever he approached the subject, he felt a new surge of pity for the newly widowed pregnant woman sitting across the table. After the baby was born, he told himself. After the baby was born, they would have to go over the company's figures and come to some agreement. Right now, though, Greg simply couldn't bring himself to evict an expectant mother from her home, even if it did belong to Ecobay.

Besides, he had come here today to discuss a different sticky subject with Holly, and there was no way he could hit her with two emotionally rough things at once. All this talk about Ecobay was his way of procrastinating while he worked up his nerve.

"Holly, there's something I need to talk to you about," he said finally, as he poured himself another cup of coffee.

"Sure, what?"

"The report on Alex's plane—you know, the one from the FAA. Well, the preliminary came in today."

Holly's hand jerked involuntarily, and coffee splashed over the top of her cup and onto the kitchen table. "Wh-what did it say?" she asked, as she grabbed a paper napkin and wiped up the spilled coffee. "What went wrong with the plane?"

"That's the problem, Holly. The FAA hasn't found anything wrong with the plane. Not a thing."

"But that's impossible. There had to be something wrong with it. Planes don't just crash into the ocean for no reason."

Greg sighed and stared at his hands. "You're right, Holly. There *was* a reason Alex's plane crashed. Of course, there was, had to be. We just don't know what it was yet. What we do know is that Alex didn't have a heart attack at the controls, or else the autop—I mean, the medical examination would have discovered it. And now the FAA can't find anything wrong with the Cessna either."

Holly wound a strand of limp brown hair around her index finger. "It doesn't make sense to me, Greg. This whole thing just doesn't make sense."

"Inspector Pruitt called me this morning."

"The guy from the FAA?"

"Right. I know he came to see you awhile back."

Holly's neck muscles tightened as she thought about her uncomfortable meeting with the fidgety man from the government agency.

"Pruitt wanted to know—I mean, he wanted me to ask you something."

"I think I can guess what it was," Holly said.

Greg chewed on his lower lip a while before he spoke again. "Could—I know you don't want to believe Alex would do anything like this, Holly, but maybe Pruitt has a point here. I mean, maybe Alex figured—hell, I might as well just spit it out." He took a deep breath and plunged ahead. "Did Alex leave you any insurance money?"

Holly's jaw became rigid and she pressed her lips together in a tight, narrow line. When she didn't reply, Greg found himself elaborating, trying to justify his blunt question.

"Look, Holly, the truth is, we both know Alex was worried half sick that Ecobay wasn't going to make it. Then there was all that trouble with his ex-wife, sort of like reopening an old wound and pouring salt in it. Maybe he thought if he wasn't around anymore, especially if he could leave you and the baby well fixed financially, you'd be better off without him. Maybe—"

"Bullshit!" Holly's expletive stopped Greg's monologue cold. She ignored the surprised expression on his face. Where he'd gotten his old-fashioned idea that women were fragile beings who didn't feel or express anger, creatures who had to be shielded and protected, she didn't know or care. But it was about time she gave him a taste of reality. "That's the worst crock of unadulterated bullshit I ever heard. From you, of all people! It was bad enough that I had to listen to this sort of nonsense from Pruitt when he was here. *He* didn't know Alex. You did!" As she spoke, Holly felt herself becoming angrier and angrier.

"Okay, okay, I'm sorry. I just thought maybe—"

"Well, you thought wrong, Greg, dead wrong." Holly felt tears stinging her eyes again, but she blinked them away. "You want to know about life insurance? Let me tell you about life insurance. Alex left me one very old policy he probably forgot he even had. It was for a whole ten thousand dollars! That's what the baby and I have to live on—if there's any of it left after I pay the mortuary bill for Alex and the medical bills for the baby. If I'm lucky, I might end up with a few measly dollars, plus our share of Ecobay Housing, whatever that's worth. Good God, Greg, do you really think Alex would leave me practically destitute like this *on purpose*?"

Greg pushed his chair back and stood up. He shook his head slowly, remorsefully. "I—all I can say is I'm sorry, Holly. I don't know what else to tell you. It's just that this thing with Alex is so weird. I can't figure it out." Feeling guiltier than ever, he made an awkward attempt to change the subject. "This woman across the circle, what'd you say her name was?"

"Pat Patterson. Lives in that big brown house." Holly angrily wiped at her eyes with the back of her hand. She was annoyed with herself for becoming weepy again, but at least this time her tears came from rage, not self-pity.

"Patterson. You say this Mrs. Patterson's planning to take you to the hospital?"

"Said she would." Holly noticed the deep worry lines between Greg's eyes softening as her words relieved him of yet another burden, and she was glad. The last thing she wanted was to add to his problems. She'd spent much of the afternoon reading about the burden the youthful Alex had taken on after his father's death—the emotionally needy young model named Celia he'd married within a few short months of the funeral. Holly had no desire to be anyone's charity project. She knew people grew to resent, even to hate their burdens after a time, even when they'd willingly taken them on. Holly had always been self-sufficient, defiantly so, even after she married Alex. She had no intention of changing. "Really, Greg," she said, "you don't have to worry about me *or* the baby. Pat will take me to the hospital when the time comes. And if she can't, I'll drive myself."

"No! That's crazy. If Mrs. Patterson takes you to the hospital, fine, but I don't want to hear anything about your driving yourself. Be sensible, Holly. Santa Rosa's at least forty minutes away. You can't risk that trip alone, not when you're in labor. If your neighbor can't take you, I want you to promise you'll page me. I can be here in five minutes, ten at the most."

Holly's eyes still blazed with resentment, but she knew Greg was making sense. For the baby's sake, she had to listen to him. "I guess."

"No guessing!" Now it was Greg's turn to show his anger. "I want your promise right now."

Holly exhaled loudly. She knew she should be grateful that Greg Garrison seemed genuinely worried about her, that he was offering his help. But all she felt was claustrophobia. She didn't want people fawning over her, not Greg, or Pat, or anyone else.

Anyone but Alex. And that wasn't going to happen, ever again.

"All right, Greg," Holly said quietly, her anger gone now. In its place she felt only exhaustion. "I'll call you. I promise."

Chapter

25

⌒

Holly turned a page in the second of Alex's handwritten journals and read an entry dated February 10, 1967. Alex and Celia had been married just over three months, and already the marriage was turning sour.

Celia threw another of her tantrums tonight. My fatal mistake was suggesting she take some credits at City College next summer. She accused me of being a "control freak." When I said I didn't want a wife who couldn't keep up with me, she stomped out of the apartment and went home to Mama—as usual. Great! What she gets there is more of how all men are scum and I'm no different. Shit! Sometimes I wonder why in hell I ever got married. I'm beginning to think Dad was right.

I just don't get it. Before we got married, Cele used to be fun and really sexy, but now all she wants to do is stare at herself in the mirror and shop for clothes we can't possibly afford. Hell, she's married to a twenty-year-old college student. How much of a shock is it that I'm not rich? I plan to be someday, but I'm sure not rich now. Between my scholarship money and my hours at Pierce & Kramer, I can barely cover the apartment and the groceries, but that doesn't stop Celia from charging stuff all over town. Won't get a job to help out, either. She acts like paying for what she buys is *my* problem, not hers.

Maybe I am a little controlling sometimes, but Cele's nothing but a spoiled brat, always demanding something, whining at me, driving me crazy with her gimme-gimme-gimme attitude. Says she's going back to modeling if I make her get a job. I don't want my wife parading around in front of strangers in flimsy underwear like she used to. I don't give a shit if it does pay thirty bucks an hour, no wife of mine is going to model.

Scares me to say it, but I think I'm getting close to the end of my rope with Celia. If things don't get better around here pretty quick, she can just go back to Mama for good, for all I care. I'm not going to let her ruin my life!

As she read her husband's written thoughts from so long ago, Holly felt an occasional flash of guilt about invading his privacy. Surely Alex hadn't intended her to see these pages. Still, she rationalized, he was gone now; what she was doing couldn't possibly hurt him. And after all, Alex was the father of her child. She wanted to be able to tell their child all about him.

As she neared the middle of the diary Alex had begun shortly before his wedding in late 1966 and continued into 1967, Holly could feel the tension in the Sheridan household growing. In the beginning, she'd been struck by an occasional pang of jealousy, reading the words a horny young Alex had written about his teenage bride. He'd described her as "the most beautiful creature I've ever seen. All I have to do is look at her and I get hot. Cele doesn't know a whole lot about sex yet, but that's fine with me. I can teach her everything she needs to know."

Holly had been neither as gorgeous as the young Celia nor as innocent sexually when she'd met Alex years later. She had been no passive female waiting for Prince Charming, either. The more Holly read, however, the more any jealousy she felt faded away. The union of Alex and Celia had been a coupling of two extremely immature young people. It was built on sexual attraction and precious little else—at least from Alex's point of view there was plenty of sexual attraction. Celia was nineteen years old, tall, slim, blond, and gorgeous; what healthy twenty-year-old male wouldn't have wanted to sleep with her? But Holly's guess was that Celia had been more interested in lifetime financial security than in Alex as a sex partner. When she agreed to marry Alex Sheridan, the beautiful Celia had clearly believed she'd found somebody to take care of her for the rest of her life.

They'd both been tragically wrong.

As she read about this volatile period in Alex's life nearly thirty years ago, Holly realized her sympathies were not always with him. As a newly married man, Alex was indeed controlling. He frequently acted as though the beautiful Celia was his possession, a beautiful trophy that also happened to turn him on. Celia was a brat, all right, but so was Alex, in an entirely different way.

During the months between February and May, Alex made fewer entries in his journal, only about half a dozen. He wrote about Celia's refusal to enroll in college to improve her mind, about her objections to entertaining his friends, about her increasing financial demands. She still had no job and wouldn't even think about getting one, other than modeling, which she knew Alex would immediately veto.

In addition to his classes, Alex took on a second part-time job to make ends meet. He was close to burning out, and he wasn't finding Celia nearly so sexy anymore.

By June of 1967, the diary entries were filled with Alex's anger over the way he'd trapped himself by marrying so young. Finally, in the middle of that month, he wrote that he'd come to a difficult decision.

> Maybe nobody in my family has ever gotten divorced before, but divorce doesn't carry such a big stigma these days, right? This isn't the fifties, and—thank God—there aren't any kids to get hurt. Celia's not even twenty. She'll get married again, probably to some rich guy who can take care of her a hell of a lot better than I can. I've had it.

A bare-bones budget was penciled into the margin of this page in the book. Alex's neatly printed figures demonstrated that he could pay Celia two hundred dollars a month alimony if he gave up the apartment and moved into his fraternity house after they separated. He assumed she would go back to her mother in Culver City. Alex would still have to work full-time in addition to taking a full load at UCLA, but he was grateful that his two major goals were still in sight—a degree in architecture and a future free of Celia. He'd made up his mind to get a divorce.

Yet Holly knew something had stopped Alex from going through with his plans for a divorce that year. In the end, he had stayed with his first wife for twenty-five years before he finally left her. If the marriage had been so terrible during its very first year, why hadn't he bailed out then, the way he'd so obviously planned?

Alex had never told Holly much about his first marriage. "I don't like to dwell on the past" was about all he'd ever said on the subject. Of course, when he filed those court papers asking for a reduction in his spousal support payments, a few bits of information had slipped out. Comments like "We never had all that much in common, Celia and I, even in the beginning." And "She had ways of making it hard for me to leave." Later, he'd confided, "Celia's made a profession out of being bitter. She's going to fight this change tooth and nail. Count on it."

Four entries written in July 1967 answered Holly's question.

July 3, 1967

Now she's really gone and done it! Damn Celia! Thinks she's tricked me into staying with her, even if I don't love her anymore, but she can think again. Promised me over and over she was taking the pill, and now she claims she must have forgot a few. How stupid does she think I am? She did this on purpose!

I told her tonight—if she has this baby, she can have it all by herself. I'm out of here. Let's let Celia have sole responsibility for somebody else for a while. See how *she* likes it.

July 8, 1967

Joe Morgenstern says his girlfriend knows somebody who can take care of Celia's problem. This guy was a medical student somewhere back east, so he knows what he's doing. Joe's girlfriend says two girls in her sorority went to him, and he took care of them just fine.

The worst part is this thing's going to cost me five hundred bucks! That's four months' rent or a quarter's tuition and books with money left over. I'll have to borrow it from Joe and anybody else I can hit up and then work extra hours this summer to pay it back.

Celia still says she doesn't want to get rid of the baby, but she doesn't want a divorce either. I promised her I'd try harder to make our marriage work, maybe even go to counseling if we can get it cheap somewhere, but only if she has an abortion. She's got her choice—it's the baby or me, not both.

July 18, 1967

Tomorrow's the day. Joe and Spider came up with the five hundred. Joe told his folks his car needed a new transmission and they wrote him a check. Don't know where Spider got his two hundred, but I'm lucky to have good friends like them.

Got to admit I'm nervous as hell about this, sick to my stomach all week. You'd think I was the pregnant one. It's probably because this is illegal. I keep thinking, what if we get caught? My whole career could go up in smoke if I end up with an arrest record.

Got to admit I feel a little bit guilty too, even if

Cele did go and get knocked up on purpose. God knows I never wanted things to turn out like this.

July 23, 1967

The doctor at St. John's says the worst is over, that Cele's going to pull through. I've never been so scared—waking up in a bed filled with blood, seeing Cele lying there white as a ghost. Thank God she didn't die. I'd never be able to live with that.

This was all my fault, I have to admit it. I made her have the abortion. She didn't want it, and she was right. That guy was a quack. The worst part is now she can never have kids, with me or anybody else.

Might as well face it. I'm stuck with Celia for good. After what I did to her, how can I ever leave?

Holly closed the journal and put it down on the coffee table. So that was why Alex had stayed all those years. Guilt. Well-earned guilt, too. He had done a terrible thing to his young wife. Still, his self-imposed penance had cost both of them the best years of their lives. No wonder Alex had never wanted to talk about what had gone wrong with that marriage. He'd punished himself for his youthful transgression for more than a quarter of a century.

As she stared out the window at the darkening horizon, Holly was filled with a bone-deep sense of sadness. Every aspect of the young Sheridans' life was tragic. Neither Alex nor Celia had been happy.

If only Celia hadn't gotten pregnant, the marriage might have ended in its first year, early enough for both of them to go on to happier lives.

Or if Alex hadn't forced Celia into having an abortion, they might have separated anyway. Raising a child alone is never easy, but Celia might have remarried and given her baby a stepfather. Or perhaps Alex would have raised his son or daughter himself.

Or if abortion had been legal and safe, Celia could have had another child with someone else. . . .

Holly jerked out of her reverie as she heard the front door open. Had the doorbell rung? She hadn't heard it.

"Hi, there! Pizza delivery!"

Holly recognized her neighbor's voice. "Is that you, Pat? I didn't hear the bell."

The taller woman barged into the living room, a large square box in her hand. "The door was unlocked and I didn't want you to get up to answer it. Brought this back from Luigi's in Petaluma for us. It's not cut yet, so we can put it back in the oven for a few minutes and warm it up. Hope you like veggies on your pizza, Holly—at least vegetable pizza *sounds* halfway healthy, right? Hey, you've been crying again. What's the matter?"

Holly swiped at her damp eyes with the back of her hand. "Nothing." She was not about to share what she'd just learned with this near-stranger. The truth was, she'd been looking forward to spending her evening alone, taking some time to think about what she'd read, trying to reconcile the young Alex of the journals with the man she married. But she could hardly tell Pat to leave when she'd gone to the trouble of bringing her a pizza for dinner.

Holly thanked Pat for the food and carried it into the kitchen. She turned the oven dial to 350 degrees, placed the pizza on the top rack, set the timer for ten minutes, and started back into the living room to wait for it to reheat.

As she emerged from the kitchen, she called out, "Tell me about your—" But her words died as she realized what Pat was doing. The dark-haired woman was sitting on the sofa, deeply engrossed in Alex's journal.

Holly moved across the room as fast as her pregnancy would allow and snatched the book out of the other woman's hands. "Excuse me! This is private!" She could feel her body shaking with rage as she carried the book into the bedroom and tossed it onto the bedspread. She felt guilty enough that *she* had read Alex's diaries; she certainly wasn't going to share them with a nosy neighbor. Pat had no right!

"Hey, sorry, Holly. I didn't mean anything."

Holly spun around and saw Pat standing in the bedroom door. The woman just didn't quit. Was there no way Holly could escape her? She bit back the sharp words on the tip of her tongue, reminding herself that, for now at least, she needed Pat. Greg obviously didn't want the responsibility of taking her to the hospital when she went into labor. Pat was the only one left.

But as soon as the baby was born, Holly promised herself, she would begin distancing herself from Pat Patterson. No way was this woman going to become a permanent part of her little family.

Not if Holly had anything to say about it.

When she got home from her Brentwood club, Buffy Lewis picked up the stack of mail from the floor beneath the mail slot and carried it into the kitchen. She tossed the letters and flyers onto the kitchen table and then poured herself a cup of coffee from the giant thermos she filled early each morning and kept handy on the Spanish tile counter.

There, she thought, as she took a big gulp and felt the hot liquid slide down her throat. The coffee quickly began to conquer her morning shivers. Buffy had been playing tennis at her club when it started to drizzle. Unwilling to stop their game in the middle, she and her opponent had continued playing until both were soaked to the skin and thoroughly chilled. At least she'd won the set, Buffy thought, but the hot shower in the locker room afterward hadn't completely warmed her up. Now, however, snuggled into an oversize white cotton sweater and soft jeans, she was finally beginning to feel comfortable again.

As she stood over the table, Buffy leafed through

her stack of mail. She quickly tossed a department store catalog and two solicitations for no-annual-fee credit cards into the trash. The last thing she needed was more credit cards. Ever since her divorce, she'd been trying to live on a very strict budget so she could keep her house and not have to get a full-time job. The rest of the mail consisted of three bills, a picture post-card from a friend taking a ski vacation in France, and a handwritten letter with a San Francisco return address.

"San Francisco," Buffy said aloud, as she ripped open the slim beige envelope. "So that's where old Celia's been hiding out." Over the past three weeks, Buffy had thought often about Celia Sheridan, wondering guiltily if their last conversation—one in which Buffy bluntly told Celia she really had to get psychiatric help—had finally ruptured their friendship for good.

Celia had left town without telling Buffy where she was going, without even saying good-bye, a move that was virtually unprecedented during the two decades they'd known each other. Celia used to tell Buffy everything, or at least Buffy always believed she did. So she must have been royally pissed off this time. It had bothered Buffy tremendously to think of Celia going off somewhere to lick her wounds, becoming more and more bitter and depressed each day; to think of her lost and alone. The truth was that she really didn't have any other friends. Without Buffy, she had no one.

The letter Celia had written from San Francisco held no recriminations, however. As she read the first few words, Buffy's face broke into a smile of sheer relief.

I'm having the time of my life here, Buff, and

I've finally taken your advice. I'm getting on with my life, and to hell with Alex and his bimbo!

For once, I'm doing exactly what *I* want to do. I sold my house to that Dutch director next door. You remember him—Pieter Vanderbilt, he does those horrible muscle-man adventure movies that make a fortune. I shudder to think what that tasteless creep's going to do to my house, but at least I made him pay top dollar. I'm going to live here in San Francisco for a while and then see where I want to settle permanently.

But that's not my best news. You'll never guess what, Buff. This is the most exciting thing I've ever done. I'm adopting a baby!

Buffy's smile faded and her jaw dropped. A baby? At Celia's age? Most women of her generation, including Buffy, were grateful when their kids were old enough to live away from home, thrilled that they finally had some peace and quiet. They enjoyed their new freedom: traveling, sleeping late in the morning, doing all the things they could never do when their kids were home. The last thing they wanted at this stage in their lives was to take on responsibility for an infant. What on earth had gotten into Celia? She read on.

I found an adoption attorney here in San Francisco, and he put me in touch with a pregnant girl. The baby's due in just a few days, and it's going to be mine. Can you believe it? I'm finally going to be a mom, at forty-eight. Better late than never, right?

Oh, Buff, I do hope you're happy for me. This is really what I want, what I've always wanted. It was only that shit Alex who kept me from having kids years and years ago. But *I'm* in charge now, and if I want a baby I'm going to have one.

Please keep in touch. I miss you terribly. This address is a new one and I don't have a phone yet, but I'll call you as soon as I do.

You'll be the first to know when my baby gets here.

Love and kisses,
Celia.

Buffy stared at the letter for a few minutes, then sank into a chair and reread it more slowly. But her old friend's words stayed exactly the same. Celia Sheridan was actually adopting a baby. At nearly fifty years of age and without a husband.

Buffy was filled with a strong sense of foreboding. Something wasn't right about this. She felt more certain than ever that Celia'd gone off the deep end that night she found out Alex's young wife was pregnant. Had she decided she was in some diehard competition with her successor? Alex wasn't even around to see it anymore.

If she'd come up with some oddball scheme to outdo her ex-husband's widow, Buffy thought, Celia could well have gotten involved with one of those black-market adoption lawyers. If she'd sold her Bel Air house, she had plenty of cash, so it was certainly possible some shyster had suckered her into buying a baby. That didn't mean the adoption would be legal, though. Or that Celia would even get the baby after she'd forked over her money.

Buffy sincerely hoped that her friend wasn't the target of a con artist. Celia's mental health was so fragile that she might never recover from something like that.

Unfortunately, there wasn't much she could do to keep Celia from being swindled, Buffy decided. At least nothing more than keep in touch with her old friend and offer her comfort if her strange plan blew up in her face.

Chapter

27

Holly opened the big carton the UPS man had just delivered. She'd been expecting it for days now, and she felt a certain burst of pleasure as she lifted the lid and began to pull out its contents. Inside were all the things she had ordered from the JCPenney catalog last week: tiny terry-cloth sleepers encased in plastic bags, two dozen cotton diapers, an assortment of booties and caps, sheets for the crib, a set of plastic nursing bottles, three crib-size blankets. Friends in Los Angeles would undoubtedly send her gifts for the baby after it was born. But because she now lived so far away and she hadn't made friends here in Bodega Bay, nobody had given Holly a baby shower. She had to buy the many things her newborn baby would need.

As she unwrapped a little white cotton knit gown with drawstrings in its hem and the ends of its sleeves, Holly couldn't help but compare it to the designer gowns her new neighbor had tried to give her. There was nothing handmade or trendy about this garment from JCPenney; it was utilitarian, nothing more. Still,

Holly felt far more comfortable with the things she had purchased. If her baby spit up all over this gown, she wouldn't have to worry about spoiling it. Nor would seeing these clothes on her child give her the uncomfortable feeling that she owed a debt she couldn't repay. This inexpensive but useful catalog delivery would never compromise her independence.

Holly was putting her purchases into the drawers of the old white dresser she'd repainted for the baby's room when the doorbell rang. As she went to answer it, she caught herself hoping that Pat hadn't come to see her again. Although it had been a few days since she'd seen her neighbor, she simply wasn't up for another of those too-close-for-comfort chats Pat seemed to love.

The window next to the front door was still boarded up, so Holly was forced to open the door to see who was ringing the bell. She hadn't wanted to ask Greg to take time off the other construction jobs to replace the broken glass. Besides, after their last conversation, she felt uncomfortable around him.

Holly opened the door a crack to see Sheriff Wills and Deputy Snyder standing on the doorstep.

"May we come in, Mrs. Sheridan?" the sheriff asked.

Holly hesitated only briefly. "I—I guess so," she said, unlatching the security chain and swinging the door open. "Did you find the man who broke in and stole my things?"

"Still workin' on it." This morning, the odor of stale liquor that typically clung to Sheriff Wills was partially masked by a spice-scented aftershave lotion. "We're here about Mr. Sheridan, ma'am."

Holly's fingers curled into two hard fists. "What is it?" She caught a fleeting sympathetic look from

Deputy Snyder; it only put her more on guard.

"Let's go on inside and sit down a minute, ma'am," the sheriff said.

Holly nodded and led the way into her living room. She hadn't cleaned house in days. The room was dusty, and old copies of the *San Francisco Chronicle* lay scattered across the surface of the coffee table. Now, however, Holly barely noticed things that under different circumstances would have embarrassed her. She dropped down on a chair, leaving the sofa for her visitors. "What's happened?" she asked, her fingernails digging into her palms as she waited for the answer.

"How come you didn't say anything about yer husband using sleeping pills?" Sheriff Wills asked. His voice held a strong tone of accusation.

"Sleeping pills? I don't know what you're talking about."

"Autopsy drug tests come in yesterday, Mrs. Sheridan. Turns out Mr. Sheridan had enough sedative in his blood to put him out at the controls. Figure that's why his plane went down. The man fell asleep."

Holly shuddered. "No! No, you're completely off base here, Sheriff. Not Alex. Alex never took sleeping medication. And he certainly would *never* do anything like that before flying his plane. This is crazy!"

"He never had a prescription for"—the sheriff pulled a scrap of paper from his pocket and read from it—"for something called triazolam?"

"Never even heard of it."

"How about some tiny white pills brand name of Halcion?"

Holly shook her head. "No, absolutely not."

The sheriff pulled a bulkier document from his pocket and slid it across the coffee table toward Holly.

"This here's a search warrant, ma'am, issued by a judge. Gives us the legal right to search these premises for triazolam."

"What? But why?"

The sheriff pushed himself to his feet. "Routine in this kinda situation, ma'am." His bloodshot eyes held no charity. "Fact is, if Mr. Sheridan didn't drug himself up with Halcion, somebody else had to do it. Maybe by putting it in his coffee or in some kinda lunch he brought on board the plane."

Holly sank back into her chair, stunned. Not only was this horrible man not doing anything about solving her recent burglary or getting her stolen belongings back, he had all but accused her of murdering Alex!

"You bastard," she muttered under her breath, as she watched him heading down the hall toward her bedroom, with Deputy Snyder close behind.

Chapter

28

Celia stood in her front bedroom and stared through the crack in the drapes for more than two hours while she waited for the sheriff's vehicle to leave Holly Sheridan's house. She was desperate to know what was going on over there. If Holly had gone into labor early and called 911, she told herself, surely an ambulance would have come to take her to the hospital, even in this one-horse town. No, this couldn't be about the baby. This visit had to be about the burglary. Yet if that fat-assed sheriff and his flunky were over there only to talk about a stolen TV set, why were they staying so damn long?

By the time the squad car pulled out of the driveway and drove off, Celia was nearly frantic with worry, imagining all her careful plans falling apart. She'd almost blown it the other night, when Holly caught her reading Alex's old diary. She'd wanted nothing more than to destroy the libelous words that son of a bitch had written about her so long ago, but she couldn't afford to let Holly become any more suspicious. Celia knew she would simply have to force herself to forget about those diaries, at least for now.

Although it took a great deal of willpower, Celia had managed to stay away from the gray house across the street for three days now, while she allowed the young widow time to cool off. She'd hoped Holly would pick up the phone and invite her over, but the call hadn't come. Yesterday, in an attempt to keep herself from going crazy while she waited for Holly to make some kind of conciliatory gesture, Celia had taken a quick trip to the San Francisco apartment she'd rented. Her visit had been fruitful. She'd spent some time with old Muriel Knack across the hall, which could come in handy later on, if she needed a witness to her pregnancy. Muriel had done her a favor, too, taking in a delivery that arrived while Celia was away.

"Oh, wonderful! I bet this is from my best friend," Celia told the older woman as she tore open the box. It bore the return address of a trendy Beverly Hills baby boutique. She pulled out a card and read it quickly. "I was right. My friend Buffy sent me this." Celia dug deeper inside the box. "Oh, look, Muriel," she said, as she lifted out a sturdy infant car seat. "Leave it to Buffy to get me something really practical for the baby." Celia felt a warm inner glow; she'd always known she could count on Buffy Lewis.

Still, it was Holly, not Buffy, whom Celia most needed right now. Waiting for an invitation to visit the house across the street, or for Holly to call and say she'd gone into labor and needed a ride to the hospital, was driving Celia crazy. And now the sheriff had been over there, doing who knew what.

After the squad car backed out of the driveway and left, Celia forced herself to wait five minutes to make sure the sheriff wasn't going to turn around and come back. Then she darted across the cul-de-sac and rang Holly's doorbell.

The door flew open. "What is it this—?" Holly stopped herself. "Oh, it's you, Pat."

"I wanted to find out what's wrong, Holly. What was the sheriff doing here?" As she saw Holly's chin begin to quiver, Celia held out her arms. An instant later, Holly had accepted the embrace and was sobbing against the taller woman's shoulder. Celia could not have felt more pleased if she'd planned things this way. She was firmly back in her chosen role of older, wiser friend.

As Holly began to tell her about the sheriff's visit, however, Celia's tension began to increase once more. So they knew about the Halcion tablets. She hadn't counted on that. She'd figured the authorities would simply chalk up Alex's timely demise to pilot error or mechanical failure, whatever causes small planes to drop from the sky. Her mind raced as she tried to figure out whether there was any way they might connect those sleeping pills to Alex's first wife.

Of course not, Celia reassured herself. Even though she'd had several prescriptions for Halcion over the years, nobody could prove she'd been anywhere near Alex for ages. She lived five hundred miles away. How could she possibly have drugged him?

"Poor Holly," Celia said, as she watched the distraught woman dry her tears. "These people actually think you drugged his coffee or his lunch or whatever?"

"God knows what they think. Or why. I tell you, Pat, this nightmare just gets worse and worse."

"At least they didn't find any evidence in your house." Celia's eyes locked onto Holly's red, puffy face. "Did they?"

"Of course not. Alex never took sleeping pills in his life, and I haven't even had an aspirin since I got pregnant."

Celia felt a brief pang of regret that she hadn't managed to plant a few leftover pills in Holly's house. She might actually have gotten the woman arrested for Alex's murder, which in her opinion, would have been simple poetic justice. Yet, if she'd done that, Celia reminded herself, she wouldn't get the baby, and it was the baby that mattered most. Holly would get her just desserts soon enough.

"I don't understand," Holly said. "If Alex didn't take those pills himself, and I know he didn't, he couldn't have, then how—? Unless those drug tests got screwed up somehow. I bet that's it. I mean, anybody can make a mistake, right? Even a crime lab."

"Did the sheriff ask you about who might want to kill Alex?" Celia held her breath as she waited for the answer. She certainly didn't want cops converging on the Bel Air house, looking for her.

"Sure, but I can't think of anybody. I mean, his ex-wife, Celia, wasn't exactly fond of him, from what I heard. But murder? I don't think she's *that* crazy!"

Celia jumped on the opportunity to deflect attention away from Alex's first wife. "I thought you told me Alex hadn't even seen his ex in years," she said.

Holly nodded. "Not as far as I know. Besides, even if Celia wanted to kill him, how would she do it? She lives in L.A. She was probably on her way to court by the time Alex's plane crashed. She certainly didn't pack his lunch that day either; I did. And *I* sure as hell didn't want my husband to die."

Celia watched as Holly fought off a new wave of tears. She saw an opportunity here and planned to take advantage of it, but she would have to choose her next words very carefully. "Holly, there *is* someone else, you know," she said.

"What do you mean?"

"That partner of yours, in the house business. The fellow with the pickup truck."

"Greg?"

"Tall skinny blondish guy who shows up around here every once in a while."

Holly nodded. "Greg Garrison. He owns half of Ecobay."

"What happens to the business if Alex isn't around?" Celia asked, watching Holly's freckled face carefully for the reaction she was seeking.

"It—I mean, we haven't decided yet. We'll have to come to some agreement pretty soon, I guess. There's one life insurance policy that goes to the company, but it's only for fifty thousand dollars. Greg might use it to buy out my interest, or else it can keep Ecobay afloat until we sell one of our houses. But I can't really see where Greg benefits very much from Alex's death. That just doesn't make sense."

"Doesn't it? Think about it a minute. You told me Ecobay was in deep financial trouble, right? So maybe this Greg guy figures the fifty thousand will keep the business going long enough to turn things around for him. Otherwise what happens? All his efforts, his entire investment in the company, goes straight down the toilet, right?"

"I—I don't know. I can't even think straight right now, Pat, but I'm sure Greg wouldn't—"

"Wait a minute. How come Greg was so anxious to convince you Alex committed suicide, tell me that? Maybe he was afraid they were going to find out about the sleeping pills, and he wanted you to think your husband took them on purpose. Or—oh, God, maybe I shouldn't even suggest this."

"What?"

"Didn't you tell me Alex let Greg fly his plane sometimes?"

"Sure, but what—"

"Think about it, Holly. If Greg had the plane all to himself, that would give him plenty of opportunity. He could have left that medication somewhere in the plane, maybe in some food he knew your husband would eat, or—"

"Stop!" Horrified and shocked, Holly pressed her fingers against her temples. "I—I don't know what to think. This is all too much for me right now."

"You're right," Celia said. "You shouldn't have to deal with this, not with the baby due any minute. It *is* too much for you, way too much. Tell you what I'd do in your place, though. I'd stay as far away from Greg Garrison as I could, at least until after my baby was born or the police figured out what really happened to my husband. I mean, if Greg's trying to take over Ecobay and he killed Alex, you and your baby could be his next targets."

Holly was too stunned to answer. Could Greg really do that? Only the ringing of the telephone managed to halt her churning thoughts. She moved slowly toward the kitchen to answer it.

From the living room, Celia eavesdropped on Holly's end of the conversation.

"Oh, hello, Greg," she heard Holly saying in a chilly voice. "No. No, I told you that's not necessary. Like I said the other day, I have everything all taken care of." There was a pause. "I—sure I hear you, Greg, but to be frank, I don't really think you know beans about what Alex would want me to do. And the truth is, *I don't want you to drive me.* That should be clear enough." Another pause. "Sure, right. If I do, I'll give you a call." Holly slammed down the phone.

"That was Greg," she told her visitor, when she returned to the living room. "He's been pressuring me to let him drive me to the hospital when my time comes. I've told him half a dozen times that I already have a ride arranged."

"Good. You did exactly the right thing. My station wagon has plenty of gas, and I plan to stick close by, night and day, from now on. Don't worry about Greg. You've got me to take care of you, and you can count on me, Holly, one hundred percent."

"Thanks, Pat. You're a good friend."

"Not only that, my dear, but I absolutely insist on feeding you dinner at my place tonight. Steak on the barbecue, baked potatoes, a salad. How does that sound?"

"Oh, I don't—"

"No excuses. I'm going to pamper you until the baby comes, help you take your mind off everything else. And step number one is, you're not cooking tonight." Celia marched toward the door. "Give me an hour to get things ready and then come on over," she said, as she let herself out of the house.

Holly sat alone on the sofa, staring into space and feeling too emotionally battered to protest.

"Guess I was hungry after all," Holly said, as she pushed her dinner plate away. When she'd arrived at the big brown house across the street, she hadn't felt the least bit hungry. The emotionally difficult events of the day had robbed her of any interest in food. But the baby had to eat, she told herself, as she forced down the first few bites of what turned out to be a particularly delicious meal. She was surprised to find that her appetite quickly returned. The steak was hard to resist, a butter-knife-tender filet mignon that was too expensive for Holly's own tight grocery budget. She hadn't eaten much meat of any kind in recent months, anyway; in deference to Alex's heart condition, both Sheridans had stuck to a largely vegetarian diet. So the steak her neighbor had grilled on the barbecue was a real treat, and in the end Holly ate her dinner with gusto, managing to finish all her meat and most of her baked potato and salad.

"How about some dessert?" Celia offered, as she reached for Holly's plate. "I've got a carton of chocolate yogurt in the freezer."

"Thanks, but I couldn't possibly eat another bite. I've already made a pig of myself. Everything was just great, Pat." Holly rubbed her hand over her belly. "Even baby here has to be full by now. Honestly, I can't remember the last time I ate so much. Certainly not . . . not since Alex died."

Celia stacked the dishes at the table and began carrying them over to the sink.

"Here, let me help you clean up," Holly said, pushing her chair backward. Celia gestured for her to stay in her seat, but Holly stood up anyway. "No, really, Pat," she insisted. "It's the least I can do, after you did all the cooking."

"Thanks, but no," Celia said. "Tell you what. You look awfully tired. Why don't you go into the guest room down the hall and lie down for a bit? We can visit some more after I get the kitchen cleaned up and you've had a little rest."

"You've got one thing right—I really am running out of steam. But it doesn't make sense for me to nap here. I'll just go home and get to bed early tonight." Holly pressed a hand against the small of her back and stretched. "With luck, tomorrow will be a better day. Lord knows, except for your dinner, this one sure has been outstandingly horrible."

Turning away from her task at the kitchen sink, Celia wiped her hands on a dish towel and stared coolly at Holly. "I want you to go into the guest room and lie down on the bed, Holly. You need your rest." She was no longer smiling.

Holly shook her head. "I told you, that makes no sense. For heaven's sake, I live right across the street. I'll go home to rest."

Celia's voice grew icier and her eyes—dark behind

brown contact lenses—were hard. "I'm not asking, Holly, I'm telling. Go lie down on the bed. *Now.*"

A warning chill crept down Holly's spine and the hairs at the back of her neck stood on end. Was she crazy, she wondered, or was it everybody else? First Greg had turned strange, and now Pat seemed to be changing into the neighbor from hell.

"I may be pregnant," Holly said, "but believe it or not, it hasn't affected my mind. I'm not senile, and I'm not a child. I can make my own decisions perfectly well—about where I sleep and everything else. Thanks for the dinner." She hurried into the front hall, opened the coat closet, and yanked her jacket off its hanger. As she began to slip her arm into one sleeve, she heard the sharp sound of a kitchen drawer slamming shut, followed by the other woman's footsteps as they hammered across the kitchen floor tiles.

"Put that jacket down, Holly, or I'll shoot."

"What the—?" Holly jerked around, an angry retort on the tip of her tongue. But she swallowed it when she saw that Pat was not kidding. The taller woman stood framed in the lighted kitchen door, and Holly could clearly see the black revolver in her right hand. It was pointing straight at her.

"Is—is that thing real?" Holly asked, in a small, frightened voice.

"Real, and loaded, and I know how to use it. Now go into the bedroom."

"What are you doing?" Holly's feet felt glued to the floor as she struggled to comprehend this bizarre situation. "I don't understand."

Celia waved the gun menacingly. "Exactly which part is it you don't understand?" She spoke slowly, deliberately. "I'll tell you one more time. Go . . . lie . . . down . . . on . . . the . . . bed. Now!"

Holly's whole body began to tremble. She dropped her jacket on the floor and forced her feet to move down the hallway toward the room at the end. "Why? Why are you doing this to me? Pat," she pleaded, "please let me go home."

Celia followed Holly as close as a shadow. When the pregnant woman hesitated briefly in the doorway of the guest bedroom, she jabbed her sharply in the back with the barrel of the gun. "Go on, Holly, get inside."

Holly surveyed the room. It seemed to be a perfectly ordinary bedroom; there was a brass double bed on the wall to her right, with a gold-framed oil painting of a vase of spring wildflowers hanging on the wall above the headboard. A pair of oak nightstands stood on either side of the bed. One held an electric clock with a lighted dial that said it was ten minutes after seven. Neither table held a telephone. The only other piece of furniture in the room was a tall oak dresser opposite the foot of the bed.

Holly felt a brief surge of hope as she saw that the bedroom's far wall was made largely of glass. In its center was a high sliding glass door, on the other side of which was a wooden deck that ran the width of the house. Perhaps, she thought, her best bet was to play along with Pat for now and then escape quietly through the balcony door as soon as her captor had left the bedroom.

"You won't be able to open that door," Celia warned, as though she'd read Holly's thoughts. "I've bolted it shut from the outside, so don't get your hopes up." She prodded Holly with the gun once more. "Go on, get inside." Holly did as she was told. "There's a bathroom over there," Celia went on, motioning with the gun toward an open doorway. "You won't be uncomfortable here, as long as you behave yourself."

Holly turned around and backed a few feet into the room, her eyes riveted to the gun in the other woman's hand. "You can't keep me here," she said defiantly. "I don't know what you think you're doing, but there's no way you can make me stay here."

Celia raised the gun, pointed it at Holly's head, and cocked it. "Want to bet? If I felt like it, I could shoot you right now," she said. "No one would hear, not in this graveyard of a neighborhood. You and I are the only ones around." She held up the gun and sighted down its barrel. "I could hit you right between the eyes, then slice open your belly with one of those nice sharp steak knives, and—well, you get the idea, don't you? Face it, Holly, I've got you right where I want you. And you're going to stay put . . . until my baby's born." Celia's eyes took on the preoccupied gaze of the obsessed as she backed out into the hall and yanked the door closed, leaving Holly alone.

As she stood there, Holly heard a metallic, grating sound. She waited a moment, then gently tried the doorknob. It swiveled freely in her hand, but she could not pull the door open. It was securely bolted from the outside.

Her fear growing rapidly, she ran to the sliding glass door that led to the deck. It was bolted from the outside too, just as Pat had warned.

She actually was a prisoner here, Holly realized. This was no joke. Her stomach began to somersault. With bile rising in her throat, she lurched toward the bathroom on shaky legs, crouched in front of the toilet, and vomited up her dinner.

Chapter

30

Greg washed his largest paintbrush clean with a mixture of biodegradable soap and warm water, rinsed it, and laid it out to dry on the newspapers he'd spread across the kitchen counter. It had been dark for a couple of hours now, but he hadn't had his dinner yet. He'd worked late on the Pelican Loop house, applying a coat of ivory paint to the living room walls, waiting for it to dry, then starting all over again with the finish coat. By the time he completed his task, he'd made up his mind. He would go to see Holly Sheridan one more time before heading home for the night.

Ever since the other day, when he'd tried to talk to Holly about whether Alex might have been suicidal, Greg had felt awful. He never should have listened to Inspector Pruitt. He should have known Holly would react badly. If only he'd used common sense before opening his big fat mouth.

Sure, he'd had tried to apologize this afternoon by phone, but Holly hadn't listened. She merely sniped at him, saying something nasty about his not having a clue about what Alex would want for her. Well, that was to be expected, wasn't it? The poor woman was hurt and angry, and he'd let her down. Greg couldn't really blame her for lashing out at him.

All he could do now, he realized, was try to put things right once more between the two of them. If he and Holly were going to work together on Ecobay Housing in the future, or if they were to come to an agreement about Greg's taking over full ownership of the company, they couldn't afford to let this rift fester and grow.

Greg was ready to apologize, to plead guilty to gross insensitivity. He held the last of the paintbrushes under the kitchen faucet until the rinse water ran clear, laid it on the newspapers, and checked the time. It was only eight-thirty, not that late, really. Surely Holly would still be up. He wouldn't risk phoning her this time; she'd probably just hang up on him again.

But if he showed up on her doorstep, Greg hoped, she couldn't get rid of him nearly so easily, at least not before she'd listened to what he had to say.

After locking up the house, Greg climbed into his truck, backed it out onto dark and deserted Pelican Loop, and headed south to Holly's place.

Chapter

31

Celia scurried across the cul-de-sac, carrying the last of the things she was removing from Holly's house. Earlier, she'd retrieved that adorable mobile she'd spent so much time selecting for the baby—the one with the brightly garbed orange-haired clowns dangling from it—along with a few more practical baby items she would undoubtedly need very soon.

Finding Alex's diaries was what had taken Celia so long. For some reason, Holly had hidden all three of them in the bottom of her lingerie drawer.

But Celia's usual perseverance had paid off. Now that she'd taken everything she wanted from Holly's house, she would never again have to set foot in the place where Alex had shacked up with his whore.

Half an hour later, Celia was sitting in her kitchen, her anger mounting as she read the libelous words Alex had written about her so long ago. What a self-centered, egotistical young bastard Alex Sheridan was back then, she thought. He was an asshole in those days, and he'd stayed an asshole all his life. Who was he to call her selfish and demanding? She'd only wanted what every woman wants from marriage: a man to take care of her, children, a nice house—

The echoing chime of the doorbell interrupted Celia's thoughts. A fraction of a second later, she heard Holly begin to scream for help from the back bedroom. Her heart pounding, Celia jerked into action. She dropped the journal on the table, sprinted across the kitchen, and punched the black button on top of the clock radio. When rock music began to pour forth from the sleek black box, she raised its volume to an earsplitting level. Only after she was satisfied that Holly's calls for help could not be heard above the music did Celia answer the door.

Switching on the front light and keeping the security chain in place, she opened the heavy wooden door a few inches and peered through the crack at the tall man standing outside. "Hello," she said. The old recording of Jimi Hendrix on the kitchen radio nearly drowned out her greeting.

"Mrs. Patterson?"

Celia nodded.

"I'm Greg Garrison, your neighbor Holly Sheridan's business partner."

Celia nodded again without speaking.

Greg raised his voice until he was almost shouting to be heard above the cacophony of drums and steel guitars. "I'm looking for Holly, Mrs. Patterson. She's not answering her door and I—well, she told me you'd be taking her to the hospital when her baby comes and I thought—I mean, do you know where she is?"

Celia's mind raced until she settled on what she thought was a plausible lie. "Holly decided to go back to Los Angeles and have her baby there," she told Greg.

The gully between Greg's fair eyebrows deepened. "Los Angeles? But I just talked to her this afternoon. She didn't say anything about leaving town."

"It was a last-minute decision," Celia said, leaning a little closer to the security chain. The pounding bass of the radio was giving her a headache. "She only decided—oh, late this afternoon, I guess it was."

"But her car's still in the garage. I could see it through the garage window."

Celia shrugged. "She didn't take her car. I drove her to the airport in Santa Rosa. Just got home an hour ago."

Greg pulled on the gray-blond stubble on his chin. "Uh-uh, doesn't make sense. I can't believe Holly would do something like that, not without telling me. And I know for a fact her doctor told her not to fly until after the baby came."

"All I can tell you, Mr. Garrison, is Holly was real upset today," Celia said. "First the sheriff comes over and tears through her whole house, looking for some kind of pills she's supposed to be hiding. She told me he practically accused her of poisoning her husband. Then, after he leaves, she gets a phone call from some jerk who's been trying to convince her her husband killed himself."

Celia's sharp eyes watched Greg's face as it registered first disbelief, then shock, then guilt. "Bottom line, Mr. Garrison, is Holly said she wasn't going to stay around here anymore, not if that's the way people were going to treat her. She was crying, practically hysterical. Called the airlines, got herself a reservation to L.A., and asked me to drive her to the airport. I didn't know anything about what her doctor might've told her. But I guess she figured she was going to do what *she* wanted to do, no matter what." Celia glanced down at the slender gold watch on her wrist. "Her plane's probably already landed in L.A.," she said.

"Did she tell you where she'd be staying, Mrs. Patterson?"

"Nope, sorry. Said she was going to some old friends, but she didn't tell me their name or address. I wouldn't worry about her, Mr. Garrison. I'm sure Holly'll be back in touch, let both of us know when her baby arrives. Right now, she's just upset. You know how touchy women can be when they're about to have a baby."

"If you hear from her, will you ask her to call me right away? Tell her I'm really worried about her."

"Of course I will." For the first time, Celia smiled at the obviously chagrined man on her doorstep. This Greg was such a fool. All men were fools. "I'm sure Holly didn't mean to worry you," she told him.

Celia closed and bolted the door, then leaned her forehead against its smooth cool surface and laughed out loud. Her headache was gone as quickly as it had come, and she felt thoroughly pleased with herself for having fooled Greg Garrison. Now she was virtually certain she wouldn't have to worry about his showing up around here again, not before she and her baby had disappeared, anyway. One very important hurdle had been cleared.

After she made sure Garrison's truck was gone and turned off the radio, Celia could still hear Holly screaming and yelling in the back of the house. She stomped down the hall and pounded her fists against the bedroom door until it rattled in its frame.

"Shut up in there, you filthy little whore!" she screamed. "Nobody's around to hear you but me. Keep up that racket, and I'm coming in to shut you up for good!"

Instantly, the big house fell silent once more.

Chapter

32

Holly lay on top of the bed, her body curled into the fetal position and her arms wrapped around her soon-to-be-born child. Her eyes were closed and her breathing was even, but she was not sleeping; she was waiting for the right time to make her move.

When she first realized she was locked into this room, Holly felt panicky. Her mind raced frantically from one fear to the next and back again. Then, when she calmed down a little, she began turning over the evening's bizarre events in her mind, trying to make sense of them.

Who was Pat Patterson, she asked herself, and why was she doing this? Was she simply one of those crazy women obsessed with having a baby, anybody's baby? Had she been pushed across some mental precipice by the recent death of her husband? Or did Pat have some specific grudge against her?

Most painful for Holly to examine was why she hadn't realized that Pat was trouble, as soon as the woman befriended her. Why she hadn't listened to her inner voice, the one warning her that this new neighbor was too smothering, too manipulating, that something might be seriously wrong with her?

Holly knew the answer, of course. She'd been so lonely, so depressed, and so desperate after Alex died that she was willing to grasp at straws. And Pat's move into the neighborhood had presented her with a very convenient straw. Now Holly knew she was going to have to pay the price for her weakness . . . unless she was somehow able to outwit her captor and save her baby as well as herself.

After the loud rock music had stopped blaring and Pat vented her fury in pounding against the bedroom door and calling her vicious names, Holly had halted her self-recriminations. There would be time for that later, she decided. First, she had to figure out how to escape from this prison.

It was shortly after midnight, and the house had been nearly silent for over an hour. The whine of water running in the pipes under the house had ceased long ago, and the only sounds Holly could hear were normal creaking noises, as the big house settled on its foundations, and an occasional *whoosh* of air that signaled the forced-air furnace was kicking in.

The escape plan Holly had devised centered on the sliding glass door. She'd tried to force it open a dozen times, of course, but hadn't been able to budge it. Still, it was made of glass, and glass could be broken. She figured her best hope was to smash the glass door and escape onto the balcony. From there, surely she could manage to climb over the wooden railing and down into the ravine, from where she could flee to safety. Waiting until Pat was sound asleep should buy her some extra time.

Holly knew enough about house construction to realize that smashing the glass door would not be easy. Such doors were constructed of reinforced safety glass to prevent breakage. Still, if she used enough leverage, she ought to be able to smash a hole in the door at least big enough to crawl through.

The tall dresser on the opposite wall would be her tool. Holly slid off the bed, tiptoed across the bedroom floor, and braced her body against the big chest of drawers. It was discouragingly weighty, almost too heavy for her to move, but Holly was desperate and her adrenaline was flowing freely. She took out the drawers, to make the huge piece of furniture as light as possible. Finally, by concentrating hard and pushing with all her might, she managed to slide it closer and closer to the glass wall.

It took Holly more than fifteen minutes to move the empty chest of drawers less than five feet. Her heart was pounding, she was breathing hard, and sweat trickled down her armpits, but finally she had her only weapon precisely where she wanted it: positioned so that one of the sharp corners on top would fall against the center of the glass pane.

After replacing the drawers, Holly took a towel from the bathroom and stuffed it against the dresser leg closest to the glass door. She didn't want the heavy oak chest to slide any further along the floor when she pushed against it; she wanted it to fall over and strike the glass door squarely.

After allowing herself a short respite to catch her breath, Holly yanked the bedspread off the bed, pulled it over her head to protect herself from flying glass, and crouched down against the corner of the chest farthest from the glass. Positioning her shoulder against the edge of the wood, she took a deep breath and then pushed upward with every bit of strength she could muster. A sharp pain coursed down her back and she felt her face reddening from the unaccustomed effort, but the weight of the dresser finally began to shift. The heavy piece of furniture teetered for a split second on one short leg and then began to topple.

Holly stepped back, huddling under the bedspread. A loud crack split the air. She waited only an instant before peering out. The dresser had broken the glass, just as she'd planned, but a sheet of clear plastic embedded between layers of glass had kept the door from completely shattering.

The crash had to have wakened Pat, Holly knew. She had to get out fast! She began kicking frantically at the plastic membrane with the toe of her shoe. The clear film bulged, but held. Panicky, Holly looked around. A long shard lying on the carpet caught her eye. Using a corner of the bedspread to protect her hand, she picked up the dagger-shaped piece of glass and used it to punch holes in the plastic.

Her breath coming in short, frenzied bursts, Holly slashed harder and harder at the plastic with her makeshift knife. It finally gave way just as she heard distinct new noises coming from the far reaches of the house. As soon as the hole in the glass door had grown large enough for her to get through, she pulled the bedspread around herself for protection and crawled over broken glass out onto the balcony.

Once she was outside, cold night air smacked Holly in the face, quickly chilling her. She had no coat or jacket and the temperature had dropped into the forties, but the bedspread around her shoulders could only slow her escape. She tossed it away, climbed awkwardly over the wooden railing of the balcony, and tried to lower herself gently onto the dark hillside below.

But she didn't have the strength to make her descent a gradual one. Her grip on the railing gave way as soon as she had climbed over it, and she dropped like a rock onto the grassy slope below. Landing hard, Holly felt her ankle turn beneath her, sending a sharp pain up her leg. The baby kicked in protest. Gasping for breath, she began sliding down the steep incline on the seat of her pants.

As she skidded quickly toward the bottom of the ravine, Holly was suddenly showered with light. It took an instant for her eyes to adjust to the change as she glanced back at the house. Floodlights now illuminated the balcony section, as well as the hillside below it. Holly could see her captor standing at the top of the hill, her feet planted wide apart and her hands on her hips. She was staring straight at the spot where Holly was crouching in fear.

Her heart pounding, Holly pushed herself to her knees, then to her feet, and tried to get away from the light. She knew she would need the advantage of darkness to have any chance of escape, but her ankle hurt more with each step and the extra weight of her full-term pregnancy slowed her. She heard footsteps coming after her, and in what seemed no more than a second or two she felt sharp fingernails dig into her shoulder and pull her around.

"Fucking bitch!" Pat's eyes blazed with fury. "Whore! I ought to kill you right here!"

Holly dropped to the ground and curled into a ball, instinctively protecting her baby from the frenzied attack. Sharp blows rained on her head and back, but

Holly couldn't fight back. Finally, the slaps and punches lessened in strength and frequency, and she heard the other woman's breath becoming more labored. Her attacker's rage seemed to be spent, if only for the moment.

"Go on, get up."

Holly turned her face upward. She watched helplessly as Pat pulled the handgun from her pants pocket and pointed it squarely at her head.

"Come on. Get up and move it, or I'll use this thing on you."

Holly managed to stand, shaking with equal amounts of fatique and terror. Then, with her captor prodding her every painful step of the way, she crawled slowly back uphill to her prison.

Chapter

33

Holly lay on the bed once again, but now she was more confined than before her escape attempt—her wrists were bound together with a stout rope that was looped around the bed's brass headboard. After prodding her up the ravine and back into the house, her captor had taken sheets of plywood from Holly's garage across the street and boarded up the broken glass door. The room was secure again. Although Holly was far too exhausted to try another run for freedom under any circumstances, her pleas to be left untethered had gone unheeded.

For the past couple of hours, she'd been dozing off and on, her body's need for rest overwhelming both her physical aches and pains and her psychic turmoil. Now, however, a sharp pain in her lower back jolted her awake. Still groggy and confused, Holly felt a gush of warm liquid soak her legs. She moaned and shifted her position slightly to relieve the gripping pain in her back.

Her water had broken. Holly knew this was a sure

sign that labor had begun. Dr. Moravian had warned her to call the hospital as soon as her water broke or as soon as her contractions were five minutes apart, whichever came first. Panic threatened to engulf her. Trussed up this way, she couldn't even use her hands to deliver her baby. Unless she got help, she and her child would surely die.

There was only one thing to do. She would have to call for help and hope that Pat wanted this baby—she'd referred to it as "my baby," hadn't she?—enough to make sure it was born safely. Perhaps, too, there was a chance the woman had regained her sanity by now and could be convinced to call the paramedics or drive Holly to the hospital. . . .

Celia laid her hand across Holly's naked abdomen. Her fingertips could easily follow the rhythmic muscle movement of the labor contraction. It was strong and Holly's birth pains were coming closer together now, a positive sign, according to the books on childbirth that she'd read and read again.

"Please, Pat." Pulling hard against the ropes that bound her wrists, Holly gasped for air between pains. "Please help me. Please get a doctor."

"I told you, no doctor. My baby's in no danger, and frankly I don't give a shit about you."

Celia forced the laboring woman's bent knees sharply apart, then positioned the floor lamp she'd carried from the living room so that it illuminated the vaginal area. She could see the top of the baby's head now. She breathed a sigh of relief. "Her head's crowning," Celia announced. "Shouldn't be long now."

Celia felt both excited and energized; the daughter she'd waited for all these years was about to be born.

Justice was so close she could almost taste it. But her anticipation was tempered by a strong dose of nerves. If something went wrong with this birth, if the baby required a cesarean section to be born healthy, she wasn't sure she could handle it. The childbirth books she'd studied didn't cover that possibility, at least not outside a hospital. She had a razor-sharp knife handy of course, but if she made her incision too deep, or if she cut in the wrong spot, she might slash the baby.

But there was no sense looking for trouble, Celia decided. Holly seemed to be in good physical shape, and God knew she was built like a peasant, with a pelvis that looked plenty wide enough for childbearing. Now that Celia could spot the top of the baby's head, her worst fears—that her awaited daughter might be breach or, worse still, that the umbilical cord might emerge through the birth canal first, choking off the blood supply—began to fade.

Holly moaned again as another contraction hit. "Please, I need a doctor. Please, Pat."

"No doctor! Just push down hard on the next contraction while I count to ten." Celia picked up one of her books and ran her finger across the section explaining how to handle an emergency home birth. "Says here," she read out loud, "'Hold your breath and tighten your abdominal muscles as though you were having a bowel movement.' Just push. You can do that. When the baby's head comes out, I'll hold it up until her shoulders are born. After the shoulders come out, the book says the rest is easy."

Holly did as she was told. She had no choice. All she could hope for now was that her child would be born healthy and that she herself would survive the birth. Her fate and that of her child were in the hands of a crazy woman, and all she could do was pray that the crazy woman could pull this off. Two lives depended upon it.

The baby was born just as the book predicted, although the birth wasn't fully accomplished for another half hour. Celia felt a genuine thrill as she held the infant's head in her hands and guided its shoulders on the journey through the birth canal. The book was right. After the shoulders came, the rest of the baby just slid right out.

She examined it. "It's a boy," Celia announced, her heart plummeting. The disappointment in her voice was palpable. She'd counted on having a girl to raise, a girl like herself that she could dress up and show off. Leave it to Alex, she thought bitterly; it was just like him to cheat her one last time. Still, this was her baby, not a purchase that could be taken back to the store and exchanged. She was stuck with a boy, so she would simply have to readjust her thinking. It would hardly be the first time.

"A boy," Holly said, in a breathless voice. "Alex's son. He—he wanted a son."

"Shut the hell up," Celia ordered. She tickled the baby's feet and scratched its back the way the book instructed, until he began to make small mewing sounds.

"Is he all right?" Holly asked. She ached to hold him, to look at him up close, to check whether he had all his fingers and toes.

"He's breathing on his own and he seems to have all his parts." Celia watched as a gush of blood emerged from Holly's womb, followed shortly by the placenta. Everything was happening just as the birth book had told her it would. She laid the infant on a clean towel and waited until the umbilical cord stopped pulsating; then she tied it off and cut it with the knife she'd sterilized with alcohol.

"Please let me see my baby," Holly begged. Her breaths were coming a little slower now. She was exhausted but tremendously relieved. Even under these primitive circumstances, she'd managed to give birth to a healthy baby! She could hear her son's small cries as he exercised his new lungs, and the sound brought tears to her eyes. If only Alex were here. . . .

"You forget, Holly. This isn't your baby, it's mine."

"No. I'm his mother, Pat. Nothing—nothing you can do will ever change that."

"Don't bet on it. I'll see this boy dead before I give him up. Better hope I don't so much as get stopped for a traffic ticket on my way out of here, or he dies."

Holly winced. She could hear bald fanaticism in Pat's voice. She had no doubt that this woman would, indeed, kill the child before she'd turn him over. Instinctively, Holly knew that further protest might well make things worse, so she held her tongue. She simply lay back against the soiled sheets and felt utter fatigue wash over her.

Perhaps ten minutes later, Holly felt herself being roughly shoved aside, the ropes on her wrists pulling tighter. Her eyelids snapped open and she realized that Pat was stripping the bloody sheets out from under her. Leary of speaking again and setting the woman off, she made no protest as Pat gathered the sheets into a bundle and tossed a fresh blanket over Holly.

She must not be planning to kill me, Holly thought. If she wanted to kill me, why would she bother cleaning up the bed?

Holly clung to that shred of hope as she watched the

other woman carry the mewling infant out of the room and then heard the terrible metallic sound that signaled the bolt on the other side of the door had been rammed shut.

Celia washed the infant with sterile water, then diapered and dressed him and wrapped him in a soft white blanket. It would be best, she knew, to have a pediatrician check him over, but she couldn't take that chance, not now. Little Patrick—she made an instant decision to name him after her family, the Pattersons—looked healthy enough. The baby was sleeping now, so Celia left him on the living room sofa while she completed her preparations for departure.

She made several trips between the silent house and her station wagon in the garage, as she loaded the last of her clothes and the baby paraphernalia into the back. When the car was nearly full, she went back inside the house for the useful gift Buffy Lewis had sent her. The infant car seat would be perfect for transporting young Patrick to his new home in San Francisco.

Celia carried the box into the living room and set it down beside the sleeping infant. She lifted the seat out and dusted off the few bits of Styrofoam packing that still stuck to it. Just as she was about to pick up the baby and settle him into the seat, the box's address label caught her eye. Her heart missed a beat. She could have blown everything.

She shook her head to clear it. She couldn't afford to let either haste or fatigue make her sloppy. With a sigh of relief that she'd caught her error in time, Celia ripped off the label, crumpled it up, and stuffed it into the pocket of her jeans. If things went as planned, she knew, this box and its label would be ashes in an hour or two anyway. But she had to figure on every eventuality. If her plan didn't work, she surely didn't want anybody finding this little piece of paper with Celia Sheridan's name and San Francisco address printed on it.

Half an hour later, Celia's preparations were completed. She positioned young Patrick in the front seat of the car, safely buckled into his car seat. He was still sleeping, with his tiny lips moving rhythmically. Then she raised the garage door, checked to see that the cul-de-sac was still deserted in the midmorning sunlight, and backed the car into the driveway. Finally, after shifting the car into park and setting the emergency brake, she got out and made one last check of the house.

Holly was making noise again, Celia realized, as she heard weak calls for help coming from the back of the house. Briefly she considered going back into the locked bedroom and silencing her prisoner with a quick bullet to the brain. But an autopsy might reveal Holly'd been shot. Hadn't an autopsy shown Alex was drugged with Halcion when his plane went down?

No, Celia decided, she would let the fire take care of Holly. When the bitch burned to death, there was at least a chance it would be chalked up to an accident. If Celia got really lucky, the authorities would believe that Holly Sheridan was safe somewhere in Los Angeles and that the charred corpse in the house was a newcomer named Pat Patterson.

The last chore Celia performed in the house on Sandpiper Circle was to pour a full can of paint thinner over the papers and bloody sheets she'd piled up in the garage. On the top of the pile, she balanced Alex's three diaries; it was only fitting, she thought, that the bastard's self-indulgent excuses go up in smoke along with his whore.

When the paint thinner had soaked into the fabric and papers, Celia placed a candle stub on top of the journals and lit it. As she backed the station wagon out of the driveway, she hit the remote control and watched to see that the candle stayed lighted as the garage door closed.

Within an hour or two, Celia figured, the house would be engulfed in flames. By that time, she and baby Patrick would be well on their way to San Francisco and a new life.

Chapter

34

Greg laid his paint roller back in the tray and picked up the small brush he used for detailing. He'd chosen a rich dark red for the front door of the Pelican Loop house, a nice contrast with its driftwood-toned siding. Still, as he put the finishing touches on the job, his usual feeling of satisfaction after he'd done a job well was missing.

As he worked alone at the construction site this morning, Greg's mind kept drifting back to his last brief conversation with Holly Sheridan. Had he really upset the poor woman so much that she'd impulsively packed up and flown to Los Angeles? He'd thought she was made of stronger stuff. And what was this story about the sheriff accusing her of poisoning Alex?

Today Greg couldn't seem to lose himself in physical labor the way he usually did on a job site. As he turned and gazed wistfully toward the south horizon, paint dripped from his brush onto his pants. The hills were greener now than in summer. Bodega Bay's winter rains had made them almost as dark as the golf course.

On most days, Greg found this vista restful, but today his mind was filled with guilt and self-recrimination.

His breath caught and he loosened his grip on the paintbrush. It fell with a clatter into the tray as he stared toward the south section of the Bodega Harbour development, past the oblivious golfers and their youthful caddies. Rising against the bright morning sky from the green and gold hills—in the vicinity of Sandpiper Circle—was a sliver of distinct gray. It looked like smoke, Greg thought, smoke far too thick to be coming from somebody's fireplace, except maybe a chimney fire.

Or maybe his eyes were playing tricks on him. Greg blinked, shaded his gaze with both hands, and looked again.

No, it was no trick; the rising gray finger had to be smoke. Greg sprinted for his pickup and raced on nearly empty roads in the direction of the smoke plume.

As he turned into Sandpiper Circle and his fears were confirmed, Greg said a small prayer of thanks that at least the burning structure was not Ecobay's nearly completed house. He grabbed his cellular phone, punched in 911, and reported that flames were shooting through the roof of the garage at 17 Sandpiper Circle.

But he couldn't stand back and wait for help to arrive. If the Patterson woman was trapped inside, Greg knew, she could be dead of smoke inhalation long before the fire trucks had made the journey from the nearest fire station.

He tried the front door and found it locked. Sprinting back into the street, he grabbed an ax from the cache of tools in the pickup's bed. Half a dozen healthy whacks reduced the heavy door to broken boards.

With a handkerchief pressed across his nose and mouth, Greg raced through the smoky house, checking each room in order. The place appeared to be empty, except for one room at the back. Strangely, the door to this room was bolted shut from the outside and secured with a padlock as well. He pressed his ear to the door and thought he heard something inside—a faint scratching sound, possibly someone's cough.

Greg used his ax a second time. The hollow-core interior door split more easily than the outside door, and in a minute or two he was inside the darkened room. He had trouble seeing in the dusky light. The windows at the back of the room were boarded up, and the smoke was now making his eyes stream.

But this time he distinctly heard a cough. "He-help. Help me." The almost inaudible plea was followed by another cough.

Greg wiped at his eyes and took in the scene on the bed. "My God, Holly, is that you?"

Within minutes, Greg had carried Holly, with the blanket wrapped around her, across the street to her own house. Emergency sirens increased in volume until the fire department sped into the cul-de-sac and began to put out the blaze. As hoses dumped gallon after gallon of water on 17 Sandpiper Circle, Holly stayed in her own house, choking out her story, bit by bit.

"I've got to get you to a doctor," Greg insisted for the dozenth time.

"No, no. I—I'll be all right. I just have to get my breath back and get cleaned up, and then I can—"

"You just had a baby, Holly, under the worst of circumstances. Another half hour, you could have burned to death! You need—"

"No, Greg! Listen! For centuries, women have been squatting in the fields and giving birth while they worked. I'll be all right, really I will. I can do this! I have to find my son before that woman gets away with him or—or worse."

"That's the sheriff's job, Holly. The sheriff—"

"No! You want to call the sheriff about this? For God's sake, that man couldn't even get my television set back, and you want to give him a shot at my baby? Hell, that stupid jerk would probably accuse me of killing my baby as well as my husband."

"But—"

"You've got to be kidding!" Holly's voice grew stronger even as she hovered near hysteria. "For God's sake, Greg, that woman said she'd kill my son before she'd give him back! She sounded like she'd freak out and kill him if the CHP stopped her for speeding! I have to believe her. I can't afford not to."

"I just want to help."

"Help! Help? You want to help, Greg, do what I ask. Give me a few minutes to get myself together, then help me find my baby. Believe me, it's the only hope I've got."

Greg sighed. He recognized the set of Holly's jaw and the determined look in her tear-filled eyes as hundred-proof stubbornness. But he really couldn't blame her. It was possible that she was judging Sheriff Wills too harshly. Still, at best the man was a drunk. Her reluctance to trust him to find her infant was understandable.

"All right," Greg said finally. "But if you start to feel

sicker, Holly, you've got to promise to let me take you to a doctor."

Holly squeezed her eyes shut and wiped the tears off her face with a corner of the smoky blanket. "Thanks, Greg," she said. "And whatever you do, don't tell anybody you found me in that house. Promise?"

Greg nodded reluctantly as Holly limped slowly toward her bedroom, the blanket that covered her nakedness clutched tightly around her.

By the time the fire across the street had been put out and the first of the fire trucks had left the scene, Holly had taken a shower and found a box of Kotex to absorb her bleeding. Every part of her battered body ached and throbbed. She knew she was running on sheer adrenaline now, that she would crash eventually, but she couldn't afford to take time out to rest. Not yet.

After examining her injuries and deciding that none required immediate medical attention, she forced herself to focus on the task at hand. She couldn't afford to give in to panic, not when her infant's very life depended on her being logical and coolheaded.

Who was Pat Patterson? she asked herself over and over again as she applied Bactine to her worst cuts and scratches, wrapped her injured ankle with an Ace bandage, and towel-dried her hair. Why would this woman steal her child? If she ever wanted to see her tiny son again, she would have to find out the answer to that question. As she began to remember little details about Pat, a horrifying possibility began to creep into Holly's mind. She yanked open her underwear drawer and thrust her hand deep inside. Just as she suspected. Alex's journals were missing.

Of course, Holly thought: Alex's first wife, Celia! She

cursed herself for not recognizing who Pat Patterson really was last night, as soon as the woman turned nasty. Sure, Celia was supposed to be blond and Pat had dark reddish hair, but the woman could have dyed her hair or worn a wig. The age was right, and the height too. Celia had to be tall if she'd once worked as a model. And there was one other thing Holly couldn't forget—the botched abortion Alex had written about in his diary.

Holly could almost understand why a woman like Celia Sheridan might do something like this. She obviously had never gotten over that terrible day in 1967 and had let her bitterness fester and grow ever since.

After dressing quickly in a loose sweatshirt and a clean pair of maternity pants with a drawstring waist, Holly pattered barefoot down the hall into Alex's office. His address book was still in the center drawer of the desk. Turning to *S*, she dialed Celia Sheridan's phone number in Bel Air.

"The number you have reached is no longer in service and there is no new number," a recorded voice told her. Of course, Holly thought. Celia had left Los Angeles. If she'd planned from the start to steal Alex's baby, she wouldn't go back where she could be found so easily.

Holly slipped into a pair of tennis shoes, threw a few essentials into a duffel bag, and went back into the living room. "I've figured out who Pat really is," she told Greg, and began to explain her theory.

When she had finished, Greg said, "Makes sense, Holly. I've got to agree. How about we call the FBI, let them take over?"

"No! I told you, that woman will kill my baby. I'm more certain now than ever. Don't you see, Greg?"

Tears welled up in Holly's eyes once more. She blinked furiously to keep them from falling. This was no time to break down again. "I don't know whether Celia took him because she really wants a baby to keep or—or just because she hates Alex so much. Me too, I guess. She had to hate me too." A shiver ran down Holly's spine, and she hugged herself for warmth. "When she saw my baby was a boy, you should have heard her voice. I don't know—maybe he reminded her of Alex. So I can't trust anyone else to find him, I just can't."

"But how are we going do it? Think a minute. You haven't got a clue where she went."

"I'll find one," Holly said, prodding her sore muscles into action. Her jaw set with determination, she limped toward the front door.

"How?" Greg jumped up and reached for her elbow to help her walk.

"I'm going to start over there," Holly said, opening the door and peering across the cul-de-sac. The fire was out now, and the major damage appeared to have been confined to the garage area. She could see the firemen reeling their hose back onto the last truck. The sheriff's squad car was nowhere in sight; for once, Holly was relieved that the man was slow to do his duty. With luck, nobody else had figured out yet that this fire was arson.

"I'm going back in, Greg, and I need your help," Holly told him. "You can keep the firemen occupied while I sneak in." She didn't want to have to answer difficult questions from the authorities, not yet. "There's got to be something Celia left behind that'll tell us where she's headed," she said. "There's simply got to be."

Chapter

35

Holly wandered from room to room in the reeking water-drenched house, searching for any kind of clue that might lead her to her baby. But Celia had done a good job of covering her tracks. None of her clothing remained in the house, and the food left on the kitchen shelves and in the refrigerator said nothing about her destination. There were no revealing notes posted by the telephone, no telltale memos in the wastebaskets, no prescription bottles in the bathroom cabinets, nothing. Even the shipping label on the empty cardboard carton in the living room had been torn off.

Damn, Holly thought, her head aching as she breathed in the potent stench that lingered in the partially burned house. She wished she could have had just one glimpse at that address label. It must have revealed something; otherwise, why would Celia have gone to the trouble of removing it? Holly lifted the flaps of the soggy carton and saw nothing inside except packing pellets. Celia wouldn't have been stupid enough to rip off that label and then leave it in the box, would she?

Holly upended the carton, spilling the packing materials onto the soaked carpet. She found no shipping label, but there was something else. Her heart skipped a beat as she spotted a small white gift card lying among the bits of Styrofoam. She picked it up and read the words printed on the front—*a gift for you from Beverly Hills Baby Boutique*—along with the store's address and phone number. Inside was a handwritten message: *For your new baby, with lots of love, Buffy Lewis.*

Who was Buffy Lewis? Holly wondered as she stuffed the card deep into her pants pocket.

Less than ten minutes later Holly had completed her search without finding anything else connected to Celia Sheridan. She sneaked out of the damaged house. Greg was still busily talking with the remaining fire fighters, diverting their attention away from what she'd been doing.

Relieved to be back outdoors, Holly gratefully sucked clean air deep into her tortured lungs. Then she crept back across the street to her own home and headed straight for the office.

She grabbed Alex's address book once more and this time turned to *L*. There was no Buffy Lewis listed, but there was an entry for a Charles Lewis with a Beverly Hills address. Holly dialed the phone number Alex had inked in next to the address.

When a woman answered, Holly tensed. "Hi, may I speak to Buffy, please?"

"This is Buffy."

Holly's knuckles were white on the receiver. "Buffy," she explained, "I'm a friend of Celia Sheridan's, and I've been trying to reach her. I called her number in Bel Air, but it's been disconnected."

"Celia sold her house."

"That's what I figured. Listen, Buffy, you and Celia were always good friends—she used to say such nice things about you—I thought you might have her new address."

"Well, yes, I do. What did you say your name was?"

"Uh, Mary," Holly said, grasping for a name, any name other than her own. "Mary Richards." As soon as the two words had escaped her lips, Holly realized that she'd not only sounded as if she couldn't remember her own name, she'd chosen the name of the fictional character Mary Tyler Moore had played on TV for so many years. Please, please don't let Buffy Lewis be a sitcom fan, she prayed.

"All right, Mary." Buffy Lewis's voice now sounded a bit more cautious. "Why don't you give me your phone number, and next time I talk to Celia I'll pass it on to her. She can contact you."

"But it would be a lot easier if you just—"

"Sorry, but the truth is I'm not comfortable about giving out my best friend's address without her permission. Besides, I don't think Cele has her new phone hooked up yet. She hasn't called to give me her number."

"Just let me have her new address, then, and I'll drop her a note."

"I said *no*, Mary. If you want to leave your number with me, I'll pass it on to Celia. Otherwise—"

Feeling cornered, Holly slammed down the phone before she could mess things up any more than she already had. Furious with herself, she pounded her fist against the desktop, then picked up the gift card and stared at it again.

Maybe all was not lost after all, she thought, as the

black print began to swim before her eyes. Maybe there was another way to get the information she needed. Holly reached for the telephone once more and dialed the phone number printed below the address of the Beverly Hills Baby Boutique.

"This is Buffy Lewis," she announced, when a clerk at the shop came on the line. "I bought a gift for a friend of mine at the Baby Boutique a few days ago— for Celia Sheridan? It—I mean, there's a problem. Celia says it hasn't arrived at her place yet, so—well, I thought I'd better check the address you shipped it to— you know, see if it's correct."

"Sure. Hi, Mrs. Lewis, I remember you." The clerk sounded young, enthusiastic. "You called in an order for one of our baby car seats and had us ship it to your friend up in San Francisco, right?"

Holly took a gamble. The box certainly had been big enough to hold a car seat. "Uh, yes, that's it," she said.

"Right. I remember writing out the gift card on that one. Just last week, wasn't it?"

"I—that sounds about right. I don't know, I'm always so bad with dates—"

"Want to hold on while I look it up, or should I call you back?"

"Oh, I'll hold, thanks."

Holly hardly dared let herself breathe while she waited for the young woman to return to the phone.

"Here it is, Mrs. Lewis, I found it," the clerk told her, nearly five minutes later. She read a Grove Street address into the phone as Holly frantically copied it down. "Is that the correct address?"

"Yes," Holly said, her voice filled with genuine relief and gratitude. "Yes, it is. Thanks. Thanks so much."

"I'm glad we didn't send it to the wrong address,

but we shipped that car seat out last Thursday. It should have arrived in San Francisco well before now. Maybe I'd better call UPS and put a tracer on it."

"Oh, no, that's all right, really. I'm sure the package will get there in a day or two. Or maybe one of Celia's neighbors took the delivery for her. I'll ask her to check around the building."

"Well . . . okay, Mrs. Lewis, but be sure to let us know if it doesn't arrive soon. All our shipments are fully insured."

Holly thanked the clerk once more for her help and reassured her that she would, indeed, let her know if the car seat didn't arrive. After she hung up the phone, she stared for a moment at the address she'd written down. For the first time since Celia Sheridan had pointed a gun at her, Holly felt a surge of real hope. This address on Grove Street had to be where Celia had taken her new son, she thought; it simply had to be.

With the scrap of notepaper on which she'd written the San Francisco address clutched tightly in her hand, Holly hurried back outside to tell Greg the good news.

Chapter

36

⌒

Celia paced the ten-foot width of the little apartment's bedroom and then retraced her steps, back and forth. The baby was sleeping peacefully now, tucked into the crib Mr. Fraser had brought up from the apartment building's basement. Celia wished she could get some sleep too. She was bone-tired after last night, but she couldn't seem to relax. She felt wired, as though she'd downed at least two pots of strong black coffee, or the way she had years ago, when she'd been prescribed diet pills that turned out to be amphetamines.

She was probably just overexcited, Celia told herself, and why not? She was finally a mother, after all these years, a mother for the very first time at age forty-eight. Why shouldn't she be too excited to rest? If only she had somebody special to share this with. . . .

Buffy, Celia thought. She could call her dear friend Buffy, thank her for the infant car seat, and share her good news. Buffy would be glad for her. Hadn't she rushed right out and bought a gift the minute she'd gotten Celia's note about the baby? Celia gave the sleeping infant a final glance and walked into the kitchen.

The wall phone next to the refrigerator had a dial tone now. Pac Bell had turned on the phone service as promised. She punched in Buffy's phone number from memory.

"You can congratulate me, Buff, it's a boy!" Celia said when Buffy answered.

"A boy! That's great, Cele. When do you get him?"

"I already have him. I'm a mother! Right this minute, little Patrick's snoozing in the bedroom. Just between you and me, I was kind of hoping he'd be a girl, but I guess I can't be choosy after all these years, can I?"

The two women chatted for a while about babies and motherhood, which gave Celia a chance to practice and embellish the private-adoption fable she'd concocted for her friends, just in case she ever decided to bring little Patrick back to Los Angeles to live.

"By the way, Cele," Buffy said, "the strangest thing. Do you know somebody named Mary Richards?"

"Mary Richards? You mean like on TV?"

"TV?"

"Yeah, remember the old *Mary Tyler Moore Show*? Mary Richards, Mr. Grant, Rhoda Morgenstern, Phyllis."

Buffy snorted. "I hardly think it was Mary Tyler Moore on the phone, Celia, and Richards isn't all that uncommon a name. Seriously, do you have a friend named Mary Richards?"

"Not that I remember. Why?" A tingling sensation began working its way down Celia's spine.

"Because a woman called here this morning. Said she was a friend of yours. Wanted your new address.

When I insisted she tell me who she was, she said her name was Mary Richards."

"You didn't tell her where I lived, did you?" Celia snapped. "I can't have—"

"No, of course I didn't. Calm down, Cele, everything's all right. All I did was tell her she could leave her name and number with me and you'd call her back if you felt like contacting her. But she hung up on me."

"All—all right." Celia breathed a little easier. "But how—? If I don't even know this Mary Richards person, why would she call you to get my address? She must know both of us somehow."

"I don't know. Maybe she's from the tennis club? Or somebody we both used to know when we were married? Did Alex and Charlie have a buddy named Richards? Doesn't sound familiar to me. The whole thing's strange, but I wouldn't worry about it. I bet she's just some slick, persistent saleswoman trying to track you down, get you to buy stocks and bonds or long-distance telephone service or something. Or—hey, Cele, you don't have debt collectors on your trail these days, do you?"

"Don't be cute, Buffy. Hey, listen, I better go. I hear the baby. If that woman calls back again, tell her I died, okay?"

"Sure, whatever you say."

After hanging up the phone, Celia stood frozen to the kitchen floor for a good ten minutes, her mind reeling. She felt more and more certain that she'd never met anyone named Mary Richards. She would have remembered if she had; she'd have commented on the familiar name. So who could it be?

The woman's calling Buffy had to be some weird

coincidence. At least Celia fervently hoped it was. Because if it wasn't . . .

Her imagination began to run wild. She imagined Holly surviving the fire and realizing Pat was really Celia, saw her somehow making the connection between Celia and Buffy Lewis, pictured her calling up Buffy. But that was impossible, wasn't it? Besides, even if Celia's worst fears were actually true, Buffy hadn't given the woman who phoned any information, right?

Unless Buffy had lied just now. Celia had reacted so sharply, so negatively, when she heard her friend say Mary Richards wanted her address. Had she frightened Buffy so much she didn't dare admit what she'd done? Celia began to wonder whether she could still afford to trust her oldest friend, the only real friend she had left.

She was probably going off the deep end here, Celia realized, but she couldn't help herself. She began to imagine the police breaking into this apartment, arresting her for murdering Alex, for trying to murder Holly, for kidnapping tiny Patrick, for who knew what else. She simply couldn't risk that happening.

By the time she had walked the short distance into the bedroom where the baby still slept, Celia had made her decision. She had no idea where they would go, where they could hide safely. What she did know was that she and the baby she'd waited so long for had to get out of this place.

Right now, before anybody else found out where they were.

Chapter

37

"There's a space," Holly said, pointing to a vacant metered parking spot a block from the Grove Street address.

Greg pulled Holly's car into the curb. At her request, he had driven from Bodega Bay while she rested in the backseat. "It's a one-hour space, though, and I don't have any quarters."

"I keep a whole stash in the ashtray," Holly told him. "And if we're gone more than an hour, so what? Worst thing is, we'll get a parking ticket." She slipped her tennis shoes back onto her swollen feet and maneuvered herself out of the car. Her ankle throbbed as soon as she put weight on it. At least it wasn't broken, she thought. If it was, surely she wouldn't be able to stand on it at all.

Despite her two-hour rest in the back of the car, Holly was exhausted, and now her breasts were starting to ache, a certain sign that her milk was beginning to come in. She was forced to draw on depths of physical strength she never knew she had simply to walk the block to Celia's apartment building.

"Here it is. She's using the Sheridan name, all right," Greg said, pointing to a line in white block letters near the bottom of the apartment building's roster. The glass door to the building's entryway was security locked, with a telephone set into a recess beside it. "How about I ring her, tell I'm making a delivery for UPS? Maybe she'll let me in."

"Okay, give it a try," Holly agreed. "Celia might think Buffy Lewis sent her another package."

Greg dialed 512, the apartment number listed after C. SHERIDAN on the roster. A series of clicking sounds came over the line, followed by ringing. He waited while the phone rang eight times. "No answer," he announced, as he hung up.

"Damn! Where could she have gone?" Holly's quick surge of optimism after finding Celia's name on the building's tenant list began to falter. Had she guessed wrong? Maybe Celia had never planned to bring the baby here after all. If she was actually living here, she couldn't simply have gone out to shop or run errands, not with a newborn in tow. "Maybe she's just not answering her door," Holly suggested. "Try another apartment, see if somebody'll let us into the building."

The fourth number Greg dialed answered and buzzed the front door open. Greg grabbed it and held it for Holly, who moved slowly and deliberately, fighting pain with each step. They rode the elevator to the fifth floor and located Celia's apartment down the hall to the right. They heard no sounds coming from inside. Holding his finger over the peephole in the door to block the hall view from inside, Greg knocked once, then knocked again, harder. If Celia asked him to identify himself, he would use the UPS story, then try to grab her when she opened the door. But no one came.

A minute or two later, he glanced solemnly at Holly, who stood off to the side with her back pressed against the wall, and shook his head.

Choking back tears of exhaustion and disappointment, Holly knocked sharply on the door across the hall. Almost instantly, the door opened a crack and an elderly woman peered out.

"Hello," Holly said. "I wonder if you can help me. I'm looking for my sister, Celia Sheridan. She lives across the hall." The old woman nodded, her sharp eyes brimming with curiosity. "I was supposed to meet her here this afternoon, but she doesn't seem to be home. I just wondered if you—"

"Celia *was* here," the woman said, opening the door a little wider. "Just had a baby—well, you must know about that, you being her sister, eh?"

"Right." Holly felt hope resurging. "I came to help her, but she doesn't answer either the phone or the door. Do you know where she went?"

"Maybe she took the baby to the doctor," Greg suggested.

"Not likely, young man." The old woman shook her finger as if scolding a stupid child. "Not with that great big suitcase she took with her."

"When did she leave?" Holly asked, feeling the wind knocked out of her again. So Celia *had* been here. Why would she pack up and leave?

"Does Mrs. Sheridan have a parking space somewhere in the building?" Greg asked. "Maybe she's still packing her car."

"Down in the basement," the woman told him. "Take the elevator. Spaces are numbered, same as the apartments. Celia's will be five-twelve. You'll see soon enough if her car's still there. But, like I said, it's not likely. Been a good hour since she and the baby left."

"Thank you very much, ma'am," Holly said politely. She took Greg's elbow and leaned against him for support as she moved slowly back down the hall toward the elevator. She could feel the old woman's prying eyes on her back the entire way.

In the basement parking garage, Holly and Greg's fears were confirmed. Space five-twelve was vacant.

"Think we can get inside her apartment?" Holly asked. "She might have left something behind."

"Not with that old biddy keeping watch," Greg said. "Must keep an eye on that hall all the time, or she'd never have known Celia left with a big suitcase."

"Maybe Celia stopped to say good-bye."

"Uh-uh, no way. If she had, the old woman would've asked where she was going, I'd stake my life on it. Nope, that woman's a snoop, take my word for it. Probably heard noise in the hall when Celia and the baby left and looked out her peephole. Look how fast she answered her door when you knocked."

"Guess you're right."

"Of course I am. She was standing right there, spying on us the whole time we were knocking on Celia's door."

Suddenly the starch went out of Holly's legs and she sagged against Greg's arm. He spun around and caught her by her shoulders. "Hey, I'm really sorry this didn't work out the way you hoped," he said, for once meeting her eyes directly. "But don't you think it's about time we called the police?"

"No!" Holly said, pulling away from him. "No cops. Not yet, anyway. I'll just have to think of something else. I have to figure out how Celia thinks, what motivates her, where she's likely to go. I'm dead certain that's the only way we're ever going to find her. At least in time."

"But—"

"*No*, Greg," Holly said. "Don't you get it? It was her, Celia! *She* murdered Alex! I don't know exactly how she managed it, but she has to be the one who drugged him. Celia was the one who wanted him dead, the only one. She murdered my husband, and then she tried to murder me. If you hadn't seen that smoke—"

Holly began to shiver.

"I know one thing, as sure as I know Celia killed Alex. I know she'll murder my baby too—Alex's baby—just the way she threatened. If she thinks she's going to lose that child, she'll snuff out his life without thinking twice.

"No," Holly said, "my mind's made up. No police. I'm going to find my son and get him back all by myself."

"You're sure you want to carry this much in cash, Mrs. Sheridan?" the bank teller asked. She was a tiny black woman in her mid-twenties, immaculately dressed in a navy suit and crisp yellow blouse. The name tag pinned above her right breast identified her as T. Parsons.

"Yes, I'm sure," Celia said. "I want it in fifties and hundreds."

"I'll have to get approval." T. Parsons sounded a bit doubtful.

"Then go get it. I don't have all day." The baby began to fuss against Celia's shoulder. She was certain everyone in the bank lobby was staring at her. She hated being so noticeable—under circumstances like these, anyway. She couldn't help worrying about what might happen if that fucking Holly had survived the fire, if the bitch had called the cops, if right now they were searching for a middle-aged woman with an infant. Celia felt cornered. She knew she would need lots of cash if she was going to hide out somewhere long enough to assess the situation. Perhaps, if she was wanted by the police, she'd have to stay hidden forever. Yet she could hardly leave little Patrick alone in the car while she went into the bank to cash a large check. Not in San Francisco in broad daylight.

"How old's your baby?"

Celia jumped. She turned to see an obese woman with stringy blond hair standing behind her in line. The woman wore a hot-pink tent dress and held a toddler girl licking a lollipop by the hand. "What?"

"I asked how old's your baby?"

"Uh, almost two weeks." If the cops had been alerted, Celia figured, they'd be looking for a day-old child. No sense volunteering that she had one right here.

"Boy or girl?"

"Girl," Celia lied, attempting to thicken the smoke screen. Nobody who wasn't changing the kid's diapers would know the difference at this age anyway.

"Lemme see, Mommy, lemme see." The small girl's lips were stained with dye from her red candy, giving her a grotesque clown's visage.

The woman bent down and hoisted her daughter onto one of her ample hips. "Baby!" the child shrieked as she reached over and poked a sticky finger at the infant's head.

Celia jerked him away from the unwelcome touch. "Do you mind?" she snapped at the mother.

"Sorry, we didn't mean anything. It's just we love babies so. My Tina's gonna be a real good mommy when she grows up, aren't you, sweetie?"

Celia turned her back to the woman and her daughter and began to drum her fingernails on the bank's countertop. What was taking that teller so long? Just as she was about to lodge a protest with the branch manager, T. Parsons came back into view, a sheaf of cash in her hands.

"Sorry to keep you waiting, Mrs. Sheridan. There's paperwork we have to fill out every time we deal with more than ten thousand dollars in cash, you know."

Celia hadn't known. Shit, she thought, expecting to see some government official come through the bank's door any minute. "There's no problem, is there? I mean, I've got far more than that in my account."

"No, no problem at all. Just government regulations." The teller began to count out the money.

The baby fussed and squirmed as his appetite began to kick in. Once again, Celia could feel eyes on her back. Were people looking at the baby or at the stack of bills on the counter in front of her? All she needed was for somebody to mug her as she left the bank with all these fifties and hundreds.

If she'd thought about it first, she realized, she would have requested a private meeting with the bank manager to get her money. With the fortune she had on deposit in this place, a little privacy shouldn't be too much to ask.

When she was certain the teller hadn't shorted her, Celia stuffed the bills into her shoulder bag and rushed out of the bank. She breathed a sigh of relief when she saw that her loaded station wagon was still parked in the twenty-minute space at the curb half a block away. Her nerves were completely on edge. She'd envisioned her car stolen; the baby snatched; cops and FBI men on every corner, each one clutching a photo of her; being knifed or shot for the wad of cash in her purse. The faster she got out of the city, with its crowds of undesirables, the happier she would be.

As Celia pulled away from the curb, the baby began to wail full blast, and by the time she reached the red light at Van Ness she couldn't take any more. "Shut the hell up!" she screamed. Startled, the baby cried even louder. A split second later, Celia felt contrite. Here she was, already yelling—swearing, even—at little Patrick, and he was only a day old.

The city was her main problem, Celia decided. In the city, there were simply too many people watching her every move. In the city, there was nowhere she could go without somebody noticing the baby. And what if they started talking about a missing baby on TV, the way they did when an infant girl was snatched from a hospital nursery in Oakland? What if they showed Celia's photograph on all the TV stations and she became a public target?

Her breathing was quick and shallow and her knuckles were white on the steering wheel. The instant the light changed, she rammed the station wagon's accelerator to the floor. The car screeched across the intersection, forcing a bicycle messenger to swerve into the curb to avoid being hit. As she headed west, Celia could hear the messenger shouting obscenities in her wake.

"Great, Celia," she said out loud. "Really great way to avoid being conspicuous." She had to get herself back under control if she wasn't going to blow everything she'd worked so hard for, everything she'd risked so much to have.

Fifteen minutes later, Celia found herself driving aimlessly through Golden Gate Park while little Patrick screamed his head off. The muscles in her neck and shoulders had turned to hardened steel. Get it together, she lectured herself, get it fucking together!

She could find nowhere to pull over and feed the

baby inside the park itself, so she headed south onto the alphabet streets of the Sunset District, finally spotting an empty curbsite on residential Kirkham Street. She parked, opened the back of the station wagon, and pulled out her diaper bag. As she fed Patrick an ounce of bottled formula, she felt eyes upon her from every window.

"Sorry I can't heat it up for you, little one," she said, as she watched the tiny lips working hungrily against the rubber nipple. "Might as well figure it out right now—you don't always get what you want out of life. Plenty of times, you just get screwed."

When the child's appetite seemed sated, Celia was tempted to beat a hasty retreat from the neighborhood, but she forced herself to minister to the rest of his physical needs first. While she was changing his diaper, using the tailgate for a changing table, he fell asleep again.

Celia knew she had to make a plan, right now. She couldn't simply drive around hour after hour with no destination, waiting to be picked up. She had to have a goal, a specific place to go. As she buckled the baby back into his car seat, she considered her options. Obviously, she couldn't hide an infant in a hotel or a motel; his inevitable cries would attract attention, not to mention the snoopy maids who came to clean every day.

If only that Mary Richards woman—was she really Holly?—hadn't called Buffy, Celia thought wistfully, she might have gone to her friend's place in Beverly Hills. She longed to see Buffy again, to ask her a few things about taking care of an infant. After all, she'd raised three kids of her own, even if they were grown up now.

But thinking about Buffy was pointless; if Buffy had

never received that phone call, she would have stuck to her original plan, hiding out in the San Francisco apartment until she was sure she was home free.

Still, maybe Buffy. . . ? Of course! Celia thought with a start. Buffy had a summer home in Lake Tahoe. She'd been there many times. That place would be perfect. The sturdy cabin was set back among the trees and was quite secluded, especially at this time of year; few people ever went there in wintertime, when there was snow on the ground. Best of all, Celia recalled, the last time she'd visited Buffy in Tahoe, she'd noticed where her friend kept an extra door key hidden. Lake Tahoe—that's where she would go! And just to make extra sure she wouldn't be found, she wouldn't bother asking Buffy's permission to use the cabin. If Buffy didn't know where she was, Buffy couldn't tell anyone.

Celia started the car again and zigzagged east to the Oak Street entrance to Highway 80 and the approach to the Bay Bridge. Now that she'd decided on a definite destination, the steel in her shoulders finally began to soften and she no longer felt compelled to keep the accelerator pressed against the floorboards. She simply kept up with the flow of traffic, disappearing into the start of the afternoon rush hour.

As she eased onto the bridge that spanned San Francisco Bay, Celia turned on the car radio and listened to the news on KCBS. She was relieved to hear no bulletin about a baby stolen from Bodega Bay, no mention of anyone named Sheridan, nothing that pertained in any way to her.

Feeling at least momentarily reassured, Celia glanced over at the sleeping baby. "Everything's going to be all right, little Patrick," she promised. "Wait and see. Mama's going to make it all better."

Chapter 39

Holly forced down the entire bowl of clam chowder and most of her salad; she knew she needed food to keep her strength up. But every time an announcement for a United Airlines flight came over the public address system, her stomach clenched and she had to fight against losing everything she'd just eaten. She and Greg were seated at one of the tables in San Francisco International Airport's Fresh Express restaurant as they waited to board the next United shuttle flight to Los Angeles. Just thinking about getting on that airplane in a few minutes was making Holly nauseous, even though the plane was a big one.

Before now, Holly'd never been a particularly nervous flier. She'd even gone up in the Cessna with Alex several times. But things had changed for her forever when his little plane nosedived into the Pacific. She would never think about flying in quite the same way again.

Now, two almost equally terrifying thoughts clashed in Holly's mind: that her plane might fall out of the sky and that her baby son might be in Los Angeles right now.

"You look awful pale, Holly," Greg said, as he buttered his third slice of sourdough bread. "Sure you're feeling all right?"

Holly closed her eyes, leaned her head back, and took a deep breath. "Just nerves, Greg. I'll get over it."

"Hey, we don't have to go to L.A., you know. There's a phone right over there. We can still call the FBI or the cops."

Holly's eyelids snapped open. "No! We've already talked about that a dozen times. I'm *not* changing my mind."

"But time's passing, Holly. The longer we wait, the farther away Celia and the baby can get, and all you've got is some half-baked hunch she might take him to her friend's house. You gotta admit, that's not a helluva lot."

"I don't need you to remind me this is a long shot, Greg." Holly had done her best to guess where Celia might have gone next, tried to make herself think the way Celia did. The only thing she'd been able to come up with was that Celia might turn to the friend who'd sent her the baby gift.

Two voices kept repeating in Holly's head. The first was Alex's. When he'd filed the court papers to modify his alimony arrangement, he'd commented that Celia's bitterness had driven away all her friends. The second voice was the one Holly heard on the telephone that afternoon, Buffy Lewis's, as she said, "I'm not comfortable giving out my best friend's address without her permission." *Best friend.* Unless Alex had been exaggerating wildly, Holly thought, Buffy Lewis might well be the only friend Celia hadn't alienated. Obviously, she'd told Buffy Lewis something about the baby. Why else would Mrs. Lewis have sent that car seat?

Phoning the Lewis woman again would be counter-productive, Holly knew. But if she went to Beverly Hills, she might find Celia and the baby there. If not, maybe she could try to convince Mrs. Lewis that the best thing for her friend Celia was to get psychiatric help. If she truly was Celia's best friend, maybe her only friend, she had to realize how mentally unstable the woman really was.

It seemed worth a try, Holly had decided, particularly when she could think of absolutely no other route to take. She shoved her plate away. "Look, Greg," she said, making a quick decision, "you don't need to stick around. I'm feeling a lot better now, really I am, so why don't you just drive on back to Bodega Bay and—"

"Hold on just a minute! I'm not trying to back out on you. Damn, is that what you think?" The frigid look in Holly's green eyes told Greg he'd guessed right. She thought he was chicken or, more likely, that he just didn't give a damn what happened to her and her baby; disappointment and contempt were written all over her face. Impulsively, he reached across the table and placed his work-scarred hand over her softer, smaller one. "I'm not very good at this kind of thing, Holly, but hell. Alex wasn't just my business partner, he was my friend, and you're my friend too. I care about what happens to you, I really do."

As soon as the words were off Greg's tongue, he realized he meant them. For the first time, he saw Holly Sheridan as more than a burden, more than just another dependent female who had to be shielded and protected. He'd even stopped watching his language around her. Holly had as much guts and as much intelligence as any three of his buddies put together. Holly was tough, a survivor. And she truly *was* his friend.

"Listen, friend," he told her gently, "let's you and me make a pact, okay? This is your baby, so you get to make the decisions. I promise to keep my mouth shut and let you call the shots. But what I won't do is let you try to do this all by yourself. Agreed?"

"Okay," Holly said, her chin quivering. "And thanks. Thanks, Greg."

Greg checked his watch. "We better get down to the gate," he said. "Flight leaves in fifteen minutes."

Holly held tightly to Greg's elbow as they walked down the jetway and onto the airplane. But despite the fear that chilled her to the bone, she never allowed herself to hesitate.

Becoming more and more frantic by the minute, Celia headed the station wagon down still another dark and deserted side road. Where the hell was Buffy's cabin anyway? She'd been driving up and down these god-forsaken ice-crusted streets for the past hour without finding the place.

Celia hadn't expected everything in the hills above Lake Tahoe to look so different in wintertime. Or for the roads to be so dark. She slowed the car to a stop at a deserted rural intersection, aimed her headlights directly toward the street signs, and squinted at them. Bluebird Lane and Parker Way, she read.

Parker Way sounded vaguely familiar, Celia thought. She turned right and drove downhill for a quarter mile until she reached another intersection, Parker Way and Curtis Drive. Curtis Drive, that was it! She remembered now. Buffy's cabin was off by itself, up the hill on Curtis Drive. She drove slowly, keeping the station wagon toward the center of the road, where the snowplow's efforts had been most efficient.

"Almost there, Patrick," she said.

The baby had been nearly silent for the last two hours; With that blanket loosely covering his tiny face, Celia couldn't even hear him breathing, and she had to admit she'd enjoyed the quiet. He'd yelled his head off all the way through Donner Pass until, completely exasperated, she'd stopped the car to feed and change him again.

This time, the baby swallowed less than half an ounce of formula before rejecting the bottle. Maybe the thick white stuff was too cold for him, Celia thought, as she sat shivering in the public rest stop's parking lot. Her raincoat wasn't warm enough for these below-freezing temperatures either; each time she opened the car door, frigid air blasted her in the face. She just couldn't seem to warm up. But maybe that wasn't all bad, she decided; as tired as she was, she needed cold air to keep her from falling asleep at the wheel.

After the baby had finished his meager meal at the rest stop, Celia tossed the extra blanket across his face, in case the chilly night air was hard on his new lungs. The best thing she could do for both of them, she decided, was to reach Buffy's cabin as fast as possible. But she'd never expected it would be after midnight before she finally turned into the cabin's snowy driveway.

"Wait here, kiddo," Celia said, as she braked the car to a stop a few feet in. The driveway hadn't been plowed, and she didn't want to venture any farther. "I'll go open up the house." She shifted the car into park, leaving the motor and heater running and the headlights on.

"Holy shit!" Celia said, as she stepped out of the car and into six inches of recent snowfall. In an instant, the frozen powder crept deep inside her loafers, numbing her toes and chilling her to the bone.

She'd expected to locate Buffy's spare key much more easily, too. She would have, of course, if it hadn't been snowy and so dark she couldn't see her hand in front of her face. Celia felt her way around the side of the pitch-black cabin by sliding her hand along the rough-textured walls and forcing her cold feet through a foot of drifted snow. After she reached the back, she crawled up six short steps and onto a rear deck that overlooked the woods.

With only the dim light of a quarter moon through cloud cover to guide her search, Celia almost missed what she was looking for. But this had to be it, she decided. This snow-covered mound at the far corner of the deck had to be Buffy's gas barbecue grill, the place where she kept her extra key.

Her bare hands stiff with cold, Celia dug through the snow until she felt the edge of the black plastic cover. Gripping the cover, she yanked until it slid free, revealing the black grill underneath. Pushing the propane gas tank to the side, she slid fingers that were quickly losing all feeling over the grill's lower shelf until she located the key.

Fearing that her frozen fingers couldn't hold the key—and if she dropped it in the snow, she wouldn't find it until spring—Celia held it clenched between her teeth as she made her way slowly back around to the front of the cabin. She breathed a sigh of relief when the key turned smoothly in the lock and the door sprang open.

She switched on the lights. The interior of the cabin was as Celia remembered it, if a bit dustier. She kept her coat huddled around her; the temperature inside the house was only a degree or two warmer than outside. But that would soon be remedied, she thought, as she twisted the wall thermostat in the master bedroom upward, setting the temperature at a soon-to-be-toasty 75 degrees.

She'd made it after all, Celia thought with a glow of satisfaction. She and Patrick would be safe here in Buffy's hideaway, at least until they found out whether anyone was on their trail.

Eyeing the bed with undisguised longing, Celia fought a strong urge simply to lie down and go to sleep. But rest would have to wait a little while longer, she told herself, as she flipped on the light switches just inside the front door. The porch and the driveway quickly sprang into clear view.

With a deep sigh of martyrdom, Celia pulled her coat more tightly around her, thrust her hands into her pockets, and forced herself back outside to retrieve the baby.

"Guess we better go on to Plan B," Holly said. "Doesn't look like Celia and the baby are here. Not yet, anyhow. And I'm afraid, if we stay out here much longer, one of these neighbors is going to call the cops."

For the past two and a half hours, Holly and Greg had been sitting in a rented car, watching Buffy Lewis's house in the flats of Beverly Hills. They were parked across the street from the address they'd found in Alex's address book, in a spot that required a residential parking permit they didn't have. This section of Maple Drive, half a block south of Burton Way and not far from downtown Beverly Hills, was an area of modest homes, at least by this town's standards. Most were one- or two-story stucco dwellings with well-tended front yards boasting the requisite maple trees. The majority also had sturdy security bars over their windows and decorative security grilles over their front doors.

Shortly after Holly and Greg had arrived at Maple Drive, a fiftyish woman with short, graying reddish hair—they assumed she was Buffy Lewis—left the single-story beige stucco house they were watching. The woman got into an older silver Mercedes parked in the driveway and drove away. While she was gone, the house appeared unoccupied. No lights were turned on when darkness fell, no one arrived or left, and no signs of activity were visible through the barred front windows. Twenty minutes ago, the woman in the Mercedes had returned and reentered the house. From what Holly and Greg could tell from their vantage point across the street, she was still in there alone.

"Your call," Greg said.

"I'll go try to talk to her," Holly said, her stomach clenching at the prospect. "With all those black bars she's got on her windows, she probably wouldn't even open the door if you came with me."

"I'll wait here, but if you don't come back for me in fifteen minutes, I'm coming in after you."

"You're on." Holly climbed out of the car and limped up the front walk. Her palms were sweaty and she felt weak with anxiety. If this was the wrong move, she knew, she could be signing her baby's death warrant. Yet doing nothing could push him toward the same fate. Saying a silent prayer that she wasn't making a fatal mistake, Holly reached out and pressed her finger against the doorbell. A moment later, the porch light flashed on, the inner door swung open, and a woman peered out at her through a thick metal mesh security door that remained locked.

"Hello," Holly said. "Are you Buffy Lewis?"

"That's right."

Close up, Holly could see that Buffy Lewis had a kind face. She was tanned a warm bronze color by the Southern California sun and wore little makeup. "I'm Holly Sheridan, Mrs. Lewis, Alex Sheridan's widow," she said. "I—I need to talk to you."

Buffy's jaw slackened. "I remember you," she said. "I saw you on the TV news after the accident."

"Sorry to bother you, but I really do need your help. It's about Alex's ex-wife, Celia. I know she's your friend—"

"Celia? What about Celia? I don't understand."

Holly swallowed hard before she spoke again. Buffy Lewis appeared to be a reasonable woman, she told herself, as she tried to calm her jittery nerves. At least Mrs. Lewis hadn't slammed the door in her face as soon as she'd introduced herself, or when she mentioned Celia's name. Besides, she'd gone this far; she could hardly chicken out now. "Please help me, Mrs. Lewis," Holly said. "Celia Sheridan has—she's stolen my baby."

"Oh, my God!" Buffy gasped audibly, clapping her hand across her mouth. In a flash, she knew what Holly Sheridan was telling her was absolutely true. All the things that had worried her now added up: Celia's never-ending obsession with Alex, the explosive way she'd reacted when she found out his new wife was pregnant, her sudden decision to sell her house and leave Los Angeles, the impulsive so-called "private" adoption. "Oh, my God," Buffy said again. "What's Celia done?"

"I brought a friend with me," Holly told her, "out in the car." She gestured toward the street. "Could we both come in and talk to you for a little while? You know Celia better than anybody, and I really think you might be able to help me find my son before—well, before there's another terrible tragedy."

Buffy just stood there, her body paralyzed and her mind racing wildly. Why hadn't she guessed? she asked herself. Why hadn't she seen something like this coming? Never particularly stable, Celia had grown stranger and stranger in recent months. Obviously she'd been planning something—something big, something completely crazy. Buffy was Celia's best friend; she really should have seen this coming.

"Mrs. Lewis, *please*. May we just come in and talk to you?" Holly repeated. "This is important!"

The younger woman's words jolted Buffy back to the present. "Yes, yes, of course." she said, unlocking the security door. "Come on in. Better have your friend move the car into my driveway, though. The police'll ticket you over there without a permit."

"You poor thing. You gave birth just last night?" Buffy was sitting at her kitchen table, across from Holly and Greg. For the past forty-five minutes, she'd been nervously kneading her freckled hands together as she listened, horrified, to the bizarre tale the two had to tell.

"Right," Holly said. "Early this morning, actually. Seems like days and days ago now, but I guess it hasn't even been twenty-four hours."

"And you haven't seen a doctor?"

"No time, not if I'm going to find my baby before— before Celia—"

"But you really should. I mean, you could get an infection."

"That's what I've been trying to tell her," Greg said, "but Holly's the stubbornest person I've ever known."

"I can go to the hospital after I get my baby back," Holly said. "I'm not sick, I'm just worn out. Besides, a doctor would ask too many questions, maybe insist on calling the police."

"At least I'm going to see that you get something to eat and get some sleep now that you're here," Buffy said, her own mothering instincts fully aroused. "You can have my guest room and Greg can sleep on the sofa. I've got some soup I can reheat, and there's some of that nice crusty Italian bread—"

"Please, Mrs. Lewis . . . Buffy. All I want from you is information about Celia. I need to pick your brain about where she'd be likely to hide. We thought she might come here, but she didn't. Have you heard anything from her, anything at all?"

"She did call this afternoon," Buffy admitted, "from San Francisco, I assumed. Sounded okay at first, I thought, just a little wired maybe—you know, hyper, overexcited. Told me she'd just picked up the baby she was adopting, that it was a boy. Sounded real happy, I thought." Buffy realized that Celia's call was clear confirmation of what these people had been telling her. The timing was right, the sex of the child, everything. "We were having a nice chat, I thought. But then, when I told her somebody'd called here to ask me for her address, she went absolutely ballistic on me. I told her I hadn't given anybody her address, but—"

"Mary Richards," Holly said, with a sigh. "That was me. I'm the one who called you. I was hoping you'd tell me where Celia was so I could find her and get my baby back. Damn! My stupid call is what scared her into leaving San Francisco. Why didn't I just tell you the truth, right there and then?"

"I probably wouldn't have believed you," Buffy said, shaking her head. "I mean, over the phone and all, who's to say it's not some kind of macabre joke? Even your coming here tonight. I mean, if I hadn't *seen* you being interviewed on TV when Alex's plane was missing, I wouldn't have recognized you. Anyway, it's my fault Celia found out about that phone call, not yours. You were just trying to—"

Greg held up his hands in classic time-out formation. "This isn't getting us anywhere, ladies. Doesn't make a damn bit of difference whose fault it is. Only thing that matters right now is this: Celia Sheridan split with Holly's baby, and we've gotta figure out where she's gone."

Buffy pushed her chair back, got up from the table, and opened the refrigerator door. She took out a white plastic Tupperware container filled with homemade potato-leek soup and scooped the thick creamy concoction into a brown glass saucepan. "Nobody can think straight on an empty stomach," she said, as she placed the saucepan in the microwave oven and set the timer. "Tell you what I think."

Buffy sat down again to wait for the soup to reheat.

"Celia might very well call me again, or just show up, if she's looking for a place to hide out with the baby. You two might as well stay right here and see what happens."

"You can't think of anybody else she might turn to for help?" Holly asked. Waiting was her least favorite thing in the whole world. She'd spent days and days doing that, waiting to hear news of Alex. Now she was being asked to do the same thing all over again for her tiny son.

Buffy shook her head slowly as she considered her answer. "Celia was always—I guess you could say she's a volatile sort of person," she explained. "She always had this deep well of anger inside, and you were never sure when it might errupt. You know, she could blow up over the least little thing. Then—well, she didn't handle her divorce very well, to put it mildly. For the last few years, all Celia has seemed to talk about is how Alex screwed her over, how much she hated his guts, him and his new—

"Anyway, the thing is, people get sick and tired of that sort of tirade. I guess I stuck by her because—well, because we go back so far together, and I was getting divorced too. But after a while, even I had to tell her to shut up about Alex and quit with the self-pity."

"So you're saying Celia doesn't have any other friends?" Holly asked. The pungent odor of onions had filled the kitchen, and she felt a sharp pang of hunger.

"Acquaintances, yes, but friends she could turn to for help right now? I don't think so." As she poured the hot soup into three bowls and set two of them in front of Holly and Greg, Buffy felt a rush of sadness. Her old friend was mentally ill, she realized. Anyone would have to be off the deep end to do the things Celia'd done—to imprison her ex-husband's widow; to keep the poor woman tied to a bed while she gave birth; to commit arson, attempted murder, maybe even—

Buffy stopped herself before her mind could take the next logical step and really examine what had happened to Alex and his plane. If Celia was responsible for that too, that made her—no, her old friend Celia couldn't be a cold-blooded murderer. Could she?

"There's her lawyer," Buffy said, as she sliced the crusty Italian bread, "but I don't think Celia really trusts the guy. I mean, they're not *friends* or anything. She treats him the way she treats her mechanic or her plumber—like an employee. No, if she turns to anybody, it'll be me."

It took almost more energy than Holly could muster just to eat her soup and a slice of bread. As deep fatigue washed over her body and her mind, the idea of lying down for a few hours in Buffy Lewis's guest room became more and more tempting. "You think she'll call here, Buffy?" she asked, fighting hard to keep her eyes open.

"Don't know, Holly. All I can say is I don't think there's anybody else Celia can go to for help right now. But—well, truth is she might not go to anybody."

"If she does contact you, you will help us, won't you?" Holly asked.

Buffy chewed on her lower lip and blinked rapidly. Celia had been her friend since her children were small. She hated the idea of betraying her. Sure, Cele had been a pain in the ass at least half the time, but they'd shared both good times and bad, hadn't they? Maybe, Buffy admitted to herself, Celia's most attractive quality had been that she'd always needed Buffy so much. And Buffy had a strong need to be needed.

"I—oh, God," Buffy cried, "I have to, don't I? I can't let Cele—look, she's my friend, but she's not well, really she's not; she needs help. I have to do whatever I can to keep her from getting herself into any more trouble. I guess that means trying to get her to give your baby back before anything—" She halted before putting her next thought into words. Holly didn't need to hear that Buffy thought Celia was fully capable of killing a newborn child if she felt cornered. Her hunch was that Celia probably had the same kind of love-hate feelings for Alex's son that she'd had for Alex himself. And look where that had led.

"Thank you, Buffy." Holly slumped back in her chair. "Thank you."

"Come on, Holly," Buffy said, taking hold of Holly's arm and pulling her gently to her feet. "I'm putting you to bed. All of us will think much more clearly in the morning."

Much too exhausted to protest, Holly allowed the older woman to lead her toward the back of the house and the seductive prospect of a few hours of sleep.

As Celia fled down the narrow street, the wail of the police siren grew louder and louder in her ears. She turned into a dark alleyway and tried to hide among the old brick buildings, but the speeding squad car kept gaining on her. Finally, as she cowered in fright behind a bank of stinking garbage cans, a police spotlight picked her out. Pinned down by the blinding light, she raised her hands to shield her eyes and screamed, "No! No! Don't shoot! Please don't shoot—"

Her own screams of terror woke Celia from the nightmare. Her heart pounding hard against her chest, she realized that the loud wailing sound she'd heard was not a police car hot on her trail after all; it was baby Patrick's earsplitting cries. And the blinding light in her eyes was not a police spotlight; it was morning sunlight streaming through the windows of Buffy's Lake Tahoe cabin. The rotten odor did not come from overflowing garbage cans either; it was simply the stench of the baby's dirty diaper. No wonder he was wailing so loudly.

Upset and tired, Celia rolled over and pulled the pillow over her head, but the infant's screams continued to pierce her eardrums. "Shit," she mumbled into the mattress. She couldn't possibly sleep with the kid making that kind of racket. Reluctantly, she threw off her blanket and thrust her bare feet over the side of the bed and into her cold, damp loafers. "Shit!" she said again.

"It's okay, little one," Celia said with a sigh, as she looked down at the baby. "Mama's here." He lay in the dresser drawer where she'd put him last night, his small face now purple with rage and his tiny hands and feet flailing the air. Wrinkling her nose in distaste, she picked him up and held him at arm's length. "Boy, do you stink!"

Celia carried the crying baby into the bathroom to change his diaper. Shivering in the still-frigid cabin, she laid him down on a towel on the cold ceramic tile countertop next to the sink, lifted his tiny nightgown, and peeled off his soiled diaper. As cold air quickly engulfed his naked body, he screamed louder still and his body seemed to turn almost blue before Celia's eyes. She turned on the hot water tap. The water never became more than passably warm, but it would have to do. She washed off the trembling infant as quickly as she could, being extra careful to avoid the blackening stub of umbilical cord on his belly, and then taped one of the last few clean diapers around him.

It wasn't until at least fifteen minutes later, after Celia had heated a baby bottle in water on the electric stove and shoved it into his frantic mouth, that the baby's racking sobs finally quieted. As she fed him, Celia carried him around the cabin. She felt warmer when she kept moving. Maybe he did too.

The wall thermostat registered only fifty-three,

perhaps twenty degrees higher than when Celia'd turned it up last night. Maybe the furnace simply took a long time to heat this house in winter, she thought, hoping that nothing more serious was wrong.

After he was burped, the baby dozed off again, warmed by the milk in his stomach and exhausted by his tantrum. Realizing that she was ravenous herself, Celia gratefully put him back in his dresser drawer bed, covered him with an extra blanket, and went to make herself some breakfast.

She found the refrigerator turned off and completely empty. Well, of course, she told herself. Buffy wouldn't leave perishable food behind when she closed up this place for the winter, would she? She searched the cupboards with little more success.

"Thanks a lot, Buffy," Celia said, her voice heavy with sarcasm. "This is all you can do for your best friend, two fucking cans of tuna?" She also found a six-pack of Diet Cokes, an unopened jar of Spanish olives, and three tea bags—the sum total of the kitchen's offerings.

She would have to make a trip to the grocery store very soon, Celia realized, as she opened one of the cans of tuna and heated water for tea. There was only one more can of Patrick's baby formula left, too, and he'd been going through his disposable diapers faster than she'd ever thought possible. At this rate, by midafternoon there would be no clean diapers at all.

After she'd choked down a few forkfuls of the greasy tuna and warmed herself with a cup of hot tea, Celia tried to take a shower, but there still was no hot water and she couldn't face standing under a tepid stream, no matter how dirty she felt. Wrapped in only a towel and shivering visibly, she checked the wall thermostat once more. Now it read fifty-one degrees. The temperature inside the cabin was dropping. Something was very, very wrong.

Forced to forgo her ritual morning shower, Celia dressed in the warmest clothes she could find, including one of Buffy's sweaters, and then searched through the closets for something—anything—warmer than her wet loafers to put on her feet. She located two pairs of Buffy's castoff tennis shoes, but they were far too small. Celia's feet were size nine and Buffy's were no larger than seven. Finally, Celia gratefully came across an old pair of snow boots she guessed must belong to one of Buffy's grown sons. The boots were big but at least they were dry, and they would be invaluable for venturing outside the cabin.

As soon as she opened the front door, Celia discovered that several inches of fresh snow had fallen during the night. She had to throw her full weight against the door to move the snow that had drifted against it. The propane gas tank at the side of the house was nearly buried too. Celia used a sturdy branch from the woodpile to brush the snow away from the tank's fuel gauge. As soon as she cleared it, she knew why the cabin was so cold—the gauge was on empty.

"Damn you, Buffy!" Celia shouted toward the brilliant blue sky. "Damn you to hell! Can't you even keep your goddamned fucking propane tank filled?"

A bird in a nearby pine tree scolded shrilly. "What's the matter?" she shouted at the creature. "Don't like my language? *Fuck, fuck, fuck!* How's that?" The bird twittered one last time and took flight.

Loading her arms with as much kindling and split logs as she could carry, Celia made several trips between the woodpile and the house. At least there was plenty of firewood, she told herself, as she moved a large supply indoors. She could always try using the fireplace to heat the cabin.

Later, squatting on the hearth as she laid a fire, she considered her options. She could call for a propane delivery, maybe even get one late this morning or early this afternoon. But that would call attention to her presence here in the Lewis cabin. Was it worth the risk?

Maybe not, Celia decided, at least not until she found out whether the police were looking for her. Of course she could call Buffy again, let her know she was here using the place. Then Buffy could call the propane company herself, explaining that a friend was staying in her cabin. Maybe, too, Buffy would know about the police. But could Buffy still be trusted? That was the question, and Celia didn't know the answer.

She lit a match and crouched in front of the open fireplace until the newspaper beneath the kindling caught. She blew gently on the first sparks until they burst into flame, and waited until they began to darken the kindling, before dusting off her stiff, cold fingers and standing up. For a moment, she warmed herself in front of the fledgling fire. Then she went into the kitchen for another cup of hot tea.

As she sipped the steaming liquid, Celia's eye fell on the electric oven. Another source of heat, she thought. She switched the oven to five hundred degrees and opened the oven door. The coils along the bottom soon glowed red, heating the area a few feet in front of the stove. Now there were two spots of relative warmth in the cabin, but the overall temperature was still dropping.

Still shivering despite her sweater and heavy boots,

Celia opened the telephone book and turned to the section marked *Gas—Propane*. There were four companies listed. With luck, she thought, the yahoo who made the delivery wouldn't even know she wasn't this cabin's owner. And if, by some chance, the deliveryman did know Buffy Lewis, she could simply explain that she was a friend using the cabin with Buffy's permission. Why would he bother to check? She would use a phony name, too, Celia decided, just in case there had been something about Celia Sheridan on the news or in the morning papers.

Once she knew when the propane man was coming, she could plan her trip to the grocery store around his delivery. Then, when she and little Patrick had heat in the cabin, plus hot water, something to eat, and a fresh supply of disposable diapers, this place really would be quite livable—despite Buffy Lewis's inconsiderate lack of hospitality.

Relieved to have made a plan, Celia reached for the telephone, pressed the receiver to her ear, and started to dial. But with only the first two digits of the propane company's phone number punched in, she stopped.

"Shit and double shit!" she screamed. She had heard no dial tone; the telephone line was dead. Obviously, that penny-pinching Buffy had had the phone turned off for the winter.

Seething with frustration and rage, Celia threw the telephone against the wall. It bounced once, then crashed loudly to the floor.

An instant later, the baby began to cry.

"I keep asking myself, where would *I* go if I wanted to hide out with a newborn baby I couldn't explain," Holly said. She took another bite of the fluffy eggs Buffy Lewis had scrambled for their breakfast. After six full hours of dead-to-the-world sleep, Holly was feeling stronger. Her ankle was no longer so swollen, and the contractions of her uterus had all but stopped. Her worst physical complaint was her hot, painfully swollen breasts. Her body had begun to ache for her baby almost as much as her mind and heart did.

"More toast?" Buffy offered, holding up a plateful of buttered whole wheat squares. The two women were eating breakfast and talking in the kitchen while Greg took his turn in the guest bathroom's shower.

Holly shook her head no. "Thanks, but I'm really getting full. What I mean is, think about it, Buffy. Could Celia just check into any old motel with a new baby? I s'pose she could, but she couldn't very well expect to keep him a secret. Babies make noise, and they need to be fed and changed—all the time."

"Maybe she's holed up in another apartment somewhere," Buffy suggested.

"You think she set up another home in advance, the way she did that place on Grove?" If Celia had arranged for more than one hideaway where she could take the baby without arousing suspicion, Holly knew she might never find her. But she didn't want to think about that. She didn't really want to think about what might happen if Celia'd gone to a motel or a hotel, either. Surely the woman wouldn't try to hide the fact that she had a baby with her. She wouldn't try to stiffle his cries. . . ? Holly choked back a sob. After what had happened to Alex, she didn't know whether she'd be able to survive another devastating loss.

Buffy shrugged. "Who knows what Celia'd do? I'm supposed to know her better than anybody, and I didn't even catch on that she was planning to steal a baby, never mind figure out what she planned to do afterward."

You have to think logically, Holly told herself. She couldn't afford to let herself fall apart. Not now. "I don't think she could camp out all that easily with a newborn baby, either," she said.

"Trust me, Celia's not the camping-out type," Buffy told her. "First class all the way, that's the way Cele likes to travel. Plenty of hot running water, room service—"

"What are her favorite places?" Holly asked. "Is there anywhere in particular she likes to go? You know, vacation spots, relatives to visit, something like that?"

Buffy refilled Holly's coffee cup, then her own. "Celia's mother died years ago, and she never had any brothers or sisters. Come to think of it, I can't remember her ever mentioning any relatives—except her mom, of course. They were always pretty close.

"When we were both married, though, sometimes we used to take vacations together as couples—Cele and Alex and Charlie and me. One year we all went to Maui, and another time we went to Las Vegas for a week and saw all the shows. I remember Celia won four hundred bucks on a dollar slot machine and then lost every last penny on roulette. Cele and Alex used to come up to our cabin in Tahoe quite a bit, too. Hah. The good old days! They're long gone."

Buffy poured a little milk into her coffee, then stirred it until the drink was a uniform tan color. "Since her divorce, though, I don't think Cele's taken a vacation anywhere. No, wait a minute. I take that back. She and I drove up to Tahoe for one weekend last summer, just the two of us."

Holly felt a pang of raw jealousy as she listened to Buffy talking about Celia and Alex as a married couple. Even after reading Alex's old diaries, in which he detailed how he longed to put his miserable marriage behind him, Holly couldn't help being aware of all the nights he'd shared Celia's bed and the many trips the two of them had taken together. Twenty-five years of marriage couldn't have been all bad. Holly herself had had only slightly less than a year of married life with Alex.

"You said Celia sold her house here in L.A.," Holly said, forcing her mind back onto the problem at hand. "There's no way she could be hiding out there, is there?"

"I don't think so. I'm sure she had to turn over the keys at settlement and—I don't know. If I were Cele, I'd hardly risk going back to my old neighborhood, even if I had a key and the house was empty, which it might not be. People know her there; they'd be curious about why she was back, about where she got the baby."

"You're right, Buffy. But damn it, where—? Say, what about that place you mentioned at Lake Tahoe? You still have it?"

"Sure do. But it's winter now, and it's probably all snowed in up there. I've never gone to Tahoe in wintertime. Do you really think Celia'd go someplace like that with an infant?"

"S'pose not. Still, is there some way you could check? Maybe dial your phone number? No! Wait a minute. Don't call. If she *is* there, we don't want to risk scaring her off again."

"I couldn't call my cabin anyway. I have the phone turned off at the end of every season."

"What about your neighbors? Is there somebody close by who could tell you whether there's any activity at your place?"

"Guess I could try to reach somebody, but I'd really be surprised if anyone's around this time of year."

Buffy pulled open a drawer of the kitchen desk, took out her address book, and dialed her three closest Lake Tahoe neighbors, one after the other.

"Sorry," she said, after a few minutes. "I bombed out. One phone's disconnected, and nobody answers the other two. Listen, if you actually think Celia might have gone to Tahoe, we could call the police and have them check the place."

"Wait." Holly still felt panicky at the idea of involving the police. She would never forget Celia's threat to kill the baby before she'd ever give him up. If the police came to the door, what would she do? "Tell me this." Holly said. "Would Celia be able to get into your place? I mean without breaking a window or something?"

Buffy thought for a moment. "I always have an extra key hidden. Yeah, I'm sure Celia'd remember where I keep it. She wouldn't have any trouble getting in."

"A cabin like that, it would certainly be private enough for her," Holly said, "and, like you said, no neighbors around to get nosy about the baby." The more Holly thought about it, the more she thought it was quite possible that Celia Sheridan had taken refuge in her friend's vacation cabin. Except for any problems the snow might present, it would be a perfect hideaway. "I don't know about the police, though, Buffy. I'm afraid, if Celia is there and the police came to the door, she might panic and—hurt the baby." Holly took a deep breath and tried to keep her fears in check.

"I know one of the local cops pretty well—George Pendergrass," Buffy said. "How about I call and tell George I'm letting some friends use my place, but I'm worried about whether they made it up there all right."

"He can't go knocking on the door," Holly warned. "Who knows what Celia—"

"No, no, that's not what I have in mind. I could tell him I don't want him to disturb my friends, just to check and see whether there's a car in the driveway. Something like that."

"Maybe you could tell him you lent your place to a couple on their honeymoon or something . . . whatever," Holly suggested, warming to the idea. "Just tell your cop friend anything, to make sure he doesn't do more than just drive by."

"All right," Buffy agreed. "Here goes." She took a deep breath and reached for the phone.

An hour and a half later, Holly, Greg, and Buffy were

in the living room, still brainstorming about how to find Celia, when the telephone rang. As Buffy ran to the kitchen to answer it, Holly trailed along behind her, hoping against hope. Her eyes were trained on Buffy's face as she answered the call.

"Thanks, George," Holly heard Buffy say a moment later. "I really appreciate your taking the trouble to drive by . . . Well, that's a big relief, isn't it? It's just, with all the snow and everything, I couldn't help worrying. . . . No, no, really, that's definitely not necessary. I promised not to disturb them. . . . Again, thanks, George. And give my best to Margie, will you?"

Buffy hung up the phone and slowly raised her eyes to meet Holly's questioning gaze. "George says there's a station wagon parked in my driveway," she announced.

"Greg!" Holly shrieked, her heart leaping with new-found hope. "Greg! Come in here quick. We found her. We found Celia!"

Her bare hands stiff against the frozen steering wheel, Celia shifted the station wagon into reverse once more and stepped on the accelerator. The big car's wheels simply spun in place, digging deeper and deeper into the the driveway's snow pack. Waiting for the early afternoon sun to melt the crust off last night's snowfall obviously hadn't helped to free the car.

Angrily, Celia pounded her fists against the steering wheel. "Goddamn son of a bitch!" she screamed, as loud as she could.

Strapped into his car seat beside her, the baby was startled awake by the sudden explosion of noise. He began to make low whimpering sounds that quickly escalated into full-fledged wails. Well fed for the moment, he wore the last of the disposable diapers and was snugly wrapped in blankets. Until Celia's outburst, he'd been resting peacefully. Now, however, his blue eyes were wide with terror.

"Shut the hell up!" Celia yelled at him. The last

thing she needed right now was a six or seven-pound brat screaming in her ear.

She shifted the car into low gear again and managed to move it forward an inch or two—downhill toward the cabin. But when she tried reverse gear once more, Celia realized she'd made the wrong move. Now the car was farther from the road than ever. It simply wasn't going to make it back up the icy incline in reverse gear. She cursed the day she'd bought the Buick; she cursed the salesman who'd sold it to her; she cursed every auto worker on the Buick assembly line.

She cursed herself. She'd wanted a nondescript American car, Celia reminded herself, and that's exactly what she got, bald tires and all. She longed for her cherished gold Mercedes; surely that trusty example of proud workmanship would never let a few inches of snow defeat it.

Over the next half hour, while the baby whimpered mournfully in his car seat, Celia tried rocking the car back and forth in place; she tried placing broken tree branches under its rear tires for added traction; she searched unsuccessfully all around the cabin for a shovel to dig out the driveway. But no matter what she did, she couldn't budge the big car from the spot where she'd parked it late last night.

She had to face it, Celia finally realized: the station wagon was firmly stuck in Buffy's snowy driveway. Unless she found a way to dig it out, or somehow managed to call a tow truck for help, she wouldn't be making any trip to the grocery store. Not today. And unless her luck changed, possibly not before the spring thaw.

Her raw frustration quickly blossoming into sheer panic, Celia snatched the frightened baby out of his car seat and carried him back inside the chilly cabin.

Chapter

45

Her knees visibly shaking and her breath coming in fast shallow spurts, Holly stood on the tarmac at Santa Monica Airport, waiting. She had nothing to do except grow more and more nervous while Greg performed his preflight check on the Cessna Skyhawk he'd rented to fly them to Tahoe City. Their only other alternatives were to wait until tomorrow morning for a commercial flight to Tahoe or fly to Reno tonight. And if they flew to Reno, they'd have to drive for another hour before they got to Buffy's cabin.

Feeling light-headed and woozy, Holly watched as Greg examined the propeller blades for nicks and climbed up on the wings to check the fuel—all the familiar things she'd watched Alex do, the very last time she saw him alive. All the terrible nightmares she'd had, every haunting vision of Alex's Cessna spiraling toward the angry waves, each heartbreaking thought about the terror her husband must have felt in his final moments, flashed through her mind once more.

You're going to do this, Holly lectured herself. You're going to get into that plane and fly to your son's rescue. You have no choice.

"You all right, Holly?"

Feeling a light touch on her arm, Holly jerked her head around and saw Buffy standing beside her. The older woman's kind, round face was a study in concern.

"Alex's Cessna was just like this one," Holly told her.

"I know this must be hard for you," Buffy said, "but remember, it wasn't Alex's plane that failed him."

"I'll be all right." Holly hoped that saying the words would somehow make them true.

When he'd finished his check of the single-engine aircraft, Greg waved his two passengers over. "All set? Let's go." He stood aside while Holly climbed slowly into the plane first, with Buffy right behind her.

Over Buffy's protests, Holly chose to sit in the backseat, directly behind the pilot. "Really, I'd rather be back here," she explained, as the engine began its ear-shattering roar. The rest of her words were lost in the plane's deafening noise.

If she rode alone, behind the others, Holly figured, they wouldn't be able to see the raw terror she knew would show on her face. They would never have to know how much it was costing her emotionally to get into this airplane, to make this flight. She fastened her seat belt with trembling fingers. Please, she prayed, don't let me be sick to my stomach.

Holly kept her eyes squeezed shut and her fingers clenched tightly together in her lap during the entire noisy, turbulent flight north. It wasn't until she felt the Cessna's wheels touch down on the small airstrip near Tahoe City that she dared look out the window again.

After Greg helped her out of the airplane and her feet touched the solid blacktopped runway, Holly felt a strong urge to kneel down and kiss the ground in gratitude.

But, being an essentially private person, she fought the urge. Instead, she simply held her chin high and walked toward the rented car waiting for them outside the airstrip's small hangar.

Holly Sheridan knew her day's ordeal had only just begun.

Chapter

46

⌒

The temperature inside the cabin registered forty-eight degrees now, although Celia was adding logs to the fire every fifteen or twenty minutes. She put on a third sweater she'd found in Buffy's bedroom and moved the baby's drawer bed to a spot on the floor near the fireplace to keep him as warm as possible.

"How're you doing down there, little Patrick?" Celia asked.

The baby's eyes were open wide, but he lay disturbingly still in his drawer, as if he no longer had the energy to cry or even move his hands and feet. His tiny lips had a bluish tinge to them, and his breathing was labored. Sucking in this cold air was probably hard on his tiny new lungs, Celia thought with a quick pang of sympathy. Still, she was grateful she no longer had to listen to him scream.

She bent down and touched his tiny hand; it was as icy as her own. "Don't you dare get sick on me, you hear?" she scolded.

Celia had to admit that motherhood was not turning

out quite the way she'd imagined. She shoved her index finger beneath the infant's clothing. He was wet again. "Never knew a baby could piss so much," she said with a sigh. All the diapers she'd brought along were gone now, and for the past two changes she'd had to resort to using dish towels. With no plastic pants for protection, the baby soaked most of his clothing every time he wet. Celia had hand-washed two of his nightgowns and hung them in front of the fireplace to dry, but they were still damp. The baby would soon be out of everything.

Using the last of Buffy's dish towels, Celia changed him once more. This time, she did her best to fashion a pair of protective plastic pants out of a freezer bag she found in a kitchen drawer. Better than nothing, she thought, but barely.

Celia knew she and the baby couldn't stay here much longer. If she didn't do something about getting them some food and heat pretty soon, they'd be found right here next spring—starved or frozen to death. Only a few ounces of baby formula remained, and Celia had already finished the second can of tuna and two of the diet sodas. The spartan feast had done little to quell the sharp hunger pains in her stomach.

Yet what could she do? She and the baby were stuck here without heat, food, or transportation, and there was no way to call for help. Maybe she could hike out of here to get help, Celia thought. From the back deck of Buffy's place, she could just make out the top of another cabin's roof through the treetops. Although she spotted no smoke rising from the chimney, there might be a working telephone over there, even some food. And maybe the place had electric heat. Perhaps she and the baby could wait, safe and warm inside, for a tow truck and propane delivery.

Celia knew she really had no choice. She would have to go for help or be prepared to die here, and she had never been a quitter. She pushed her feet back into Buffy's son's sturdy boots and put on her raincoat over her trio of sweaters. In case she might have to break into the other cabin, she thrust a hammer and screwdriver from Buffy's tool kit into her coat pocket, then opened her purse and took out the .38 revolver she'd used to herd Holly Sheridan into her bedroom prison back in Bodega Bay. Had it been only the night before last? It already seemed like ages ago. Celia pushed the gun deep into her other coat pocket. There was no telling what she might run into at the neighboring cabin, and she wasn't going to take any chances.

When she was dressed for the outdoors, Celia wrapped the baby in a couple of bath towels and then in the two small blankets from his bed. "Come on, mister," she said, as she hoisted him up off the floor. "You and I are going for a little hike."

If she died somewhere out there in the drifting snow, Celia decided, at least she was going to take Alex's son along with her.

"Slow up when you go around this next curve," Buffy said, as Greg drove the rented car down icy Curtis Drive. "It's the next driveway on the right."

"That's it! That's the car she had in Bodega Bay!" Holly shouted from the backseat as she spotted the Buick station wagon. It was mired in a snowdrift a few feet off the road. "Thank God she's still here."

"Looks like she's gonna be, too, for a good long while," Greg said. "Wagon's gonna need a tow to get out of that drift." He drove past Buffy's driveway and stopped at the side of the road about fifty feet beyond it. Here, trees blocked the view of the cabin and, Greg hoped, Celia's view of them as well.

"I better go in alone first," Buffy said, "see if I can talk to her."

Holly leaned forward and gripped the shoulder of Buffy's red ski jacket. "Be really careful, Buffy. She's probably still got that gun."

"Thanks, Holly, but I'm not worried. I'm Celia's oldest friend—she'd never pull a gun on me. I'll just tell her I decided to come up for a few days of skiing or something, act surprised to find her here. I don't think she'll see me as a threat. Remember, I'm supposed to think she legally adopted this baby."

"Well, okay," Holly said. "Just try to keep her away from the windows on the front side of the house if you can. Greg and I will give you five minutes or so; then we'll creep up on the place and wait until you give us the signal."

"Better make it ten," Buffy told them. "I'll ask to hold the baby. That way, I can get him safely out of the way while the two of you deal with Celia."

While Buffy hiked down the snowy driveway to the cabin, Holly stood waiting next to the car, more frightened and anxious than ever, now that her baby seemed so near. But her hopes plummeted a few minutes later, when she saw Buffy coming back toward the road with a puzzled look on her face.

"She's been there, all right," Buffy told the others. "There's still a fire burning in the fireplace, so she was there until recently. But Cele and the baby are gone."

It took Celia nearly fifteen minutes to reach the cabin she'd spotted through the trees. In some places, the snow she trudged through was knee deep. Once, she tripped and fell face first into a snowdrift, losing her grip on the baby. He went flying, landing flat on his back and sinking deep into the soft snow. But she managed to right herself and dig him out with no apparent permanent harm done. Now, she could hear small whimpers—tiny kitten sounds—coming from inside his cocoon of towels and blankets.

The cabin she found was deserted. As she circled it, Celia saw no sign of lights inside, and there was no car, not even any tire tracks, in the unplowed driveway. Like Buffy's place, this one was closed up for the winter, with both its front and rear doors securely locked. She laid the baby gently on top of a snowbank and pulled the screwdriver from her coat pocket.

As a light snow began to fall, Celia wedged the screwdriver between the front door and its frame, then pried sideways, again and again. All she managed to do was splinter the wood a bit; the door remained firmly locked. This sort of thing always looked so easy on television, she thought, kicking the solid door in sheer frustration. At this rate, she would have to dismantle the door splinter by splinter before she got inside.

"The hell with this," Celia said, a few minutes later. There had to be an easier way to break into this place. Leaving the baby where he lay on top of the snow, she walked around the wooden structure, looking for a better way in. On the west side, she found it.

Thrusting the screwdriver back into her pocket, Celia took out the hammer. She shielded her eyes, then used the hammer to break out a windowpane. Reaching inside carefully so as not to tear her coat sleeve on the jagged glass, she felt around for the window lock. "All right!" she said, as it slid smoothly into the open position.

But as she began to raise the sash to climb inside, a deafening burglar alarm went off.

"Oh, shit!" Celia said, falling back as the ear-shattering ringing continued. Was there anyone around to hear? She'd seen absolutely no one since arriving last night. Still, for all she knew this alarm was connected to the local police station. Cops could be on their way here right now. She needed help, but the last thing she wanted was to try bullshitting her way around a bunch of police.

Celia hurried back to the front of the house and grabbed the terrified, squalling infant. She could feel his small body shivering through his thick covering. She looked around in sheer panic. Should she head back to Buffy's and try to hide there until this goddamned alarm stopped? It was loud enough to wake the dead, but maybe it had an automatic shutoff.

No, Celia decided. There was nothing for her at Buffy's, and her original idea had been a solid one. There had to be another place around here where she could find food and shelter and, most important of all, a working telephone.

She squinted into the distance. There it was, she thought—another chance. Perhaps a third of a mile downhill from here she could see another small house, this one painted a gaudy barn red.

Gripping the infant tightly against her chest, Celia turned away from the route back to Buffy's and began another trek downhill.

Chapter

49

"What's that ringing noise?" Holly asked, cocking her head toward the woods behind the cabin. She and Buffy were standing in the driveway while Greg checked out Celia's stranded station wagon. They'd already looked through the cabin. It was obvious that Celia and the baby had been there, and just as obvious that they'd gone.

"Sounds like some kind of burglar alarm to me," Buffy said.

Holly walked back to the cabin and climbed the stairs onto the back deck. Shading her eyes against the snow's glare, she peered off into the distance, in the direction from which the ringing noise seemed to be coming. She could just make out a distant rooftop through the trees. Far easier to spot from this vantage point was a trail of footprints in the snow. They led in precisely the same direction.

"Come on," Holly said, excitedly gesturing to the others to follow her. "I think I see where she went."

The three trudged through the snow toward the

nearest cabin, having an easier time of it than Celia had had. It was snowing harder now, but Celia had had to break the trail and, unlike her pursuers, she'd been walking with an infant in her arms. Still, Holly stumbled and fell more than once. Clearly, she hadn't yet regained her strength after giving birth, and the hike through the snow was particularly grueling.

At one point, Buffy took over the lead and Greg attempted to pick up Holly and carry her. "No, Greg," she protested, wrenching herself free. "You'll just exhaust yourself. I can make it on my own, really I can. I just have to go a little slower." She said nothing to the others about the feverish feeling that was rapidly stealing over her body, nor about the cramping in her uterus, which had returned with a vengeance.

Just do it, Holly lectured herself every time she felt she was beginning to falter. Get up and get on with it! Forcing herself forward with little more than sheer determination, Holly was right on the heels of her companions when they reached the edge of woods and stood looking across the clearing toward the second cabin.

As Holly, Greg, and Buffy stood there, trying to decide what to do next, the alarm stopped ringing. A deathly silence descended upon the woods.

Chapter

50

When she reached the little barn-red house, Celia didn't waste time trying to pry open the front door with the screwdriver. Instead, she immediately smashed a window in a rear bedroom and got ready to flee once more if another burglar alarm went off. But this time she was in luck. The only sound she heard was the distant ringing of the alarm at the cabin she'd just left. She set the baby down on the cold ground, climbed in through the open window, unlocked the front door from the inside, and went back outside to get him.

With the baby balanced on her hip, Celia quickly surveyed the house. From what she could tell, it hadn't been occupied recently, but there was a plentiful supply of canned goods in the kitchen cupboards—a variety of soups, baked beans, evaporated milk, a tin of Spam. Equally important, a moment after she turned up the thermostat, the forced air furnace began to blast forth precious warm air.

There was a telephone here too, and when she

picked up the receiver, Celia heard a dial tone. She never thought she'd be so grateful for a few small luxuries like these, but after spending last night in Buffy's cabin, she now felt like she'd died and gone to heaven.

If only that alarm would stop ringing at the cabin up the hill, Celia thought, as the house quickly began to warm up. She removed the outer layer of blankets from around the baby and tried to rub some color back into his tiny blue-white fingers and cheeks. She couldn't help worrying that the alarm had already summoned the police, that they were already on their way, that they would go door-to-door, looking for anything suspicious.

"Think we better hide out here for a while, little Patrick," she told the chilled and listless infant, "at least till we see whether those nasty old cops are coming to get us."

Celia decided to wait before phoning for a tow truck and a propane delivery for Buffy's cabin, perhaps until tomorrow. There was plenty right here for her to eat, and she could warm a bit of that evaporated milk for the baby, spoon enough of it into his mouth to keep him satisfied until she could buy more baby formula. Things would be much better tomorrow, she told herself. At least, by then she'd know whether she was going to have to deal with the police.

As the temperature of the room rose, the baby's eyelids fluttered and he dozed off. Celia carried him into the main bedroom and laid him in the middle of the double bed, feeling grateful for a short reprieve from constant mothering. As she was arranging the blankets around the sleeping child, the burglar alarm suddenly stopped ringing. Celia stiffened, not knowing whether she should be grateful or even more worried. Had the alarm been on a timer after all? Or did the sudden quiet mean that the police had arrived and switched it off?

Celia had no idea what might happen next, but she fully intended to be prepared for it. One thing she did know: If the police arrived and tried to arrest her for breaking and entering or any other crime, she would not go peacefully.

She hurried back into the living room and grabbed her coat from where she'd thrown it across a chair. She pulled her .38 revolver from the pocket, checked to make sure it was fully loaded, and then sat down on the sofa and waited in the eerie silence.

"If Celia was here, that alarm probably scared her off," Buffy reported. "I found a broken window on the other side of the house. Looks like she tried to break in and set the alarm off, but I don't think anyone's in there now."

"I see more tracks over there," Holly said, pointing out the trail through the snow. "Maybe she decided to try another cabin." Her small discovery infused Holly with another needed jolt of adrenaline, just enough to keep her on her feet and moving despite her rapidly deepening fatigue.

The trio followed the trail through the woods. When they reached the clearing at the bottom of the hill, they found a small red house with lights shining brightly through the front windows.

"I'll go knock on the front door," Buffy offered, "and see if Celia's in there."

"Good," Holly said. "Try to keep her occupied, Buffy. Greg and I will see whether we can get into the house from the rear side, maybe take her by surprise."

* * *

Despite the chill in the air, Buffy's palms were sweaty as she knocked on the front door of the red cabin and called out, "Cele. Cele, you in there?" In spite of her bravado in front of Holly and Greg, Buffy knew that some part of her old friend's mind must have come completely unhinged. Otherwise, she never would have done such terrible things. Celia's altered mental state changed all the rules of their friendship, and Buffy honestly couldn't predict whether her old friend would now turn on her as well. "Cele? Open up, please. It's Buffy."

The door opened a crack. Buffy hardly recognized the haggard-looking woman who peered out at her. It wasn't just the messy hair and smeared makeup that were so unlike the old Celia Sheridan, it was the deep stress lines around her mouth and the dead look in her eyes.

"Hi, Cele," Buffy said. "Can I come in?"

Before she opened the door further, Celia tucked the revolver into the waistband of her slacks and pulled layers of sweaters over it to hide it from Buffy's view. "What are you doing here?" she demanded, unsmiling.

"I just came up to my place for the weekend and—well, obviously I saw you'd been staying there." Buffy stomped the snow off her boots on the front steps and stepped into the entryway of the little red house.

Celia moved half a step backward. "I didn't think you'd mind, Buffy. It—it's not like you ever come up here in winter."

"It's not that I mind, Cele. I don't. You can use my place anytime you want, you know that. It's just—you might have asked me first."

"It was kind of a last-minute decision, and then there

wasn't any heat or food, and my car got stuck in the snow, and I had to—" A look of raw suspicion crept into Celia's eyes. "What are *you* doing here?"

Buffy pulled off her gloves and rubbed her hands together briskly. "Lord, it's cold. I'd kill for a cup of coffee."

"*Why*, Buffy? Why are you here?"

"Thought I'd try some skiing."

"You, skiing? You're putting me on. You've never skied in your life."

"New Year's resolution, Cele. I'm going to get into shape if it kills me. So what's it going to be? You going to keep me standing here with the door open or you going to ask me in?"

Moving slowly and silently around the darker side of the house, Holly and Greg peered into window after window. They located the kitchen, a bathroom, and two bedrooms. One of the windows in the first of the bedrooms had been smashed, undoubtedly by Celia when she broke into the house. But it was what Holly spotted in the second bedroom that made her heart leap. At first, she thought it was simply a pile of blankets tossed onto the center of the big bed. But as she looked more closely, she saw a bit of movement among the blankets, then a tiny fist being raised.

"That's him," she whispered to Greg, as sharp pains coursed through her full breasts. Holly ached to hold and nurture her child. "There's my baby, Greg! Thank God, he—he's still alive. I was so scared—" She choked back a sob.

"It's going to be all right, Holly."

"There must be some way for me to get into that room without Celia's catching me," Holly said. "I'd like to sneak the baby out of there. I think that'd be a whole lot safer than confronting her."

"Might work," Greg said, "as long as Buffy can keep Celia occupied in the front part of the house. I can boost you up through that broken window and climb in after you. But we don't know the floor plan of this place—might have to pass right by the living room to get to that other bedroom."

"I have to try, Greg, but you stay outside. That way, if I get caught, you can still come in after us."

"Okay." Greg slid the broken window open as quietly as possible, then boosted Holly up onto the window ledge. She balanced there precariously for a moment, tightly gripping the window sash, half in and half out of the room. When she'd caught her breath again, she carefully lowered herself onto the bedroom floor. The heavy boots Buffy had loaned Holly for the trip north made crunching noises as she walked across the window glass littering the hardwood floor.

Tiptoeing in the boots was impossible, Holly quickly realized, so as soon as she'd moved past the broken glass, she slipped them off. She opened the door leading into the hallway very slowly, praying that its hinges wouldn't squeak and advertise her presence. When the door made no noise at all, she exhaled in sheer relief.

For once, she was in luck, Holly thought. Leaving the bedroom door open to facilitate her escape with the baby, she sneaked into the hallway and stole slowly along the bare wood floor. But as she reached the bathroom, she heard voices coming from the front of the house.

"—see him later," Buffy was saying. "Don't wake him up now, Cele, really."

"We won't wake him. Come on, Buff, just take a quick little peek. I want you to see my Patrick."

As she heard footsteps approaching, Holly froze, then ducked into the bathroom just as the two women entered the hallway. She hardly dared breathe for fear that Celia might hear her.

As she cowered behind the partially open bathroom door, Holly heard Buffy's voice, now coming from the larger bedroom. "Just adorable, Cele!" she said. "But don't you think we'd better let him sleep while he can? The way I remember it, you don't get all that much quiet time when they're this little."

Thank you, Buffy! Holly said to herself. Get her out of there.

"You got that right," Celia said. "Haven't had two hours of sleep since I became a mother."

"Come on, Cele, let's go see if there's any coffee in this place. I think we could both use something hot to drink."

When the women's voices had faded out of her hearing, Holly ventured back into the hallway. Her heart beating wildly, she peeked around the archway into the living room. She could see Buffy standing with her back to the living room, looking into what was probably the kitchen. She couldn't see Celia at all; she must be in the kitchen making coffee, Holly thought gratefully.

In her stocking feet, Holly skittered past the archway and into the bedroom where the baby lay surrounded by blankets and towels. She reached over and stroked his downy hair with her index finger. She'd never felt anything so soft in all her life; it was like touching a cloud. Holly spread one of the blankets out on the bed, lifted the sleeping infant onto it, and wrapped him tightly. He would need all the protective covering he could get, once she got him outside.

As she wrapped the second blanket snuggly around him, the baby began to squirm a bit, making small mewing sounds.

"Hush, sweetheart," Holly whispered. "Hush now, Mama's here to take you home."

When the infant was securely bundled up, Holly lifted him off the bed and held him close for a moment, gently kissing his forehead and breathing in his wonderful baby smell. There was no way she could possibly live without this child.

Suddenly a door slammed, rattling the house and jerking Holly back to the present danger. The bedroom door she'd left open! The draft through the broken window must have blown it closed. Damn! Holly thought. How could she have been so stupid?

The startled baby let out a quick yelp, then began to cry as Holly spun around and headed toward the hall to make a run for it. But she was too late. Celia stood blocking the doorway, a look of raw hatred on her face.

"So that's what this is all about!" Celia's face quickly grew red with rage. "Buffy, you fucking traitor! I thought you were my friend!"

Buffy moved closer to Celia and touched her gently on the arm. "I *am* your friend, Cele. Because I'm your friend, I'm trying to save you from yourself. Can't you see that?"

Celia jerked away from Buffy's touch and, in a single motion, reached under her sweater and brought out the .38. "Go on, get over there, stand next to the bitch," she ordered, gesturing with the gun. Buffy didn't budge. "Move, or I'll shoot you right here."

"Cele, you wouldn't—"

Celia raised the gun and fired a bullet into the ceiling. The baby shrieked in terror, and the stench of burned gunpowder filled the air. "Next time I'm not going to miss!" Celia screamed.

Buffy's mouth fell open in shock, but she moved obediently across the room toward Holly. "Celia," she pleaded, "please, just think a min—"

"Shut the hell up!"

This time Buffy did as she was told. The woman standing in the doorway with the gun was no longer anyone she recognized, no longer anyone she could reason with.

"Bring my baby over here, bitch," Celia said to Holly.

Holly stood her ground, patting the wailing infant's head to comfort him. "He's my baby, Celia. Nothing can ever change that."

"Come on, do what I tell you, you fucking whore! I swear to God, I'll kill you. And if you make me, I'll shoot right through him to do it. If I can't have him, nobody will."

"But—"

"I'm giving you a choice, you fucking home wrecker. Hand that baby over to me now, and he lives. Otherwise"—she cocked the gun once more—"otherwise he dies right here, along with you."

Holly swallowed hard, trying to figure out a way to buy time. "All right, Celia," she said, struggling against rising panic. "All right, you win. He's yours. I can't let you hurt him. Just let me hold him for one more minute. *Please.* I know you lost your baby too; you know how hard—"

"Shut the hell up! You don't know anything about

me, and I don't want to know anything about you. Bring my son here!"

"Okay, okay, I'm coming."

Holly moved slowly and deliberately toward Celia as the baby's panicky screams increased in volume. She kept talking as she moved closer, maintaining eye contact with Celia all the while and taking extra care not to let her face react to the blur of motion she could see just beyond the woman holding the gun.

"All I ask is that you promise me one thing, Celia," Holly said, pressing the child more tightly to her chest. "Promise me you'll take care of my son, that you'll love him. If I know he's got somebody who really loves him, dying won't be quite so—"

Celia raised the gun and took aim at Holly's forehead. "I told you to shut the hell—"

Holly dove to the right as Celia squeezed the trigger. As the shot exploded, Greg tackled Celia from behind, knocking her forward. The bullet whizzed past Holly, lodging in the far wall.

Celia hit the floor hard, losing her grip on the gun. As Greg straddled her, she stretched her long fingers toward the spot where the gun had fallen. But Holly moved faster, kicking the weapon away before Celia could grasp it again.

Still holding the terrified infant clasped to her breast, Holly swooped down and snatched the gun off the floor.

"It's going to be okay now, little one," Holly murmured to the baby through her tears. "Everything's going to be okay."

"I won't need that thing," Holly said, as she saw the wheelchair the nurse's aide was pushing into her hospital room. "I can walk just fine, thanks."

"Hospital policy, Mrs. Sheridan," the aide replied. "All our patients get a ride out to the curb when they check out."

Holly shrugged. Whether she and her sleeping son walked or rode on their way out of Tahoe Community Hospital didn't really matter to her. During the past two days, both mother and child had been thoroughly examined by the staff doctors and pronounced healthy. Now Holly was anxious to get back home to Bodega Bay and start living the rest of her life.

The aide took the baby from Holly's arms while she put on her coat. As Holly was transferring herself into the wheelchair, Greg entered the room.

"All ready to go?" he asked. "I've got the car parked right out front."

"Timing's perfect, Greg. I just finished signing the

two of us out of here." She settled herself into the wheelchair and took the baby out of the aide's arms.

"Did you talk to the police again?" Holly asked Greg a moment later. The aide was pushing her wheelchair toward the hospital's front door while Greg followed close behind. "Is it okay for me to leave town and go back to Bodega Bay now?"

"No problem," Greg told her. "Celia's still locked up in the local jail, and the police here are in touch with the Sonoma County cops. Only thing is, I hear she's hired herself a high-priced defense attorney. He's trying to get her released on bail."

"*Bail?* After everything she did?" Holly was indignant.

"Lawyer promises she'll check herself into a locked psychiatric facility if she gets bail, claims what she really needs is a good hard shrinking, not prison."

Holly stiffened. After two days in the hospital with little else to think about, the raw horror of the past few weeks had sunk in thoroughly. Any sympathy she might once have felt for Celia had quickly withered. "Celia's far more than a kidnapper," Holly protested. "She murdered Alex, I know she did."

"Don't worry," Greg said, as he opened the passenger door of the rented car and helped Holly inside, "you're not the only one who thinks that. Sonoma County District Attorney's office already has an investigation going."

"Plus kidnapping, attempted murder, arson, and probably half a dozen other crimes, I hope," Holly added. She craved reassurance that Alex's ex-wife— whatever her motives and whether she was truly crazy or not—would never again have an opportunity to harm her or the baby she loved so much.

"One more thing," Greg said, as he climbed behind the wheel of the car. "I talked with Alex's attorney this morning."

"Bryce Cannon." Holly smiled and waved good-bye to the nurse's aide, who was still standing on the curb with the empty wheelchair.

"Right, Cannon. He says to tell you he's been in touch with the life insurance company that had the big policy on Alex, the one where Celia was still beneficiary. Cannon says the insurance company's investigators are gonna poke around a little themselves, see if they can give the cops an assist in convicting Celia of Alex's murder."

"Insurance investigators? Why?"

"Because the insurance company hasn't paid Celia's claim yet, and it's against the law to profit from killing somebody. If Celia's convicted of murdering Alex, she doesn't get a dime of the insurance money."

"But what—I mean, they can't just keep all that money, can they? Alex paid—"

"If Celia's out as beneficiary, Cannon says the insurance money'll go to Alex's estate—which means you and little what's-his-name here."

"Alexander," Holly said, gazing at her sleeping son's face. "His name's Alexander." Her heart filled with love and gratitude every time she looked at her perfect little boy.

"So you decided to name him Alexander," Greg said, pulling the car away from the curb. "Good choice, Holly. Alex would've liked his son to be Alexander Sheridan, Junior."

Holly looked over at Greg and smiled, gently placing her hand on his sleeve. "Alexander's not a junior, Greg, not really. Alex's full name is—was—Alexander

Bryant Sheridan. I'm naming this little fellow Alexander *Gregory* Sheridan—after both of the fine men responsible for giving him life."

Surprised and pleased, Greg blushed red beneath his deep tan. "I don't—I mean, thanks, Holly. I—well, just thanks."

"No, I thank *you*, Greg—for my son's life and my own. I'll always be grateful to you. Now, if you don't mind, I really do want to go home."

Holly knew that the life she was returning to would not be without its unknowns, without its risks. It would be very difficult, raising little Alexander Gregory Sheridan all by herself, without a father's help.

Still, as she journeyed through the snow-capped mountains, back toward Bodega Bay and the interrupted dream she and her husband had shared, Holly felt a surge of newfound hope. She had her health, she had a wonderful son, she had a loyal friend in Greg Garrison, and she had an important business to run.

For the first time since the day she waved good-bye to Alex's little plane as it disappeared over the Pacific horizon, Holly Sheridan began to feel optimistic about the future.